© **Max Lamira**

**Published by**

# © 2021 Saguenay, Quebec, Canada

## Credits:
*Kindle publishing*

## Cover credits:
*Word 2 Kindle*

## References:

*Erich Von Manstein book*　　*Lost Victories 1958*
*Heinz Guderian book*　　　*Panzer Leader, 1952*

# FOREWORD

Dear readers, I welcome you back to the blitzkrieg Alternate Series. We take to the story right where it left off, at the end of 1943. The year is now 1944, and "Fortress Europe" is being assailed from every side. The German Reich will be hard-pressed to fend off the powerful Red Army forces or the incredible Allied air superiority.

I have often wondered what would have happened if the Third Reich had been able to develop its war machine un-hindered by the Allied destruction of its industrial base, and also with the unlimited oil of the Middle East. In the Blitzkrieg Alternate Series, these two conditions are a reality. One could only speculate on the numbers of ME 262 jet fighters Germany could have pumped out of its factories. They did, historically, make 1294 of them amidst Hitler's hindrance and all the difficulties caused by their demolished factories and dwindling oil supplies.

While the war would have been still ultimately lost because the Germans were fighting the whole World, it would have lasted a lot longer, and we would have seen a very different direction taken. What if the Luftwaffe had been able to negate Allied air superiority?

As to the other wunderwaffe weapons (wonder weapons), of which a flurry came to fruition in 1944 (historically) but too late to have any impact on the war. One again might ask what they could have done with some numbers, like the Royal Tigers (Tiger II), with its nearly impervious armor? Or the German air to sea guided missiles (Fritz missile) against ships that sunk an Italian battleship late in the war?

We will explore these possibilities together in this exciting new chapter of the series. The Reich will be hard-pressed, will retreat, but won't die just yet. Far from it, in fact.

# PROLOGUE

# Wunderwaffe
## The first flight of the Messerschmitt ME 262, January 1st, 1944

The incredible aircraft was lifting off gently off the Lechfeld airfield, located in Bavaria (southern Germany), about 20 kilometers south of Augsburg. To the people on the ground, it made a magnificent noise, and quite different from a propeller-engine aircraft. It almost sounded like distant thunder, or of a long roar in the large blue sky. As it lifted off, it left small white contrails in the cold January air.

The plane quickly climbed in the sky, in a wide arc. Too quickly it seemed. The small crowd of people gathered outside by the control tower wasn't speaking, they were speechless. Hermann Goering, new Fuhrer of the Reich, was standing and looking quite satisfied. The plane turned around, and in what seemed an instant, roared over the airfield at incredible speed. The Nazi leadership was witnessing the first operational flight of the jet-powered engine ME-262.

Also present were a flurry of Luftwaffe officers, from the likes of Albert Kesselring to the new commander of the air force after Goering acceded to ultimate power, the very competent Marshall Erhard Milch. The latter had pushed hard for the ME-262 to finally take to the skies.

The plane had shown great promise in the first test flights in 1942, but Hitler had plagued the development program with his indecisions and other considerations like he'd wanted to have the plane as a bomber. But upon his arrival in the top position, Milch had put every ounce of his newfound influence to make the project a reality. And since it was a Luftwaffe project, he received the full backing of Hermann Goering.

The plane roared again over the gathered men. It turned on itself and made some fancy maneuvers. The whole thing was about showing the top men in the Reich what the plane could do. And all presents were unanimous. It could change the balance of power in the air and tip it back toward the Axis.

One man was also standing there, a little apart from the crown. It was the minister of industry and armament, Albert Speer. Seeing the plane roaring in the sky above him, he was already calculating how many of those wondrous machines he could make. Petrol would not be a problem, they had plenty. Resources, the same. And they had the factories to make them. He smiled outwardly. With these planes, maybe they could sweep the Allies out of the skies.

# The Stalingrad breakthrough
## More disasters on the Volga

After being pretty much stopped by the German counter-offensive in late December 1943, Zhukov had also had his victory over Rommel's Middle East army. Our army group, while being able to return to Stalingrad, was in terrible shape. The Soviet tank corps and the riffle army that had been sent against the German army group had had so much success that it even could enter the outskirts of the city, right by the Volga. As the Romanian forces had melted away on the flanks, the Stavka quickly recognized that they had a golden opportunity to shake the Axis frontline to its core.

While the Wehrmacht was busy licking its wounds in the centre of the front and looked worryingly at the Don and Southern Volga situation, the Red Army threw in all its reserves and new units into the cauldron of fire.

By January 10th, the Russians had cleanly broken thru the front on Don's south side, representing the left flank of the Stalingrad position. During that same time, an attack was conducted on the city of Astrakhan, at the mouth of the Volga, and by the Caspian Sea. The city fell within a day since it had only been held by a division of French SS volunteers that retreated in disorder after being severely mauled by superior forces.

With no real instructions from OKW at the time (that was still trying to get a grip on the situation thousands of miles away in Berlin) Rommel, did not need any grand strategic thinking to see that Stalingrad was threatened. Indeed, the whole Don, Lower Don, and Caucasus theaters were threatened with total collapse. There wasn't much in terms of troops behind the lines. Simply said, no reserve to speak of since everything had been used in re-establishing the situation created by the fall-early winter Bagration offensive. Indeed, considerable forces were still needed by Manstein that, while he had established a somewhat stable frontline, was engaged in furious combats with the Yvan's all over his area.

On the 11th, just after the terrible news of the Russian breakthrough in the north and the fall of Astrakhan, Rommel ordered a full evacuation of the city that would be left for the Red Army. It was either that or stay in place and be encircled and ultimately destroyed. Rommel also had in mind the survival of his forces to fight another day, from a better position.

The Russian, for their part, sent more and more troops to the area. Army Group South commander, Von Kleist, tried as best he could to plug the gaping holes in his frontlines and called for reinforcements.

*The new Mareth Line*
**January 15th, 1944**

# THE MARETH LINE IN 1944

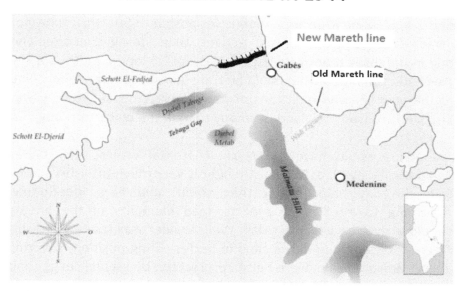

Silently tapping on his cigarette that dimly lit the surrounding dark about him, Walder looked over the small ridge he was standing on. They'd taken the position a day earlier, as per the general evacuation of Tunisia, that had gone well, in retrospect. They'd spent their nights driving hard and hiding during the day from the damned Allied planes. Several close calls with the enemy that had broken thru to the Mediterranean sea as well, but for the most part, what was left of his heavy panzer battalion was safely behind serious fortifications.

The Mareth line was a system of fortifications built by France in southern Tunisia in the late 1930s. The line was intended to protect Tunisia against an Italian invasion from its colony in Libya. The line occupied a point where the routes into Tunisia from the south converged, leading toward Mareth, with the Mediterranean Sea to the east and mountains and a sand sea to the west.

Since it faced the wrong way, German and Italian engineers had decided to build a new Mareth line, located a little north of the French line, near Gabes, on the Akirit river, that emptied in the Mediterranean Sea (right flank). At the same time, its left side was covered by a large saltwater lake called the Shot-El-Fedjed. The place was a near-perfect defensive position, but this time for invaders coming *from* Tunisia. A river, then strong concrete, and dug-in defenses that at its largest was not 15 km in width. So, the Axis had dismantled what could be transported from the French line to the new line and built tons of new emplacements. Artillery was also shipped from Italy and Germany to man the place correctly.

The Allies would have to attack in frontal waves, and it was generally believed, as Walder thought it very much after his survey tour the day before, that they could hold here indefinitely. According to intelligence reports, lead elements of the enemy should arrive the very next day. Well, Walder was ready. All of his Tigers had been dug in the sand in perfect firing position, covering every angle. They were also protected by sands bags and camouflaged properly from air attacks. He thought that it would take the devil himself to dislodge Panzerarmee Afrika from this fortification.

**Back in Tripoli, January 15th, 1944**

(...)The events which led to my return – for the third time- in Tripoli must be described in detail, as they are a testament to the courage, skills, and determination of the German fighting soldier. Again, I must emphasize how dedicated were the soldiers under my command, facing such odds and overwhelming difficulties(...)

(...) Our position at the end of December 1943 was far from satisfactory. While our forces maintained some offensive and defensive power semblance, it was continually losing strength from the multitudes of attacks from the air. Regardless of the gallant and mighty effort the Luftwaffe put into the skies, the Allies still were able to inflict an over-abundance of attrition on our forces. Camouflage and protection from the air quickly became of paramount importance to any sane field commander.

Furthermore, and compounding the problem, the Allies enjoyed a vast quantitative superiority over our forces on the ground. The army of Afrika I had under my command was a potent force. But it was fighting at a horrible estimated 1:4 ratio, which was not sustainable, especially for the fact that OKH and OKW, even the Italians, for god's sake, had no more reinforcements to send us. Indeed, the Reich and its allies were trying to fend off a disaster in the east. In doing so, the Axis used up all the available and trained reserves of the ground forces.

So, the meeting held in Milan between me, theater commander Rundstedt, and OKW chief of the general staff Halder (January 2nd) didn't linger too long on the apparent necessity of evacuating the entirety of Tunisia. To do so, the Regina Marina would sortie, with all available transports, to ferry about half of Panzerarmee Afrika back to Sicily. Then again to Italy, while the rest of the force, that was already concentrated in the south, would retreat to a new defensive line near Libya.

Back in Tripoli the very next day, I issued the necessary orders for the evacuation moves to happen as fast as possible. I also stressed the importance of moving only at night (to avoid Allied airstrikes) and leaving a strong rearguard on the still somewhat quiet frontlines (the Allies seemed busy with consolidating).

The southern part of the retreat went well, most of the troops safely behind the new Mareth defensive line by January 14th. The northern evacuation was a little bit harder since the Allied air force reacted quite strongly to seeing the Regina Marina near Tunis. Large air battles then happened between the Axis air force and the Allied air armadas' combined power. In the end, the Italians were less a couple of capital ships and plenty of damaged ones. Still, they were able to evacuate over 100 000 Germans, 85 000 Italians, and even a Spanish corps (25 000). These forces would come in handy for the hard fights ahead in 1944 and 1945(...)

## Carinhall, private retreat of the Fuhrer
### January 12th, 1944

Goering thought, foggily, that he had never endured such pain. It was, quite understandably, excruciating. If the man had been a little more aware of his surroundings and actual situation, he would have remembered that this was not the first time he was in such pain. He'd tried to dispel his Morphine spell addiction many times over the years.

The Fuhrer was a drug addict since the beerhall putsch (Munich putsch) in 1923. During the struggle leading to their ultimate failure, he had received a bullet in the groin. Seemingly innocuous at the time, the injury would plague him for the rest of his life. For at the beginning, he had been under such pain that the doctors had prescribed morphine to abate it. He had become hooked on the substances and never really shook it off.

His new position as Fuhrer of the Third Reich had first thrilled him to no ends, but rapidly the crushing weight of leadership pressure made him take more and more drugs, to the point that one day he realized that something had to be done about it.

He had ordered his SS bodyguards and Heydrich himself to surround Carinhall and sever his link to the drug the hard way. By total abstinence. Only food and medical care were brought to him, even if he clamored, no ordered and threatened, for his fix.

The whole ordeal had started four days ago and would last probably another four or five, after which he would still have the craving but would stop having such pain. During his half-conscious moments, he remembered why he was there and steeled himself to finish it. And then a minute later, he was back into the deep pain cave and would beg for a fix.

## Halifax, Nova Scotia, Dominion of Canada
### January 22nd, 1944

Churchill was on the large and impressive harbor installations of the city of Halifax. Dubbed the largest military naval facility in Canada, it boasted naval shipyards that we're busy building new ships of war for his majesty's navy. It was also the central hub for the western wing of the British Isles and Ireland invasion.

From Halifax would set forth an armada of the likes had not been seen in human history. Hundreds upon hundreds of ships would sail under the combined flags of the Allied nations operating them. Battleships, aircraft carriers, submarines, destroyers, and cruisers would all be dedicated to protecting the most important cargo of all within the fleet, the infantrymen, airmen, and tankers that would do the fighting in Ireland and retake the ground lost to the Axis in 1940.

Most of the ships were already in the harbor and would be ready to go soon. Looking at all the assembled masts, Churchill was overwhelmed by the numbers of them. Never in his wildest dreams had he imagined that so many ships could be built and then gathered in one venue for war.

Soon, he would be aboard the newly built battleship Canada, that had sailed forth from Quebec city(it had been constructed in the Levis shipyards). He would see to the honor guard and also talk to the sailors with words of encouragement. Then the meeting with American general Eisenhower, the overall commander in chief of the Iceland-United Kingdom theater, on the details of the Allied landing in both Ireland and Scotland.

It would be the grandest naval invasion in the whole history of humankind.

## Oval office
## Washington D.C. , January 23rd , 1944

It was finally time, thought the US president satisfactorily. In front of him was a glowing report on Pearl Harbor and the Pacific theater's overall situation. According to the paper in front of him, Admiral King (overall navy commander) and general Macarthur (army commander, Pacific) said that everything was ready.

The Japanese would never know what hit them. The multitude of naval reinforcements of 1943 and the ones en-route from the latest productions would make for a vast fleet of ships that could challenge and defeat the Japanese imperial might at sea.

In his report, King had outlined that the first operation would encompass the liberation of Johnson's atoll, Midway Island and Wake Island. He was also of the mind that Yamamoto would not resist making a sortie with the Jap fleet. It would be a fight to remember, but America could afford the losses it would probably take there. Hundreds upon hundreds of new navy pilots were in the pipeline, as well as over ten carriers that should roll on the waves no later than mid-end 1944.

For himself, Macarthur had described in detail the "island-hopping" campaign he had devised. The strategy called for circumventing Japanese strong points by interdicting them from the air with their large bomber forces (B-29'S, B-17's, even carrier strikes)) and only landing on the islands that they could use for their planes to make bombings further away. Once isolated, these Japanese strong points (like the Truk atoll in the southeast Pacific) would wither and die, especially when the Jap navy would be defeated, since then they would receive no reinforcements.

Finally, the submarines, able to project to Australia with the liberation of Hawaii, would sail and attack Japanese shipping that brought the precious resources (oil, rubber, steel) to Imperial Japan.

Roosevelt leaned back in his chair, rocked it slightly, and lit an excellent cigarette. He inhaled deeply, in the satisfying manner of a happy man.

# CHAPTER 1

# Extracts from Von Manstein's 1958 book, LOST VICTORY
## The winter 1943-1944 campaign

(...)While we were fighting for our very survival in the center, the Eastern Front's southern wing was simultaneously the scene of a struggle at least as significant. The issue was not just about the fate of a city and the beleaguered units retreating with every possible difficulty, but of the entire southern wing and ultimately all Caucasus.

This struggle was spared the tragedy of defeat, being ultimately marked – for one of the last times in World War II- by a brief glimpse of victory. In the face of an enemy whose manifold superiority offered him every chance of success, the German command had to improvise again and again, and the fighting troops to perform unparalleled feats(...)

(...)Though its end was marked by neither the fanfares of victory nor the muffled drum-beats which accompanied the many soldiers that gave the ultimate sacrifice, this battle still deserves recording. As a withdrawal operation, it must inevitably be devoid of glory. Yet the fact that, far from ending in defeat, it offered the Supreme Command one more chance of achieving at least military stalemate was possibly more than an ordinary victory.

To appreciate the significance of this decisive campaign on the southern wing and the magnitude of the dangers it involved, we must briefly consider the operational position at its inception.

In the winter of 1942-1943, Russia's military resources had only sufficed to halt the German attack on Moscow and the German campaign as a whole. Then, in the Summer of 1943, the tide had again surged over the USSR's capital, only to ebb by itself by the simple fact that the Reich was at the end of its operational capability.

At the beginning of 1944, the enemy, at last, felt strong enough to wrest the initiative from us. It had already given a big blow with the Bagration offensive, and now it would try to send the killing stroke while we were momentarily stunned and out of balance. The question subsequently was whether that winter would bring the decisive steps toward Germany's defeat in the east.

There were two reasons why the Soviet high command could hope to attain this goal in the south of the Eastern Front. One was the Russian forces' extraordinary numerical superiority; the second was the favorable position it found itself in operationally due to the German errors of leadership associated with sending Army Group South toward Saratov and an area that couldn't be adequately supplied.

Let me give a short account of the strategic situation at the start of that winter campaign in South Russia. The German front ran a somewhat straight line from occupied Leningrad, down up to the Don Bend, near Stalingrad. There it was broken by sizeable Soviet formation having created a large salient after their victory over the Hungarian army on the Don and Rommel's retreat from the city he could have defended if he had not lost most of his offensive force in some fool errand in the Russian steppes. The center of the front, pivoted by Moscow, Tula, and the line in front of Voronezh, was still the stage for very heavy fighting. The Russians weren't getting thru our re-constituted defenses there, but they were trying.
Then, there was the grave and unmanageable breakthrough of a Soviet rifle corps at Astrakhan by the Caspian Sea shore. Unmanageable because there was no reserve to speak of to send to

try to block their advance. Indeed, the Soviet High Command would not fail to send more troops through that gap if we didn't address it most energetically.

The enemy, whose armies formed a "Moscow Front," a "Voronezh Front," a "Southwest Front," and a "Caucasus Front," had not only superior forces in the line but also robust reserves behind these army groups further back in the hinterland. From my standpoint, their numbers might have been unlimited. It would not have made a difference since anyway. The front was only so large as the number of units you could cram in it. And the line was full of Soviet troops. And always more than we could kill. Sometimes even more than the ammunition we carried to battle.

This contrasted strongly with the Axis position, which, apart from Moscow's north to Voronezh, did not entertain a continuous line of troops handling its defenses. This meant for all instances and purposes that the Russian forces could and would continuously find and exploit holes or gaps between our units.

Hence the importance of my "fire brigades" battalion concept in the mobile strategy tactic. Operate the line as best as we could, and then counter-attack strongly with highly-mobile forces when the enemy broke thru where we weren't there.

During these grave times, a conference was called in Smolensk, where the 3 top men from OKW flew in to discuss strategy. Kleist, the Southern Army Group commander, was also called, as was I. We met on the 20th of January when the situation was a dire as could be. The whole front was deeply jeopardized, and now the enemy was not even 200 kilometers from Rostov, at the mouth of the Caucasus, and threatening Groznyy in the center of it. From Kleist's own words over the matter, we were but a week from complete collapse.

Losing Rostov, and consequently, the Caucasus would have dire consequences for the Reich and its allies. This meant that the land link between the Middle East and the refineries in Germany would be severed. The precious oil would still travel thru Turkey and by boat from Alexandria. Still, the Reich's needs were significant for the substance, and we had just completed the necessary rail modification and repairs (with armies of Russian prisoners of war) for it to roll northward. It also meant losing the oil wells of Maikop and Groznyy, two other quite productive areas – and a lot closer to the fatherland-. What would stop the USSR from launching offensives against the Middle East once it re-conquered the Caucasus? The scarcity of our military units in Persia, Turkey, and Iraq made it very likely that we would lose the theater altogether.

While we were all getting to the meeting, Kleist had not been idle on the grave matter at hand. He had been able to cobble up together a scratch division from scattered units across his command and railed them to Groznyy, so at least a military unit would be in place to receive the Russian Riffle corps bearing down on it. Reinforced by the remnants of the French SS volunteer's division, it was hoped it would hold for the time it took for us to re-establish the situation.

With its battered infantry corps and panzer division, Rommel was making good speed toward Rostov. Kleist remaining units under his command were also gathering in the city to fight to the finish with the immense forces coming down the don river.

At the meeting, the three men representing the High Command were very forthcoming and accommodating to find a solution. A very refreshing sight from the bad times of Hitler, Keitel, and Jodl. We all decided that units would be transferred to Kharkov to gather the necessary offensive forces for a counter-attack at the right flank of the Russian armies bound to besiege Rostov.

Ribbentrop had already been ordered to fly to Ankara to ask the Turkish government to release one or both of the two corps it maintained for civil order in its own country. They would be badly needed in the defensive line we discussed organizing in the Caucasus mountains. The Middle East command, already barebone thin from the successive depletion of its units because of other fronts needs, was again deprived of an additional division to man a line operated from the Caspian Sea to the Black Spain in the high mountains of the area.

I was named in charge of the counter-offensive from Kharkov and would need to take several of my most robust units out of the battleline near Moscow and Voronezh to make the newly named "Army Group Don" a reality. Halder also proudly announced that he had received the Fuhrer's approval to release the last reserve corps in Germany, consisting of 3 new SS divisions that had been earmarked for Africa by Goering. Now that we were evacuating the area there, fewer forces would be needed. We even also talked about railing two of the divisions that would eventually land in Italy. And there, for the first time, I heard Walter Model talking about the possible evacuation of the British Islands to shore up our defenses elsewhere in Europe. I remember being appalled at this admission by the general but thought it might not be possible to avoid it. A desperate measure by any means, but potentially the only solution we had at the time, according to the manpower figures and the units we badly needed to fend off the Russian hordes or the Western Allies that were bound to push hard on Spain and Italy.

We all left with only one possible outcome if we failed in this winter campaign: Germany was throwing its last reserves in the cauldron, and there could be no mistaking what would happen if the Soviets bested us in this struggle for survival.

# The Battle of Midway
### Somewhere between Wake Island and Midway Island, February 7th to 11th 1944,

One could say that the party was over for the Japanese Empire. Any observer would have been able to see the crushing (and still growing) US fleet quantitative and qualitative superiority.

The fleet sailing somewhere between Midway and Wake Island was simply enormous. It was the most significant concentration of naval power to date in history. First, there were the veterans of the war so far, that had survived from the many battles of 1942 and 1943. Aircraft carriers Saratoga, Enterprise, Wasp, Yorktown, Hornet, Essex, and Lexington II, accompanied by their smaller escort and light counterparts; Bogue, Independence, Princeton. They were protected by the powerful battleships California, Tennessee, South Dakota, Colorado, West Virginia, the French Lorraine, and many cruisers, light cruisers, and destroyed that numbered in the hundreds. All were afloat this day for the showdown with the Imperial navy.

What made the fight one-sided was that an appreciable number of reinforcements had since joined the veterans. Namely, the aircraft carriers Yorktown 2, Bunker Hill, Intrepid, with their smaller counterparts (escort and light carriers) Belleau Woods, Cowpens, Casablanca, Monterey, Casablanca 2, Casablanca 3, Langley, Bataan. Also present were the pristine and modern, following battleships: Alabama, Iowa, and several others. And then a flurry of lighter vessels as well.

The armada had over 1300 embarked carrier planes. It was more than enough to swamp the Japanese fleet that hadn't changed much since the start of the war. It still had the competent carriers Akagi, Zuikaku, Shokaku, Soryu, and Hyryu, which were helped out by their lighter counterparts Junyo, Unyu, Ryuho, Chiyoda, Hosho, and Kaiyo, making for roughly 650 to 700 carrier planes total. But it was a far cry from the American offensive capability.

They were protected by the same array of battleships (the ones that had survived so far) than at the war's start, namely the Yamato, Musashi, Yamashiro, Mutsu, Ise, Kongo, and Haruna, plus about 75 vessels of smaller sizes and types.

So, one could not blame Yamamoto for his less aggressive stance than in past engagements. Yes, he had the large airfields full of planes in Wake and Midway (about 400 more) that he could call on for attacking and supporting his fleet. Still, the admiral had no intention of first positioning himself in a way where the battle would be joined entirely or trying to get a gun duel like he had the year before in Hawaii. Japan simply could not take the casualties.

Roosevelt's warning to Japan had come through. He had covered the sea in steel and might. Furthermore, the American intelligence service was "reading Japan's mail" and had broken their naval codes, so knew pretty much what the enemy planned and where it moved. Admiral Nimitz, confident with all its powerful armada, launched a first devastating 1000 planes strike on Midway since he knew that Yamamoto's fleet was 1500 kilometers away. Then about three hours later, the fleet's numerous battleships shore bombarded anything that was left moving, so by the middle of the 7th, the whole Island had been neutralized, and the 4th marine division could land on the Island to reclaim it. Some fierce battle would surely be coming their way as the Americans had learned – the hard way- that Jap soldiers did not surrender, but in the end, the outcome was not in doubt. Then on the morning of the 10th of February, the large American fleet was in sight of their next objective, Wake Island. By that time, Yamamoto had positioned himself properly and maintained radio silence, so the US Navy would have to detect them if they wanted to find him and his ships.

Wake Island was not under radio silence as it was useless to try to hide land, and so after the multitude of seaplane search units went in all probable direction where the American fleet could be found. They detected it and relayed the American's position on broadband and in the clear since they knew that the combined Japanese fleet was in the vicinity and thus received their communication.

By 10h30 on the 10th, the brave multitude of Japanese embarked carrier planes were lifting off toward the eastern horizon. Their target was the US fleet that they found flying over it a couple of hours later. They were joined, or more or less followed, by a large airstrike from the planes on Wake island. Over 500 planes dived or dropped torpedoes on the 1st US carrier task force.

Furious dogfights ensued, and planes fell on both sides, their flaming debris hitting the sea at full speed or blown up in the sky. While the Japanese had the edge in quantity, their fearsome zero planes, known across the Pacific for their powerfulness, had met their match with the US Wildcat planes (F3F model). It had better engines, better climbing capability, better armor, and more powerful guns. The kill ratio was well in favor of the American flyers, but the sheer size of the Japanese raid (over 600 planes) overwhelmed the air and flak defenses, so they planted many torpedoes and bombs into the US capital ships that day. Both heavily hit by three torpedoes each, the Enterprise and Yorktown ended up sinking in a fury of fire and explosions a couple of hours later, while the Essex, receiving a torpedo and three bombs on its deck, was heavily damaged. For itself, the Saratoga survived the ordeal with only one torpedo in its flank, with a list to starboard, but still able to process plane operations. The Japanese flyers left the area victorious and with a shattered US fleet.

They'd lost over 150 planes in the raid, but no matter. It represented a great success. Unfortunately for the Japanese, they had only crippled the first US task force. The second, third and fourth were still afloat, and in the interval, had also launched a rugged, all-destroying strike on Wake Island. They'd also detected one of the Japanese task forces containing the fleet carriers Akagi and Hiryu, protected by ten cruisers, 20 destroyers, and the battleships Musashi and Mutsu. They didn't linger too long in sending a strike with 350 planes toward the task force.

The Americans timed their raid perfectly, it seemed, for they arrived just at the time that the almost gasoline-empty Jap planes were landing back on the decks of both carriers and the light carrier Chiyoda. Another very short but intense dogfight ensued. Several American dive bombers got thru the combat air patrol fighters' line to plant several torpedoes in both the Akagi and Hiryu. The Akagi, receiving five of them, exploded on the fourth and fifth one since the explosions had reached the ammunition magazines. A large pillar of fire climbed high in the sky, followed by dark-grey smoke, showering debris all over the sea. A large loomed large over the churning, debris-riddled sea. The Hiryu didn't fare much better. After receiving four solid hits, it sunk three hours later, amidst fire, confusion, and gushing water from the gaping holes produced by the American weapons. The Chiyoda also disappeared from the waves. Musashi received one torpedo, shrugged off by its armor, and the rest of the task force was lightly damaged.

On the night of the 10th, the American battleship and landing task force arrived at Wake, only to shell it to oblivion during the night, rendering the airfield inoperable. On the 11th in the grey morning that ensued, the numerous marine forces (5$^{th}$ marine division) landed to slug it out with the shell-shocked Japanese defenders. The fight would be brief but sharp. By the 12th, the Island was flying the stars and stripes again.

At dusk on the 11th, the Japanese fleet detected an American task force again. Yamamoto decided to gamble and sent in all remaining planes from Zuikaku, Shokaku, and Soryu on the grouping of ships that seemed to contain several smaller aircraft carriers and a massive battleship. The admiral knew that the pilots would have some difficulties finding their home carriers again with the fading light, but he decided it was worth it. The 200 or so Japanese planes arrived at 4 PM over the American fleet centered on the new super-battleship Montana, escorted by the light carriers Cowpens, Casablanca, and Belleau Wood. These scrambled their planes and slugged it out with the zeroes and Val bombers but were unable to fend off the plane strike, that succeeded in  sinking the Belleau Wood and Cowpens, also planting three bombs into Montana, that pretty much shrugged it off with its powerful armor.

On the way back, a couple of squadrons of Japanese planes did not find their carriers, and so the strike itself returned with less than 100 aircraft.

During that night, Admiral Yamamoto decided to retire to Japan at full speed, having received the reports that the game was up at Wake and Midway, while there had been no more news of Johnson Island for a while. The Americans found the Japs again on the 12th in the morning and launched one last strike that damaged the Zuikaku and the Soryu and sunk two Cruisers (Takao and Aoba).

The battle of Midway  was over, with some sense of Japanese tactical success, but a clear American strategic victory. The three islands (Wake, Midway, and Johnson) had  been liberated, and the Heavier  losses on the  US navy side did not matter since  they had a

lot more coming up down the production line. The Japanese had lost two fleet carriers that would hardly be replaced, widening the gap in  carrier forces disparity. Also,  most  of the last experienced pilots left to Japan were gone(the fleet was returning to home waters with less than 100 of them), and their replacement would never be as good. The fact of the matter was that Japan did not produce enough experienced pilots compared to the Americans.

# Status of capital ships on both sides at the end of February 12<sup>th</sup>, 1944

| | |
|---|---|
| BB Yamato --- | BB California --- Heavily damaged |
| BB Musashi --- moderate damage | BB Tennessee --- |
| BB Yamashiro --- | BB South Dakota lightly damaged |
| BB Mutsu --- | BB Colorado --- moderate damage |
| BB Ise --- | BB West Virginia --- lightly damaged |
| BB Kongo --- lightly damaged | BB Lorraine --- |
| BB Haruna --- lightly damaged | CV Saratoga --- lightly damaged |
| ~~CV Akagi --- sunk~~ | ~~CV Enterprise --- Sunk~~ |
| CV Zuikaku --- light damage | CV Wasp --- |
| CV Shokaku --- heavy damage, heading for Japan | ~~CV Yorktown --- Sunk~~ |
| CV Soryu --- heavy damage, heading for Japan | CV Hornet --- Moderate damage, being repaired |
| ~~CV Hyryu --- sunk~~ | CV Essex --- heavy damage |
| ~~CVL Chiyoda --- sunk~~ | CV Lexington II --- undamaged |
| CVL Junyo --- | ~~CVL Belleau Woods --- Sunk~~ |
| CVE Unyu --- | ~~CVL Cowpens --- sunk~~ |
| CVL Ryuho --- | BB Montana --- lightly damaged |
| CVL Hosho --- | CV Yorktown II --- |
| CVE Kaiyo --- | CV Bunker Hill --- |
| | CV Intrepid --- |
| | CVE Casablanca --- |
| | CVE Casablanca 2 --- |
| | CVE Casablanca 3 --- |
| | CVE Casablanca 4 --- |
| | CVL Monterrey --- |
| | CVL Langley --- |
| | CVL Bataan --- |
| | BB Iowa --- |
| | BB Alabama --- |

## *Wolfsschanze, East Prussia*
### *Masurian Woods, Fuhrer bunker, February 15th, 1944*

Hermann Goering, presiding a meeting of OKW for only the second time since his accession to power the year before, looked sharp. He had lost weight, had his keen, smart look restored, and looked the part of a warlord.

According to rumors, the Fuhrer had been able to get rid of his drug habit(for now). The result was striking. Gone were the haggard looks, empty eyes sockets, far away attitude. Back was the sharp, intelligent, and strong man that came to power in Nazi Germany years before.

He had already had a meeting with Albert Speer, the minister of armament, who left a meeting with his leader a happy man for the first time. They had agreed to take some steps to rationalize production and make sure that the ME 262 would come to be produced in great numbers. A very efficient administrator, Speer would make sure that the jet fighter (that could, in most minds, change the course of the war in the air) would be present in sufficient numbers on the battlefield.

Another signal that things had changed was that Goering had decided to hold the meeting at the Wolf's Lair, Hitler's symbol of power and organization. The place was superbly suited as a war HQ, and Goering wanted to show that he was back in business by holding the meeting there.

Notwithstanding these facts, Hermann was still the same, vain man, that lusted for power and position. He would always be more of a problem than a solution for Germany and its war effort. But he had come to realize that he had achieved the Apex of leadership in Nazi Germany and didn't need to pursue it as blatantly as before. The Reich's success as a whole – and not just Goering little Empire and Luftwaffe- would be his glory and power now. So, once in a while, he would show a brief glimpse of sharpness like that day of February 1944.

He had called all the leading generals of OKW (Oberkommando der Wehrmacht) and OKH (Oberkommando der Heer), Kriegsmarine, and Luftwaffe. It was to be a crucial meeting. During the three hours it was held, several key aspects were agreed on. First of all, the Reich would immediately stop building any ships, except for the ones already under construction. The Kriegsmarine had grown exponentially but had failed to be the strategic weapon of decision Hitler and Raeder had sought. It had been unable to fend the Allies in the North Sea, so now they were poised to land in Scotland.

The fleet's resources would consequently be allocated to the Luftwaffe, Goering pet project since the 1930s. The move was seen as sound for everyone except Raeder since they needed planes. A LOT more planes. ME 262 would be mass-produced, along with several other new jet planes coming along the development line.

In the last part of the meeting, the subject of the country's over-extension had been discussed. Walter Model, from OKW, had presented the facts for the Eastern front. The Russians were attacking at the ratio between 5:1 to 7:1, and it was getting worse. The pre-war production estimates of the Abwehr were wildly off the mark. The Russians had an incredible production capability, probably 7 to 10 times greater than the Axis. All the territory they'd lost in 1942 and 1943 amounted to no effect on their ability since they had moved most of it over the Urals, quite out of the Wehrmacht reach.

While they didn't produce that much quality, they did have the numbers. As good as the Tigers were, they would always be swamped by 6 to 10 T-34's. The Russians also had built excellent planes in the Sturmoviks and were fielding them in ever greater numbers. So, the real problem was that the eastern armies would not be able to hold the flood of Soviet soldiers, tanks, and planes forever. While attrition was a genuine problem for the Reich, it did not seem to be an issue for the USSR that had an endless stream of fresh meat to throw in the cauldron of fire.

Model had then argued for the German command to evacuate a couple of areas of the conquered territories to free up forces to fight the Russian hordes and try to reach some military stalemate because there were no more doubts about the incapability of Germany to conquer Russia. It was brought about by the ratio of forces, production capability, numbers of enemies, and logistics. Finally, they did also have the powerful Western Allies to fight, after all).

So, in the end, one suitable theater of war could be evacuated with some sense of short-term gains: the British Islands. The battle order was twenty division of infantry and two armored in the United Kingdom, and another five (one armored) in Ireland. These forces were relatively fresh, at full strength, and experienced. Besides, argued Goering and Paulus to support Model's views, once the Allies invaded Scotland and Ireland, more troops would need to be sent to the Islands to keep them, something that the Reich was incapable of doing.

"The decision has been reached," had grandly announced Goering, that only two divisions and some security forces would be kept in the United Kingdom and one in Ireland. The rest would be ferried across to France and Germany, to be railed to the Eastern front. The Kriegsmarine, strong enough or not, and ready or not, had been entrusted with fending off the Allies from the islands. A task it was not equipped adequately to do. But in the end, there was no choice, as much for Raeder that grudgingly approved of the plan, as for shoring up the Reich strategic position. All the forces freed up from Tunisia's evacuation that had needed to be ferried to Europe would be sent at best speed to the Eastern Front. The 4th panzer, 11th, 12th heavy panzer battalions (to be refitted with King Tigers tanks that were shortly becoming operational), 13th and 18th motorized division 131st, 145th, 222nd infantry divisions, and finally the SS Das Reich mechanized division. Numerous Spanish and Italian forces were now either in Southern Italy or Spain, but these would have to stay in theater, Franco wanting his troops back in Spain for the expected attack on his homeland.

On the production front, an unprecedented effort had been demanded of Albert Speer and the OKH to field more divisions. The Fuhrer had asked for 20 more infantry, five motorized, and five armored by the end of 1944, notwithstanding the reinforcements that the actual forces would need.

The situation was dire for the Reich, but there was still some hope. Several new weapon developments, along the lines of the revolutionary ME 262, would soon come to the production lines. Guided air to sea missiles, weaponized rockets, a canon of unimaginable power and scope, new tanks like the King Tiger were forecasted to be invincible on the battlefield. Some new bomber projects, some jet-powered, one 6-engined to bomb Amerika (with three working specimens already), and other wondrous things.

But for these weapons to have the miraculous impact the Reich leaders thought they could have, Germany would need to win some time. For if things went to a head in the east, the Reich would be swamped before it could retaliate in kind.

The assembled men in the room were confident. They had an entire industrial base, unlimited oil, and could harness a continent's resources and then some for their war machine.

## The Battle for Rostov part 1
### Frontline, February 14th, 1944

Artillery shells and explosions were swamping the ground. The Russian shelling had been going on for hours. The Axis had also been doing the same from their far-away positions in response. One just hoped that the enemy would not land a shell directly in its foxhole. With remnants of Romanian and Hungarian divisions, the German forces were sheltering as best they could in their foxholes or wooden bunkers on the outskirts of Rostov. A heavy battle had been taking place ever since the Red Army had broken thru on the Don and advanced to the town itself.

Rostov was the key to Axis land access to the Caucasus, for it was the last defensible position that linked it with the Ukrainian plains. Army Group South commander had rushed everything available. The 174th infantry division had so been moved by rail from Kharkov. It had been resting and refitting from the epic battles that it had fought near Belgorod. Several other battalion and regiment-sized units also were moved to the city for the desperate defense. The Russians had shown up with a full Rifle Infantry army and a powerful tank army, making life difficult for the men trying to hold on to the ground. At a ratio of 1:7, the Axis was hard-pressed to defend.

Fortunately for them, there was two heavy panzer battalion in defense of the city and a multitude of artillery and 88mm anti-tank guns. Earmarked initially for reinforcements to Stalingrad, it had never got there in time, and now that city was in Russian hands.

The Germans also had several regiment-size artillery units as well as a couple of Italian ones. So, all in all, the defense was not so bad, well supported by guns. It also seemed, for once, that the Luftwaffe had the mastery of the sky. Even if uneven because of the disparity

of forces, the fight was one that the Axis seemingly could handle, for the time being, well-entrenched as it was.

The soldiers hunkering down in place and hoping not to be hit by a shell on its head also expected the Russian assault to begin shortly, as it had been for several days. The Yvan's had the same tactic. Bomb the area to oblivion, then bomb it again, then send overwhelming numbers at the enemy. So far, the Axis forces had been able to repulse – or annihilate- all the waves of humans coming at them. Ammunition and supply, for one of the rarest occasions on the Eastern Front, were plentiful, so there was no way the Russians would be able to send more men than the Axis had bullets, for a change.

For Rostov was the central supply hub for the Caucasus and the Caucasian rail network's essential node. All the supplies that had initially been earmarked for Stalingrad and the rest of the units on the former Don-Volga frontlines had been stockpiled in the city for weeks. Without a final destination, because the Axis did not control those areas anymore, the army logistical types had accumulated it in place.

Rumors had it that a full corps was coming up from Germany to relieve the beleaguered troops heroically defending the city and that a powerful counter-offensive was being prepared. If only they could hold another week or so, had told them their commanders...

# Henchel tank factory
## Kassel, German Ruhr, February 20th, 1944

The Henschel und Sohn of Kassel (south of Hanover) in Germany had always been intimately involved with the Wehrmacht armored might. It was first established in the early 1800s as a builder of locomotives, and during World War, I undertook armament manufacturing. By the Second World War, the company was producing locomotives, tanks, diesel engines, trucks, airplanes, and artillery pieces. The tanks it manufactured included the Panzer I, II, III, Panther, Tiger I, and Tiger II.

Henschel was comprised of three general engineering works in and around Kassel. Werk I in Kassel was devoted to locomotive assembly and gun production. Werk II in the Rothenditmold area consisted of a large foundry, boiler, and other locomotive component shops. Werk III in Mittelfeld was primarily devoted to tank assembly and component manufacture.

The Mittelfeld Werkes were situated on both sides of a railway line running north and south. Looking north, those buildings on the left side of the railway line were used for manufacturing locomotive components and truck and engine repair. The main storage area for tank components was also on the track's left side, including sheds that held Tiger hulls and turrets. On the right side of the track were four main shops numbered 1, 2, 3, and 5. (Shop 4 was planned, and Speer had made sure it would be built by the end of 1944.). Tiger manufacturing took place in shops 3 and 5. An average of 18 to 22 tanks was carried at any one time in the factory and approximately 25 undergone final assembly every week. A far cry from the hundreds a Russian factory could pour out every week, but there was a notable difference in building quality. The Germans were known for precision building, and it showed in their war machines.

Unfortunately for them, so far in  the war in the east, quantity had been paramount over quality. But with the Tiger II and their smaller Tiger I brothers, things were about to change.

Henschel was at the epicenter of an extensive network of firms that produced components for the tank and transported them by rail to Henschel for final assembly. To give an idea of the network's scale, the armor plate for hulls and turrets were made by Krupp in Essen in Western Germany. Many of the 88mm guns were built by DHHV in Dortmund, not far from Essen. Engines came from Maybach in Friedrichshafen, well to the south near the Swiss border. The transmissions they would be connected to were built by Adler in Frankfurt, halfway back to Essen. Getting the completed turrets to Henschel was somewhat easier – Wegmann Waggon Fabrik (that was making them) was also based in Kassel.

Albert Speer, minister of armament for the Reich, was currently touring the crazy busy factory with his cronies. He wanted to emphasize the importance of the current Royal Tiger production to the workers, especially to the factory managers and the Henchel company owner. The Reich needed these machines of war.

He had toured the parking grounds for the finished machines a little earlier in the day and was amazed at the new panzer's size. The Tiger II was the Tiger I's successor, combining the latter's thick armor with the Panther medium tank's armor sloping. The tank weighed almost 70 tonnes and was protected by 100 to 185 mm (3.9 to 7.3 in) of armor to the front. It was armed with the long-barrelled 88mm long-barreled anti-tank cannon. It was thought to be almost impervious to any frontal attack and would fight nicely against the big machines the Red Army put up in the field.

As for the Allies, their lighter tanks would feel like paper to the

Royal Tiger's gun. Furthermore, the enemy's tanks puny guns would fire shells that would mostly bounce off the German panzer's incredible thickness. There were reports of heavier, better-gunned armor coming down the line for the American and British, but Speer thought it would not be a problem. If they could field these incredible machines of war in sufficient numbers on both fronts, it would be trouble for the enemy and incredible hitting power for the Wehrmacht.

Now, if only he could make the war industry produce more. He estimated that the Kassel factory would yield over 1000 in 1944. Not enough to stop the Allied masses by any means, but definitely enough to stiffen the spine of many a panzer unit.

# The Battle for Rostov part 2
## Frontline, February 27th, 1944

THE CAUCASUS SITUATION, FEB 27TH. 1944

LEGEND:

| | |
|---|---|
| Army-level Russian infantry units | |
| Corps-level Russian infantry units | |
| Army-level Russian armored units | |
| Corps-level Russian armored Units | |
| Corps-level German Infantry units | |
| Division-level German infantry units | |

The arrival of the 1st SS corps gave some new to the beleaguered city that had been resisting the assaults of the Soviet forces. They went directly from the rail depot, which was still held by the Axis, to the frontlines, mostly as infantry soldiers without their heavy weapons. For such was the emergency of the situation. The SS soldiers still at least had their riffles. They also carried submachine guns and big MG-42 heavy machineguns. General Blumenritt, one of the commanders on the scene, sent them all at once on a counter-offensive right into the center of the city to fend off a sizeable Russian advance that had happened the day before.

They went at it with all the fanatism and determination of the elite troops they were. The German artillery continued to pound the

Soviet forces to no ends, while their enemy counterparts also did the same. By dusk on the 27th, the fresh SS forces had retaken most of the lost ground and repulsed the Red army rifle division that had mastered the area earlier.

The fight had been going on for more than 15 days by now, and the Russians had occupied, inch by inch, and with a lot of spilled blood, the eastern and central part of the city. They could even see the Black Sea coast from their position. They were so close to victory. Rostov itself, one of the beautiful Russian towns before the war, had much suffered since the struggle between the USSR and the Third Reich. First, the German had stormed it in 1942 during their Barbarossa operation. They'd also bombed it many times before taking it. Now, the fight of two large armies was happening directly in its midst, creating so much destruction that not many buildings were still left standing or undamaged. From the pilots of both sides, that fought and died in the skies above, the whole area only seemed to be a pile of poorly strewn grey-dark rubble where smoke, explosions, and fire gushing out from everywhere.

All the while, the outlying troops had spilled across the countryside, taking a large swath of territory from the Axis. During that interval, Maikop had fallen, without hope of any counter-attack. The Soviet forces were nearing the base of the Caucasus mountains, where the last-ditch Axis defenses were being prepared. The Turkish had sent their last two corps to man some defensive line, helped by remnants of many a German, Italian and Romanian units that had been able to retire in some capacity (most were badly depleted) to the mountains.

The reality of the matter was that it was more than doubtful that the Axis would be able to retake the Caucasus north of the mountains and east of Rostov with the current state of their forces.

The best they could hope for was to push back the Russian attack from Rostov and establish a river line defense on the Don River, east of the city. It seemed like the mountains would be the new border in the south if the Axis succeeded in blocking the Soviet troops from further advances.

With the added strength of the SS corps and vigorous efforts by the Luftwaffe and numerous artillery pieces, the fight for the city had finally taken its toll on the Russian offensive that was showing signs of petering out.

Everyone on the German side hoped that the Wehrmacht would soon be ready for the offensive rumored for the last few weeks.

## Mareth Line
### Tunisian-Libyan border, February 28th, 1944

Fire! Yelled Walder. He was atop his turret, watching the large dust cloud that was swirling up in the air with the flurry of Sherman tanks driving on their position. The 88mm anti-tank shell seemed like a flash of light that quickly attained its destination: a poor Sherman tank penetrated cleanly by the Tiger round. The hole in the front of the tank glowed a bright red. A second later, the tank commander or some other American opened the hatch, leaving the way for a pillar of flame, followed by a soldier covered in fire, that crumpled awkwardly on the side of the tank.

All around them, rounds after rounds of artillery shells were falling, making the panzer's armor trickle with the noise of flying shrapnel. Two Tigers had been hit directly on the cupola, destroying them outright. All around them, other tanks were firing, making for what seemed like a gigantic firecracker show. The anti-tank guns PAK 43, all hidden safely behind the prepared bunkers of the Mareth Line, also added their fire to the maelstrom. He wondered why in hell, the Allied general wanted to attack again after the many other assaults that had been bloodily repulsed.

Having entrenched not far from the Axis defensive positions, the enemy had launched yet another attack after six hours of shelling from its numerous artillery pieces. So far, the German guns and grit were holding them at bay.

Not an hour before, the Mareth line had also endured a large air raid by the Allies. Utter devastation had been the results, but most bunkers had held, except those hit by a bomb that landed directly on them.

Walder wondered how long they would have to hold here, probably until they got swamped by superior numbers. This had seemed the norm now since the middle of 1942 in any of the fronts he'd fought. For him particularly, this would be his last days in the area, if he survived, of course. He had received his transfer papers to another stint on the Eastern Front, to command a new heavy panzer battalion. According to rumors, it would be with a new type of tank, the Royal Tiger, a 70 tons beast that he could hardly wait to get his hands on.

The war in the east was not going well, and while the one in Africa hadn't gone well either, at least they had somewhat stopped the Western Allies at Mareth's fortified line. He had heard thru the vines that the situation on the Eastern Front was genuinely worrisome. The Russians had hordes upon hordes of men and tanks with which they were swamping the Reich's braves forces.

He'd received his transfer papers from Guderian himself, as the general had also been recalled to Berlin for some other assignment that he still didn't know yet. Both of their guesses had been Spain, where the Allies were expected to land in force soon. Their hunch proved to be right, at least for the general.

Looking again with his binoculars at the dusty cloud, he didn't see as much movement as before. Many Allied tanks had been eliminated. The rest probably had had enough. He took the time to look around the German position itself. Alas, he could see many dark spots along the line of half-buried Tigers and other panzers. Many roasting fires of flesh were unmistakably fueled by human flesh, making for a horrid scene. And finally, several dark smoke columns pointed to destroyed German bunkers, machine gun nests, or panzers. And above all, the smell. The damning "sweet" smell of death and burning bodies.

But, the Mareth line was holding and would be for a long time still.

## "It was like being pushed by angels"
### First operational flight of the ME-262 jet fighter, February 28th, 1944

The reference to the impression of flying with angels had been made by Adolf Galland, German fighter ace, over the radio, to his men, upon taking off from the Spanish runway in Southern Spain. They were near Seville, where the central supply depots for the Axis armies in the area were located.

The German high command was expecting, any day now, an enemy landing, for this was, for the Allies, the next logical step. They had reached an operational limit in French North Africa. Without the ships to get supplies to the frontlines, the troops arrayed in Tunisia could hardly be expected to force the way into the Mareth line and even less to cross the sea to Sicily by foot. It could only stay in relative impotence, stuck there. The Allies needed ships to continue advancing in the Central Mediterranean and land in Italy to knock it off of the war. On the other hand, the Axis needed the Allied fleet to stay in the Atlantic. If not, this would mean trouble on the continent and an interruption of their numerous oil tankers bringing the substance into Naples harbor.

The Western Powers could only achieve this by the re-conquest of the sea's mouth at Gibraltar, where the Axis had heavily mined and gun-manned the straight with numerous artillery pieces. With the place reconquered, the way to the Mediterranean Sea would be open again.

They had tried to force their way with a powerful fleet but failed. They needed to take control of Southern Spain's ground to eventually assault the fortified positions that straddled the straight with enough firepower to destroy them.

The Allied air command had been blanketing Southern Spain with bombs in numerous bomber strikes to soften the defenses for when they attacked with their troops. By day, the American B-17's were pounding the cities, defensive positions, and anything else they could get their eyesight on. At night, the British took over operations with their Wellington and Halifax bombers.

They did so with relative impunity up to that fateful day of February the 28th, 1944, where the numerically and quantitatively superior American Mustang P-51's battled for the first time against what would become the most famous fighter of World War Two, the Messerschmitt 262 jet-propelled airplane.

Galland, one of Germany's highest-decorated ace, had been more or less removed from the frontlines in the last two years or so, promoted to positions of training and organization for the Luftwaffe. But he'd been so impressed by the performance and speed of the new fighter that he'd wanted in on its first mission. Hitler would have never agreed to it, but Goering was made of a different sort and understood the itch a fighter pilot could have, and so gave Adolf Gallant his blessing for a return to operational fighting.
As it happened, the first fight in the skies for the German jets would be filmed, as the American had brought a camera crew for propaganda and to shoot a recruiting movie. One could see all was quiet in the film, with usual crew chatter in the inner plane's radio. Suddenly the camera settled sharply right (it was located B-17 gunner canopy) in a quick turn around motion. Then had started the surprised shouts of the tail machine-gunners with a "what the hell was that." As a response, a ME-262, with its characteristics long nose and engines on each wing, was seen on film rocketing into view, for a fleeting, quick instant. The plane was going, after all, at over 825 kilometers per hour, while the top speed of the best

America had (the P-51) was barely a little over 700 km. The typical bomber went at just above 500km per hour. It seemed that the B-17 was still in the air while the German Jet fighter flew by. The film recovered several months later (it had miraculously survived), stopped there, as the bomber housing it was hit multiple times by the two auto canons of a ME-262, and went down in flame to spill itself on the rugged Spanish countryside.

For his part, Galland was making the most of his superior skills and was looking to get to 100 victories, as he had had 96 before being dismissed by Hitler in December 1942 over differences of opinions and put on the pilot training effort.

He had been sidelined by the old Fuhrer but intended to prove to the new one that he could still be relied upon to slug it out and win against the enemy. He lined up behind an enemy bomber that seemed immobile while at the same time merely outrunning a P-51 that had put itself on its tail. He loosed a series of canon bursts on the B-17, hitting it on its upper fuselage and completely exploding the rear gunner's canopy. The bomber pretty much opened like a tin can and disintegrated into mid-air.

A bit to his left, he could see another Luftwaffe pilot splitting a bomber wing with precision, making the enemy tumble down in grey-dark fires, with parachutes spewing out of its sides.

Galland's fighter, (no by God, he thought happily) his flying angel, just came across a lingering P-51 that was angling upward to take altitude. He caught to it in an instant, before the American could hide in the big white cloud looming close, and fired three bursts (the first two missing as the tracers arced around the enemy), the third hitting it on its tail and obliterating it, sending yet another Allied machine to its doom on the ground below. He shot past the falling fighter, looked back for an instant to see a parachute jutting out of the pilot's canopy.

The macabre German dance around the Allied bomber formation continued for another three or four minutes, killing another twenty-five US bombers and shooting down eight Mustangs. At that moment, the American squadron leader, that had just been shot down but still able to radio to his mates, ordered them to turn back and retreat before he crashed to his death.

The final tally of the day for the "Angel Squadron," as it would come to be called, was thirty-two B-17 and twelve Mustangs shot down.
No bombs would fall on Seville or on any spot in Southern Spain that day. The Germans had found a way to nullify western air power. On his way back to the airport, Galland was lost in his daydreaming. That of an all-conquering Luftwaffe with its jet fighters. If only German industry would provide enough of them to have a real impact on the war.

Throughout 1944 and 1945, German fighter production would concentrate on making jet fighters. It had the oil to fill its tanks, so the Allies would be in for a rough spot until they caught up technologically.

## Rommel at his best
### Crossing the Don, March 1st, 1944

"Enough is enough," said Rommel in his calm, usual manner. He stood up, knuckles still resting on the maps strewn about on the table in front of him. "We cross the Don here," said, putting his finger to the south part of the city. The general wasn't known for his placidity, even in defensive warfare. And he had had quite enough of retreating and hunkering down. Just not his style. And he had been doing so ever since his ill-fated offensive in the Volga Uplands beyond Stalingrad.

"Captain Luck," he said in his firm voice, addressing the commander of the first recon battalion of the 7th division. The man has been with the general for most of his battle since his first campaign in France. The officer stepped forward in front of the crowd of other men assembled in Rommel's makeshift HQ. "We will cross near the Vorochilovski bridge." The Germans had mined the bridge upon their arrival weeks earlier to block the Soviets from having easy access across the river. It wasn't destroyed yet as it had been untouched by enemy airstrikes, and also, the Germans held both banks of the river near it.

"We know Manstein is launching Operation Winter Storm today, and so we will help him," said Rommel with his characteristic smile. Everyone in the room knew that their mobile forces weren't strong enough to hope for any serious breakthrough on their own. But with the brunt of the attack being applied north of Rostov by Manstein's powerful and newly named Army Group Don, all the officers present could see that their general wanted to do the unexpected, again.

No one, not even OKW, expected Rommel's forces to attack, and it was precisely why the famed general wanted to do it. Rommel had

had a string of uninterrupted victories from 1940 to just recently when the army group under his command had been beaten back from Stalingrad from its foray into the Volga Uplands and offensive on Saratov. That defeat had stung the famous man to the core. But in the eyes of most of the men assembled in the room that worshipped him, it was hardly the legendary general's fault. The supply situation had been so dire that the units had to stop to await reinforcements and simple commodities like food and oil every two days or so. They were also insufficiently covered on their flanks by sub-quality troops, namely Romanians. Not necessarily bad soldiers, but the troops could not do much because they did not have the heavy weapons to fight off Russian tanks. They'd only had their wits and bravery, which was most often than not insufficient on the Eastern Front.

So, the real problem had been the Soviet attack on the Romanian corps covering the offensive's right flank. The supply situation had then compounded the disaster.

Captain Hans Von Luck, panzer commander of the recon battalion, clicked his heels and acknowledged his general's orders. Rommel then gave a flurry of instructions to the other officers.

Five hours later, the general was overlooking the crossing, being in the front as always, posing as a target on the Don's bank. He was standing erect, directing his troops, like he didn't have a care in the world, while people on his left and right fell, wounded or dead. He was beside his faithful recon man Von Luck, and they were discussing the problem of not having any smoke shells to cover the dingy boats trying to cross the Don. Everyone that went in the water was blown sky-high by Russian artillery. And so, Luck had called Rommel to ask for instructions. The response had been that the general came directly on site, and in a quick, snap-decision, ordered the three large silos of grains that were still standing half erect / half crumbling near the shore to be set afire. The tons upon tons of grain soon caught into a mighty fire that created so much smoke that the Germans were able to cross the Don, well covered from the Soviet's artillery and machine guns fire. "Here's your smoke, Von Luck' "had said the unorthodox general going about the next emergency that needed his attention.

Two hours later, a pontoon bridge was also completed while the infantry took hold on the other bank, and a stream of panzers (a mix of older Panzer IVs and new Panthers) started to come across. The Germans only had about 110 tanks left, and Rommel had decided to use them all in his counter-attack. They were a little on the soft side with no Tigers to stiffen their spine, but it would have to do, had thought the general.

Everything hinged on Manstein, making such an impact that the Soviets would need to send all available forces toward Army Group Don in the north to fend it off. At the same time, Rommel's leftover army group could wreak havoc behind the lines.

The battle for the opposite bank of the Don was sharp but brief. Three hours into the engagement, about half the panzer force was already rolling east and north to try to roll-up the besieging troops that would be hard-pressed to continue their attacks on the city. He would force them to defend from his counter-attack or make them retreat. With again the excellent Von Luck in front as a recon unit, the other half of the forces would drive straight east, as fast and as deep as possible, with orders to storm the city of Veselyy by any means possible. If this could be managed, the whole Russian supply situation would be un-hinged, as supplies inevitably passed thru this vital road junction. It would create a significant problem for the armies rampaging southward near Maikop, as much as the ones in front of Rostov.

On the 2nd, most of the Russian forces in front of Rostov were disengaging as best they could. Several Russian regiments and battalions simply surrendered under the pressure of units attacking from the city and the south along the river's bank. Rommel's attack was a complete success.

At that time, the Soviet southwest theater commander was also in dire trouble as Manstein's attack had come as a powerful un-welcome surprise. The Russian offensive had finally petered out, after a thousand miles advance from the Uplands to the edges of the Ukraine.

Apparently, the Reich could still bite vigorously, and the Soviets would learn about it the hard way in the next few months of battle.

## Somewhere in between Canada and Ireland
### Raider hunting, March 4th, 1944

They'd finally found the bastard of a ship that had been preying on Allied sea lanes. The German raider Courland, a 25 000 tons "pocket battleship" or heavy cruiser, had sunk several Allied ships making the naval routes south and north from the USA to Canada.

The German raider, 37 knots of pure speed and armed with three triple 300 mm turrets, was a dangerous foe. He was paired up with what the Germans called a wolfpack or U-Boat gathering attacking in groups. This particular group of Kriegsmarine ships had been prowling the waters for months, and the Bonaventure, along with an escort of ten destroyers, three cruisers, and two battleships, had been tasked to eliminate it.

It was a severe problem for the fleet that would eventually sail to invade Ireland and the United Kingdom. The German naval group was also preying on bigger ships like cruisers and even battleships since it had not just a cruiser but ten U-boats.

So far, the group had sunk over 120 000 tons of regular shipping, the cruiser Agamemnon (British), and four destroyers. It had had even an encounter with a task force headed by the battleship Malaya and two cruisers. It had ended with the U-Boat sinking the two cruisers and Malaya retreating at full speed north, severely damaged.

So, it was with great satisfaction that Seafire pilot Gaston Lamirande had lined up, from quite far away, on the broadside superstructure of the German raider. The damned Germans had been a real thorn in the Allied side for months. Goebbels propaganda had been blaring its exploits all over the radio waves. Everyone in the Western Power's camp was fed up with the raider. But now it was time for its reckoning. A recon flight had spotted the

Courland, and the Bonaventure had been close enough to be able to send an airstrike to try and destroy it.

Gaston was flying just 5 meters above the waves. It was almost like he could touch the sea, and if he wasn't careful, he could hit the water. But upon his torpedo attack training, there was no helping it. They needed to be dropped low in the water, and that was the maneuver he executed.

The distance closed unerringly fast. Lamirande felt sweat trickling down his face and back. Then seemingly out of nowhere, flak explosions around his plane. Looking closely, he could see the flash and brief glimpses of the red tracer shells coming his way. His speed and angle of attack was a challenging shot for the ship's flank gunners. For all the long seconds they blazed away at Gaston's plane, they either fired their explosive charges behind or too short. Lucky Gaston didn't get a scratch on his aircraft. Several of his squadron mates didn't have the same luck. The plane on his left and right both got downed and crashed hard in the sea to disappear almost instantly in the depths.

And then it was time. He pulled on the release arm for his torpedo on his naval-attack mode Seafire plane (it was called the Seafire-N1 variant), and off it was. Gaston immediately pulled up to swing his plane hard left to avoid flying over the Courland since that was a maneuver that had killed many a pilot. For a flak gunner, if there was a position that he could pin down with absolute accuracy, it was undoubtedly just above his ship. A plane flying just over would quite literally sly into a wall of fire.

The torpedo plunged hard and fast in the water to disappear to a depth of about 2 meters. It activated its built-in engine, and off it went toward its target. The Courland captain, experienced in these matters, called for a turn hard to port  and dropped his vessel's speed to nothing. He hoped that the torpedo would pass in front of the ship.

But, alas for the Kriegsmarine man, the torpedo hit amidship in a rugged, ear-splitting explosion. The ship shook violently, as most onboard were thrown to the floor, momentarily stunned or even hurt (and some seriously).

Gaston's torpedo had opened a gaping hole in the ship's hull, and almost immediately, tons upon tons of water gushed in the interior of the vessel. Simultaneously, the fire of the explosion raced through the Courland's compartments like balls of fires in the metal hallways. Many sailors were burned alive.

About 20 seconds later, the ship was hit by another torpedo, this time from Gaston friend's, August McIntyre. It crashed in the back of the boat and destroyed the rudder and internal engine. Lamirande, taking advantage of the hit and the fact that most sailors, panicked or dazed, were not busy operating their flak guns, made a strafing run on the decks of the ship. He riddled it with bullets, wreaked havoc on its wooden deck, and killed several Germans.

By then, the ship had a perceptible list, and it was apparent it would be sinking unless a miracle happened. The Courland's career was over, and the U-boats captains all around could only watch in impotence from their periscopes the fate of their fellow seamen.

Gaston, August, and the rest of the squadrons seven planes roared one more time over the stricken ship, wagged their tail in triumph, and flew away toward the Bonaventure. Lamirande signaled for the Allied ship not to come to pick up survivors since many of the men in the squadron had seen periscopes.

Another good day's work, smiled Lamirande inwardly. Life was good

# Extracts from Von Manstein's 1958 book, LOST VICTORY
## The Rostov Counterstroke, March 1st to March 7th

OPERATION WINTERSTORM MARCH 1ST TO 7TH 1944
Manstein and Rommel encircle the Soviets

LEGEND:

| | |
|---|---|
| | Army-level Russian infantry units |
| | Corps-level Russian infantry units |
| | Army-level Russian armored units |
| | Corps-level Russian armored Units |
| | Corps-level German Infantry units |
| | Division-level German infantry units |
| | Division-level German panzer units |

(...) After all the preparations of the last ten days and the concentration of forces to the new "Army Group Don" formation for which I was at the head, the disposition of troops at my command to restore the Caucasus situation was as follows. 2nd panzer division, 7th panzer division, 3rd ss panzer division "Aryan," SS mechanized division "Death's head," 28th and 31st motorized division, three divisions of Hungarian, Turkish and Bulgarian troops (to guard the rear and supply lines) and three sturdy, experienced German infantry divisions transferred at no small risk from the still fierce battle in Army Group Center's sector (replaced by two new divisions railed from Germany).

With these quite substantial forces, we were to check, send the Russian back across the Don, and tentatively restore the whole German situation in the Caucasus. The spring thaw was almost upon us in these southern parts of Russia, so even if not entirely ready, I decided to set forth toward destiny. Besides, according to the last reports I'd received at the time, the city of Rostov was days from falling.

Then, by the afternoon of the 1st of March, while my force was driving hard south-east toward the Russian positions in Rostov and north of them on the Don, I received news of Rommel's providential breakthrough south of the city. As I knew the man, it was a desperate gamble, and I would not have approved it in anything but the circumstances we were in at the time. This quite surprisingly successful foray into enemy territory would form the basis of the stunning victory we achieved several days later and divide the Russian's attention in two opposite directions.

By the morning of the 2nd of March, lead mobile elements of the Death's Head and Aryan divisions were already heavily engaged with the enemy 40 km north of Rostov. I called in the Luftwaffe for one of the significant strikes we had planned that day. While the air force was scattered and quite inferior in numbers to the Russians, it was still capable, with the appropriate concentration of troops in a specific area and the right timing, to be quite useful to us.

The flight of Stukas (about 300 of them) demolished the two Soviet tank divisions racing to attack the two SS vanguard divisions. When the Death's head finally broke thru the riffle divisions facing it, the rest of Army Group Don arrived and swamped over the Russian positions.

The 7th panzer and the two motorized divisions entered the gap created by the SS  and plunged south-east toward the northern outskirts of Rostov. On the morning of the 3rd of March, the Russian commander  had started  to disengage his troops from their besieging position around the city. Still, it was much too late, since my forces were already storming the town of Novocherkassk north-east of Rostov, while Rommel had taken the city of Veselyy further east.

The conditions were then ripe for one more large encirclement operation. On the 4th, the forces in Novocherkassk had to cope with a severe counter-attack from the retreating Russian rifle corps that had previously been assaulting Rostov. The Soviet troops were desperate in their attack and launched waves after waves, that we blunted with the Luftwaffe and our excellent defensive positioning. We also were helped by the besieged forces in Rostov that made a sally and attacked the retreating Red Army troops in their rear. The engagement was fierce but brief, and by the end of the 4th of March, we had utterly broken the enemy that would surrender in troves in the following days.

On the 5th, I ordered the SS Death's head and the Aryan panzer SS to drive toward Rommel's forces that were coming hard in a hook north. The weather was sensibly warmer, and it was apparent that rain and melting snow would soon be upon us.

It was for the better since the weather held long enough for us to complete the encirclement, and by mid-morning on the 7th, heavy rain poured down across the bleak Russian landscape. While it put a stop to our incredibly successful offensive, it was, in retrospect, for the better, since the spring thaw prevented the two larges armies (one rifle and one tank) that were coming from the Stalingrad area to bear down on us.

Our counteroffensive's final tally was two Soviet Rifle corps, one tank corps, and one motorized division. In all 125 000 men and tons of burning tanks were vanquished. The victory prevented the Soviets from completely swamping our southern wing, and the Wehrmacht was able to re-establish a semblance of defense in Rostov and north of it in Belgorod.

Unfortunately, for the overall situation, we still lost big strategically. The Russians remained master of the Caucasus north of the mountain range. Maikop ended up falling mid-March, and Grozny followed not many days after. The forces in the mountains were able to hold the line (mainly because of the spring thaw), and OKH also sent back the 1st, 2nd, and 3rd mountain divisions in the area (thru Turkey and Armenia) to hold it correctly with the Turkish corps and remnants of other Axis units. The Reich had lost its land link with its Middle East dominion.

It would prove, for the future, disastrous. We were never able to regain a foothold in the region in the next few years of the war. Instead, we kept losing ground to relentless Allied attacks that eventually reclaimed the entire area, to the great dismay of the Reich's war effort.

But for now, at the start of 1944, things looked like they were improving for us on the Eastern Front. Tons of reinforcements were earmarked to arrive, mainly from Southern Italy and the British Islands' planned evacuation. Halder had also promised new units from the training grounds in Germany.

We also started to hear about the coming of the Tiger II to the front, which, it was believed, would make the difference in this great war of attrition. And finally, the first squadrons of Jet fighters had started to fly over the Moscow skies in March and had made mincemeat of the Soviet airplanes that dared to come close to them (...)

## Somewhere in Oklahoma
### Elk city, March 9th, 1944

U.S. Route 66, or U.S. Highway 66 (U.S. 66 or Route 66), also known as the Will Rogers Highway, the Main Street of America or the Mother Road, served as a primary route for those who migrated west, especially during the dust bowl(major drought) of the 1930s. The road supported the economies of the communities through which it passed.

Being a famous or well-known road, and with limited maps and knowledge of the USA, Skorzeny had elected to take this path to his target in New Mexico. According to the Fuch papers he had read, the whole secret atomic project thing was being developed in a location there. As the recovered information from the NKVD buildings had been damaged, some information was missing, primarily where the project was explicitly located in New Mexico.

The going had so far been uneventful for him, as the Americans were of a careless sort. It almost seemed like they didn't know there was a war on. Life was going along as it always had before, especially in the southern states. Military types could be seen everywhere, and it was apparent that the country was bustling with activity. Still, the S.S. commando man was amazed at how easily he had been able to roam without being questioned. He and his men had landed in the dead of night in the Carolinas at the beginning of January 1944 and had fanned out in different directions. The goal had been to meet up in Elk City, the non-descript small town they had all agreed on at the start of the mission. Out of the ten men that had landed, so far, five had arrived. Three by train in the last few days, one by horse and walking, and one had been with Skorzeny, his good old reliable man, Sturm. He did not speak good

English like Otto, but they'd decided he'd play the part of a simpleton that couldn't talk.

They'd bought a farm delivery truck, Hammer and Sons, after walking for several days in the wilderness. They'd brought a lot of money with them, so it hadn't been a problem. The truck was full of eggs and so had represented the perfect cover for the German commando men. They just drove on the main road and pretended their delivery was into the next few towns. They rarely stopped, only for gas. They slept mostly in the wild, avoiding hotels. So far, so good, no one had questioned them on anything. And they'd eaten a lot of eggs.

There were still five days for the other men to make it to the rendezvous point. He would wait, then move on to New Mexico, and try to find this secret place where the U.S. was supposedly trying to build a super bomb.

# CHAPTER 2

## Panzer Lehr Division training and assembly grounds
### Munster, Lower Saxony, Germany, March 20th, 1944

The Panzer-Lehr-Division (in the meaning of armored training division) was formed as an elite German armored division. It had been formed in 1943 onwards from training and demonstration troops (*Lehr* = "teach") stationed in Germany to provide additional armored strength for the East's desperate situation. The goal was to form a new division that would have an elite status from the start. It would have some impact on the next panzer troops' training, but high-command was taking several veterans from the frontlines to be brought up as new instructors, like injured or personnel needing leave. On the 8th of March 1944, the division was officially designated as the 130th Panzer Division. However, it would go on about the war to be usually referred to as the Panzer Lehr Division. It was, at that point in the war, the only division to be fully equipped with tanks and with half-tracks to transport its mechanized infantry.

Furthermore, the tank in its midst would be comprised of the excellent and reliable Panther tanks (1 regiment of 128 units), Tiger (1 battalion of 128 units) Panzer IV "H" with the side protection for the tracks (1 battalion of 128 units). As an added strength, it would have the incredible, 70 tons monsters Royal Tiger, or Tiger II as a heavy panzer battalion (40 units fresh off the factory in Kassel). Complementing was a full regiment of panzer grenadiers, coming with their full complement of Hannomag armored transports. And to top it all, a battalion of mobile anti-tanks (40 units) in the form of the brand new Jadgtiger, a turretless anti-tank machine with the 88mm gun and same armor as the Tiger II (built on the same chassis). It would be one genuinely fearsome unit. To protect it were two regiments of *Flakpanzer* IV "*Wirbelwind*" (whirlwind), a newly developed self-propelled anti-aircraft gun that promised to be very effective against aircraft (200 units).

The commanding officer for the unit would be the excellent and reliable general Fritz Bayerlein, former chief of staff for Rommel up until the conquest of Astrakhan in 1943. From there, he had been recalled to the Reich to build up the Panzer Lehr Division.

The general was waiting by the train station for pretty much the last piece of the gigantic puzzle representing the buildup of a German panzer division. The commander of his heavy panzer battalion. The man came with heartfelt recommendations from Heinz Guderian himself, with whom Bayerlein had corresponded since the start of the war (they were good friends since the officer school days). The man also had been under Rommel's orders in the 7th division in the French campaign, and while he was a relatively unknown figure at the time, Bayerlein remembered the steady tanker he was.

The heavy panzer battalion would be the masterpiece, as well as the cornerstone of his elite unit. The Tiger II was a beast of war. The Tiger I's successor combined the latter's thick armor with the armor sloping used on the Panther medium tank. The tank weighed almost 70 tonnes and was protected by 100 to 185 mm (3.9 to 7.3 in) of armor to the front. It was armed with the long-barrelled 88mm KwK 43L/71 anti-tank cannon. The chassis was also the basis for the Jagdtiger turretless anti-tank vehicle. It was believed that it would perform incredibly well on the Eastern front and prove impervious to any guns the Western Allies fielded at that moment.

The general had needed an experienced man in charge of the heavy battalion since it would be his masterpiece. Captain Erich Walder that had been promoted to colonel for this very reason, was the chosen man.

Still lost in thoughts, Bayerlein's attention was brought back to the present with the train's screeching halt at the Munster station. The long black train on which only one passenger coach was attached rolled to a halt. The rest of the train was dedicated to reinforced railcars(that had been needed to move the super heavy Tiger II) that would be loaded up soon since the Panzer Lehr was going east to face the Russian masses.

Stepping out was a handsome, black-uniformed man with a serious attitude. Bayerlein knew from the pictures on his file that it was Walder. The man walked up to him. "Welcome, Colonel Walder," said the general. Erich responded with a smile and a Nazi salute. "Thank you, herr general," he said in a crisp voice. "still trying to get used to the new rank," he finished with a smile.

The two men walked up to the black Mercedes staff car that was waiting outside of the station. They quickly got into it, and the driver sped off at a brisk pace toward the armored troop's school (panzertruppenshule), located three kilometers away.

The training school's entrance was protected by large metal gates and a sturdy stone wall. They opened upon the Mercedes approach. Souvenirs then washed over Walder. This is where he had been trained, in what seemed a lifetime ago, before the war. "I received my tank officer's instruction training here, herr general," he ended up adding. Bayerlein looked at him with a thin smile. "Well, colonel, then we can say that you have completed your loop. The panzer Lehr will be the most powerful panzer division in the whole Wehrmacht". The general gave him a file full of papers, which Walder opened promptly. "Three regiments of panzers, tigers, Panzer IV's and Panthers. One full regiment of Panzer grenadiers coming with their Hannomag armored transports. One battalion of heavy anti-tank newly developed Jadgtiger. Two regiments of flakpanzer IV Wirbelwind for air protection. And finally, the masterpiece" Bayerlein paused for effect. Walder looked up at him with a thin smile. "The heavy panzer battalion. Wait until you see the new beasts!" he finished with obvious enthusiasm.

# Extracts of Heinz Guderian 1952 book, Panzer Leader
## Yet another command, March 20th, 1944

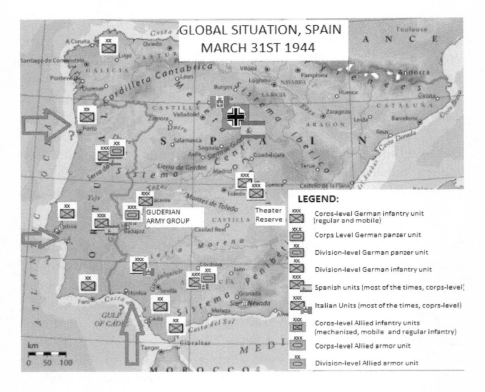

GLOBAL SITUATION, SPAIN
MARCH 31ST 1944

LEGEND:

Corps-level German infantry unit (regular and mobile)

Corps Level German panzer unit

Division-level German panzer unit

Division-level German infantry unit

Spanish units (most of the times, corps-level)

Italian Units (most of the times, coprs-level)

Corps-level Allied infantry units (mechanized, mobile and regular infantry)

Corps-level Allied armor unit

Division-level Allied armor unit

My arrival at Rundstedt's HQ was somewhat anti-climatic, as the large, recently constructed bunker in Seville was bustling with activity. My recent transfer from Africa to the Iberian peninsula had everything to do about the urgency of Spain and Portugal's situation. We'd managed to bring about a military stalemate in Tunisia. Now that my offensive services were less needed in that area, another general, better suited with defensive skills, replaced me in Tripoli. At the same time, I was called to greener pastures, literally speaking.

The whole ride on the Condor transport airplane had been quite long, boring, and uneventful. It gave me the time to familiarise myself with my new command. I was not to replace the theater commander but work in collaboration with Rundstedt concerning all the mobile forces available in the Peninsula.

Contrary to my other command transfers, I had not been recalled to Berlin first. I found it difficult for it would have given me time to see my wife and have some downtime. But as explained in my orders from OKW, the situation in the Iberian Peninsula was dire, and I needed to take command.

For the task at hand, I had a pretty sizeable force at my disposal, notably the 5th panzer division (mostly composed of Panthers), the 11th (Panzer IV's), two heavy panzer battalions of Tigers, and the Wiking SS panzer division (with panthers). Also very intriguing was the recent arrival of a super-heavy panzer battalion in the form of 40 tigers II. With over 70 tons of might, these panzers were immensely rugged and would make mincemeat of Allied armor.

Completing the scene was an Italian division, the Celere, with their sub-par tanks, but still useable for recon and missions against infantry. The Spanish 1st armored, composed of Panzer's I and II's, for the same purpose as the Italian Celere. Adding to my offensive command was the 2nd panzer grenadier division, a fully mechanized unit that had just been created. It was nicely equipped with Hannomag armored transports and had about 100 PAK 43 anti-tank guns, which would come in very handy, with enough power to destroy any tanks the western enemies could throw at us. Speaking of an anti-tank role, I would also command three mobile guns battalions, one of Elephants, one of Jadgpanther (turretless panther's chassis with 75mm guns), and one of Stug III (lighter, but still useable against the light and Allied medium tanks). Two more motorized divisions completed my order of battle (the 44th and 167th).

As I understood it, and according to the orders I was able to read on the flight to Southern Spain, I would be in full command of the mobile forces in a sort of independent control from the old general. At the same time, he would retain the overall theater command and lead over the 4 Spanish corps, the Italian army, and the 15 German divisions entrenched in one area of the other in the Iberian Peninsula. I was to exercise the full judgment of my panzer skills in counter-attacking in "the utmost vigor" the Allied landings and push them back to the sea.

On my arrival at the Rundstedt HQ, I was taken immediately to his office. He greeted me warmly, as we had not seen each other since the fateful days were he had overturned one of Hitler's orders so that the attack could proceed on Dunkirk. This was the discussion starter, as I had never had the chance to thank the man face to face for his quick action that almost cost him his career and had sidelined him for a while, but that had sealed the fates of the British and French land armies.

We quickly moved to a bottle of schnapps for good measure and talked a long while about the great campaigns we'd fought together. He then asked me many questions about the numerous battles and campaigns id done since we sort of "parted ways" after the French campaign. He admitted that he had been following my exploits all over the map. We talked and talked; the general waved away all the staff officers that came to his desk for questions, orders, or paperwork to sign.

When several hours had passed, Rundstedt could no longer delay the obligations of command that had accumulated to dangerous levels and told me we would talk some more about specific planning and disposition of forces for my command over breakfast the next day. In the meantime, he invited me to review my troops (Wiking SS was stationed just north of Seville).

The very next day at dawn, I was woken up (I'd slept in one of the bunker's "guest rooms") by a colonel (a Bokoritzky if I remember correctly) and taken to the general's office for a business meal. We started right where we left off, but this time talked more about the present situation. Rundstedt had a large map of the Iberian Peninsula pinned on the concrete wall in his office, which immediately became the focus of our attention.

He told me he was expecting a landing in Portugal, as this was the Allies' obvious choice. The south was too heavily fortified, and also Portugal offered more options for landings, and a certain distance from Spain so from the bulk of the Axis forces. He suggested I station my troops just north of Badajoz, where I would be in a perfect position to strongly counter-attack if the Allies chose Lisbon or, more surprisingly, Southern Spain. If Oporto was the target, Rundstedt had a solid German division defending the town and positioned enough artillery to hold several days. One of the Spanish corps was placed just 70 km south, with the light armor division Spain sported. They would be able to intervene rapidly and block the Allied landings until I arrived.

After careful reviews of the reports and other probable angles, roads, and state forces, I agreed with him within two hours for the overall plan. Badajoz it would be. The next few weeks would prove eventful and would test the German troops' resolve to its limit, for the Allies were coming at us with their full might.

## Casablanca strategic conference
### Morocco, March 24th, 1944

The stage was set, thought Churchill between 2 big puffs of his cigar. Roosevelt was talking about the final date for the Iberian Peninsula invasion. It was to be on April 1st, 1944. Operation Anvil would involve a powerful fleet and ten divisions for the first day of the landings. More troops would follow later. The Allies had started to evacuate some of their soldiers from Tunisia, as it was apparent that it was a strategic dead-end without Spain. The Mareth line also had proved impenetrable and physically impossible to outflank because of the Mediterranean Sea and the Rugged ground south of Tunisia. The invasion would be the biggest in human history to date. The Axis had an estimated fifteen German divisions (three armored, four Mobile infantry), one Italian army (six divisions total), one Italian armored division (the Celere light tank division), and four Spanish corps(fifteen Spanish divisions). Many fortifications were also present in the southern part of Spain, making a landing in that area quite problematic.

The Allies would eventually throw in a total of 35 divisions in Spain and Portugal, and a storm of might and steel. Thousands of planes from the British and American air forces would be involved and all the big guns of the fleet. Several ships from the North Sea fleet had also sailed to Portugal's coast for the operation to bolster the attack. A large American landing fleet was at this moment sailing from six different harbors in the United States. Churchill didn't think the Allies could fail, apart from the fact that the Germans had recently employed a new, fearsome weapon. A fighter so fast that the Allies seemed like sitting ducks against them. The fighters had effectively put an end to the American day bombing campaign. The losses had been too significant.

The British statesman listened to General Marshall talking about the plan to overwhelm the German jets with quantity. The Allies would send so many escorts with their bombers and troops that they were bound to destroy the ME 262's. Some tactics had been quickly developed by several of the American aces, where they took up altitude and plunged hard. With this move(helped by gravity), they could briefly attain speed equal and even more significant than the Germans. A couple of victories had been scored that way against the jets before the Allied high command ordered a stop to the day raids.

Churchill thought that all of these discussions were fine. Still, there was nothing better than a faster plane to respond to the current German technological developments in his old warhorse experience. He'd already started to do something about it. The British had been developing Jets as well before being invaded. He was working on re-starting the program in Canada.

General Montgomery then took up the presentation to discuss the agreed-upon landing sites of Oporto and Lisbon. Obvious choices for the Axis that had positioned several units in both areas. While obvious, the enemy had not fortified the area much, instead of continuing on its southern fortress buildup. The Germans did intend to make a stand in Gibraltar, for it was the key to the Mediterranean Sea, and losing it meant unraveling their whole strategic position. With Allied ships in that sea, Italy would be in dire trouble. The oil tankers would eventually stop coming to Naples since the Regina Marina (Italian Navy) could not hope to stand against the combined might of the Anglo-French-Americans.

Churchill then looked at Roosevelt, that, lovingly inhaling his cigarette, also was looking at him with his deep, intelligent eyes.The two men had had many discussions the night before in the grand hotel and had argued intensely on the Scottish landing operation. The British prime minister wanted the landing to happen now, amidst his resistance fighters' reports of Axis troops evacuation to mainland Europe. The troops, ships, and planes were also ready in the Faroes, Canada, and Iceland, but the Allied high command had elected to do each operation in sequence.

Churchill believed that the combined Allied navies should have been employed aggressively to catch the Axis off guard and prevent them from transferring their troops. In his view, it was evident that if the Germans were taking such measures, they desperately needed the soldiers in Russia. To him, it meant that they were nearing the bottom of the barrel, so required intense pressure to be applied.

And so, the Allies should have advanced their timetable. But the old bulldog had found no support from De Gaulle's, that was set on the Iberian operation, his perceived first step toward the liberation of the French homeland, and a stalemate with Roosevelt that was not in agreement.

"The operation, gentlemen, starts in 7 days", finished Montgomery loudly. "Good luck to all." And the sudden ruffle of papers and moving of chairs shot Churchill out of his daydreaming. The meeting was over.

Churchill stood up, smashed his cigar into the ashtray, and walked up to admiral Tovey, the admiral in charge of the British fleet for the operation. He needed to discuss strategy with the man since, as former first sea lord of the admiralty in the first World War, he had some suggestions to make...

## Stavka meeting
### Kuibyshev, Siberia march 30th, 1944

Looking quietly at the map before talking, Stalin contemplated the enormous success, and disastrous ending, of the Caucasus campaign. What had started so well as an offensive of strategic, war-winning proportion had petered out in the cauldron of Rostov, where the Red Army forces had been caught napping (in a manner of speaking) attacking the city. The damned (but admittedly very competent) general Manstein had again saved the day for the Germans. Several more Soviet forces had been encircled and destroyed.

But, Stalin's wrath about it was past now. He had been well satisfied with the execution of Magosvky, the general in charge of the southern front offensive. For good measure, he had also tasked Beria to send five random divisional commanders to the Gulags, just to put some spine into the others. Some had protested and rightly so since they had nothing do to with the defeat, but that was not what was necessary. In the big picture, the soldiers and officers knew a high price to pay for failure, even for the people doing their job. He didn't need to explain the why since, for him, it was apparent. You could do your job well, but if others around you didn't, well, it was also your fault for not trying to fix the situation or for just being involved in the defeat in an overall manner. In another smart move, he'd ordered the NKVD to double the number of political officers to the Caucasus units.

On a strategic level, as was explained by Zhukov, it was a great success for the USSR. While the losses at the end of the operation had been regrettable, it was undeniable that they were now master of the theater. They had locked the Axis out of the Caucasus by solidifying the front at Rostov. The mountains blocked the southern units. Then again, Zhukov was confident that the Red Army would overwhelm these positions over time, even though they were in excellent terrain for defense.

"So, what now, comrades?" shot Stalin suddenly, totally surprising the men in the room. Nikita Khrushchev had been talking about the state of the Soviet industry and what it would produce in the next year to supplement the masses of the Russian hordes already in the field.

The other people in the room, mainly generals, shifted uneasily in their chairs. Stalin NEVER talked in the Stavka meeting, and everyone that had an ounce of knowledge about the terrible man knew that it couldn't possibly be a good sign.

Only Zhukov, the ever-brave man in front of the dictator, seemed calm. "What can we do for you, comrade Secretary-General?" he said in a questioning matter, being careful to put as much respect in his tone as he possibly could. Stalin bored his eyes into his best general. His anger flared inside him for a moment but subsided immediately. He was paranoiac, for sure, but hadn't maintained himself at the head of the Soviet Union just with that skill. He needed Zhukov, he reminded himself. After the war, now, it would be a different matter...

"I want results, my dear comrade General," he said in his calm voice, then moving slowly to lit his tobacco pipe. Inhaling some smoke, he leaned back in his chair and put his hands on his big belly. A characteristic of the man when he was either thinking of was being displeased or uncomfortable. No one dared speak, even Zhukov. The man knew Stalin's limit.

"The state is providing much to the army," he said, pausing for effect. "Yet, the German I invaders are still unbroken." He looked calmly at the glowing-red burning tobacco in his pipe. "We need more results and faster," he finished. No one talked yet. They knew he wasn't done. To interrupt Stalin without permission meant a trip to the Gulag or death. It was, however, challenging to know when he was done talking.

"Well!" he said in a raised voice. Most in the room seemed like they'd jumped from their chair in fear. "I am done talking, now propose a solution! I want the Fascists gone from the Motherland".
Zhukov finally had his permission to speak." Comrade First Secretary," he started with all the poise he could muster without showing his fear. This was a dangerous moment for the general. The dictator was in a bad mood. "I am certain that with your leadership and benevolence, we can win the day, especially with all the great war materials the people are providing the army." He paused for a perceptible 2 or 3 seconds to see Stalin's reaction. The man continued to smoke his pipe silently, looking for all he cared like a grandfather relaxing at a table. "We need to press our advantage as soon as the spring thaw is over. I think we attack here", he pointed with a hard knock on the map laid on the table." Kharkov-Belgorod."

At that, Stalin's eyes lifted. "Why," he asked simply. Zhukov took a deep breath and finished: "Because, Comrade First Secretary, this is where the Germans do not expect us. They think we will push again at Rostov or Moscow, even press our advantage in the Caucasus." Stalin was listening intently. "If we attack and storm the Kharkov-Belgorod area, the Rostov position will become untenable for the Axis, as well as all the industrial and coal-rich Donets basin."

"Explain your plan, General," said Stalin questioningly. His mood seemed less restless now. "We start with a powerful attack in Moscow here and make the enemy believe that this will be our main focal point. We move plenty force North of the Don Bend as quietly as possible, and 2 to 3 weeks into the Moscow attack, we strike."

For another 2 or 3 minutes, the general talked. Stalin went back to his usual self, which is silently listening to the meeting. He knew he had instilled some severe fear into Zhukov's mind. He laughed inwardly. He had no intention of getting rid of him in any way. He needed him. But there was no harm in showing him who was the boss, once in a while. The dictator of the USSR much-believed in this tool to keep his iron grip on Mother Russia.

## Reich ministry for armament and production
### Berlin, April 1st, Albert Speer's office

A mess. An unshakable, un-fixable, ugly mess. He crumpled the paper that he had just read on his desk, and threw it angrily in the bin. Albert Speer was not a happy man. He worked relentlessly, day and night, into making the Nazi war machine more productive.

He was sitting in his lavish ministry office, with expensive furniture's, magnificent pictures adorning the walls. There was even a couple photos of him and Hitler in some Nazi ceremony, shaking hands. A grand painting was hung at the center of the big fireplace, that commemorated the great Nazi rally in 1939. There he had had the idea of the "pillars of light", where he had pleased his Fuhrer and Nazi audience by bringing dozens of large anti-aircraft searchlights, that he had put in a vertical position. When night had fell and at the start of Hitler's speech at the Nuremberg rally grounds, he had lit the searchlight, and they had seemed like pillars of light reaching for the skies. Hitler had been so impressed by it that he commissioned one of the best German artists to have the commemorative painting done and given it to Albert.

His desk was full of paperwork, reports, things to be signed, for Speer was an important man in the Reich. The man was responsible for armament production. But his job was difficult. Nazi Germany was a collection of realms within the realm. There was Goering Luftwaffe, Himmler's SS, the Gestapo, the Kriegsmarine, the Army. All vied for position, power and resources. Nothing had been done to coordinate a national effort. That was just the way Hitler had liked it. Everyone competed with everyone so that he could stay safely on top of it all.

And then there were the industrialists. They all had their  agendas, done to try and coordinate some semblance of national priority. This created many conflicting situations, like the Jet program, for instance. While the ME 262 was a startling example of German engineering and success, the Reich had entertained and financed at least four different projects from other arms manufacturers. Not very efficient. Speer estimated that in this particular example, the ME 262 fighter, as revolutionary as it was, could have been fielded a year earlier if things had been done to rationalize the process and get the competing companies to work with some semblance of collaboration.

He was currently trying to convince two competing industrialists, Porsche and Henchel, to work together to improve and rationalise the Tiger II production. He was also discussing with other factories to stop making several types of panzers and mobile anti-tank guns into one or two models. But none of the protagonists either wanted to abandon their projects nor share their designs with the others. Speer needed the Reich to concentrate, to make more materiel of war. It was quite obvious, from what was arrayed against them on both eastern and western frontlines, that the Axis would need to produce a lot more if it wanted final victory. No tactical prowess would change the inescapable fact of modern war. Who wins is the one with the most guns.

Him and his staff had made some figures and analysis, and it was believed that the Reich should concentrate on only 3 models of panzers. Mainly the Panthers, the Tiger and the Tiger II. Everything else should be phased out. But there were gigantic financial interest backing the panzer IV production, or other R and D project, like the ridiculous Maus 120 tons tank prototype that was being built, or the fact that some factories still produced panzer III's that didn't have the guns nor the armor to stand up in any fight these days except against the medium tanks that the Western Allies still fielded.

A multitude of auto tracked anti tanks guns were being produced in at least eight different factories, The Stug III, the Jagdpanzer IV, the Jagdtiger, Jagdpanther and plenty others. While these guns were good in terms of production rationalizing because they didn't need a turret produced but still sported the power of the 75mm and 88mm guns, the Reich needed to concentrate on one or two. It was a simple matter of logic. Less models meant less parts to produce to maintain the machines operational, more optimisation in production. Standardisation. Higher production figures...

But, alas, tons of powerful interests worked against him to block the solutions. He had had many talks with the most powerful industrialists, like Messerschmitt, Heinkel, Porsche, Junker, to name a few. None of them had wanted to collaborate.

So far he had not been able to move the new Fuhrer in doing something about it. The man simply did not care for it, since he was also reaping a lot of benefits from the system. Goering was a very rich man, and liked to get his cut. He also had many friends in these industrialists and did not want to indispose them.

So, there was no real solution for now, apart from trying to make things work as best he could. At least he could increase production for the relevant stuff the Reich was building, like the ME-262 and the Tiger tanks (I and II). That could be achieved by making more factories for them and allocating strategic resources.

He called his two main staff people to discuss the new plans for adding a couple more factories for Messerschmitt, with state-subsidised funds and slave labor. After all, there was the timely arrival of over 100 000 Russian prisoners of war to allocate to the Reich's production in the next few months...

## The Allied invasion of Portugal
### April 2nd, 1944

In the dim light of the morning of the second of April, 1944, two large fleets approached Portugal's coast. They came after the Allied air armadas launched massive bombardments into the targeted landing zones. Both areas were still smoking from the thousands upon thousands of bombs that had rocked them. Piles of rubble, large fires, crumbling buildings destroyed Axis defenses.

The two landing zones, the first near Oporto, just north of the river Douro, and the second near Lisbon, did not get much reprieve from the relentless Allied firepower. Both big fleets, sporting close to ten battleships each, started shelling them with their powerful big guns. And so, the area, and both cities, still had had to endure the pounding. Not many soldiers or civilians had dared stay outside, as the incredible destruction was overwhelming.

The Axis tried to intervene with their planes, especially their ME-262 Jet powered fighters, that simply made mincemeat of their enemies. But, unfortunately, the Allies had so many bombers and fighters (thousands) that, even with an incredible kill ratio of about five to six planes for every Jet on each one of their sorties, some still got shot down, and the Allies maintained the mastery of the skies by their sheer numbers.

The troops started landing in significant numbers around 9 AM. In contrast, two American and one Canadian parachute division landed in a scattered area north of Lisbon, much helping the confusion that the Allies sought to create. The 167th German division tasked with Lisbon's defense soon had its hand full trying to fend off the paradrops, the landings, and the pounding from the air and sea. By noon, Lieutenant-colonel Stengel, commander of the unit, radioed to Seville (HQ) that he would not be able to block the Allied landings that were already happening.

In Oporto, the Axis defenses fared a lot better. Rundstedt decided to concentrate much of his airpower in that area for the first parts of the morning, and so the troops received some support and could move without being destroyed from the air. The Spanish corps and armored division quickly set for the landings site near the Douro, and so by 11 AM, the Axis was heavily contesting the Allied landings. The three leading divisions that had landed were confined to a narrow 1.5 kilometer of beach and shoreline, frantically trying to dig in to protect themselves from the enemy attacks.

Rundstedt and Guderian also decided, contacting each other over the radio at noon, that the reaction forces near Badajoz would wait before intervening. The Allied air mastery was too dense, and both men predicted that if Guderian moved, his units would be relentlessly pounded from the air. He would stir his forces at dusk and counter-attack with all his strength at dawn on the morning of the 3rd. With this, it was hoped by both men, they would hit the Allies in the best way possible.

It would also prevent the Allies from bombarding the German counter-offensive with their battlewagons. The Allied airpower would still attack with its multitude, but Rundstedt promised Guderian the entirety of his air strength to try to fend off the Allies. They knew that casualties caused by enemy planes would be horrible, but there was no choice. The Axis needed to counter-attack in the strongest manner possible in the first hours or first day of the landings or face ultimate defeat in the Iberian Peninsula.

## Aircraft carrier Bonaventure, air squadron 22
### Sky near Portuguese shores, April 2nd, 1944

The large fleet that had been operating in the North Sea and that had been involved in the campaign for the Faroes had been sent south to support the Iberian Peninsula operation. The powerful armada, centered on the carriers Furious, Ark Royal, Argus, Audacity, Bonaventure, the small American Langley, and the escort carrier Sangamon, plowed the warmer waters off Portugal. It was escorted by the numerous big guns that were also tasked with bombarding the shores and defensives Axis positions (Renown, Prince of Wales, Ramillies, Valiant, and pristine new US navy battleship Indiana).

As the carriers were holding much to the rear of the big ships that had approached within 25 km of the coast, Gaston Lamirande and his squadron flew over the big gathering of battlewagons that were all lined up in a log file, hammering away with their big guns at the distant shore. From his altitude, the pilots could only see the bright flashes of their large naval cannons firing. Smoke also enveloped the large guns, remnants of earlier shots fired. The battleships had been at it for a while. Looking further east, toward the distant coast of Portugal, Gaston could see the specks of lights created by what must be the gigantic explosions created by the large naval shells. Most of them were above the 320mm caliber, so he shuddered at the impact and detonation that each resulted in when it hit the ground, buildings of Axis defensive positions.

Still looking east with great attention, something else caught his eye. Small, tiny dark specks in the sky. The sure signs of enemy planes coming to meet them. He radioed his squadron mates to brace for a fight. Another ten to fifteen seconds and they would be upon them, he had estimated. Not five seconds later, they were almost there already. Something felt amiss; the enemy had arrived much too fast for his taste. In a flash, he understood. The fighters coming hard at them must be the much-talked-about jet planes the Germans had started to field in March.

Extensive briefings about them had been held in the carrier's mission meeting room in the last week, especially the tactics to employ against them. It was still early in the process on how to fight them. Yet, American airmen had been able to best some of the jets by attacking from high up and in a downward plunge, which would enable their propeller-driven fighters to emulate the ME 262's speed for a few seconds.

At the same time as pretty much every fighter in his squadron, he pulled his altitude stick up to gain as much as he could before the enemy would be upon them. The main problem was that the seemingly lumbering Seafires were slower than normal. They had been outfitted for a bombing mission. The machines would not be able to climb as fast as the fighter-outfitted version in the raid. They did not rise as fast and were much too slow for the oncoming enemy.

After about 600 meters of climbing, Gaston, looking down thru his canopy, saw that the enemy fighters were streaming hard toward the fighter-bombers below. He was one of the lucky guys that still had been outfitted without bombs so that he could defend himself on better terms than the poor blokes several hundred meters below that were struggling to climb as fast as their fighter counterparts.

He thought it odd to see the weird shape of the 262's and also that they left a fading white contrail of smoke behind them. He dropped his stick again, to plunge  as fast as he  could toward the attacking

Germans. It would be a close-run battle. The Allied planes had what seemed like a definitive quantitative superiority, but it was said that the jets could dance around their enemies. Lamirande would just have to see about that for himself in the next few minutes.

One hour later, Lamirande was trying, amidst every difficulty, to line up his damaged Seafire in line with the Bonaventure's deck. The plane was lumbering along, engine petering out, smoke jutting out of it. The aircraft was severely shot with gaping holes in the wings. He had his mask on, smoke being prevalent into the canopy. Its window was cracked in many places, remnants of either enemy shells fragments or pieces of his plane.

The five minutes or so that the battle had been joined with the German jet aircraft had been the most challenging dogfight of Gaston's war so far. After the initial rush of altitude-helped attack by the Seafires, the squadron was exposed to the ME-262's speed, and the enemy made mincemeat of both the fighter and bomber-configured Seafire.

Not many airmen from the Bonaventure came back to tell their tale. What had saved them was the relative short autonomy of the Axis planes, that could never linger too long in a fight, their gas tank emptying rapidly, especially when dogfighting. Lucky Gaston (yes, he'd been lucky again) had been saved by the fact that the tailing ME-262 that had badly shot up his plane had had to abandon the wild pursuit it was engaged in since Gaston had flown full speed in a large cloud, and that the German had no more autonomy to search and destroy him. When he flew out of the cloud expecting more enemy fire, he was greeted with a gratefully empty sky.

The ME-262 had disappeared as fast as they had appeared. The British airstrike from the Bonaventure had been wholly broken, its remnants coming back with great difficulty to its deck. Gaston's plane wheels finally touched the landing area. He thought for a fleeting moment that he needed to get out of his Seafire as fast as possible. The plane was fast catching fire.

Some of the techs on the deck helped him get out of the Seafire while other seamen were pouring water on his machine to prevent the fire from spreading everywhere. He was alive again.

## Extracts of Heinz Guderian 1952 book, Panzer Leader
## The counter-attack, night of the 2nd of April 1944

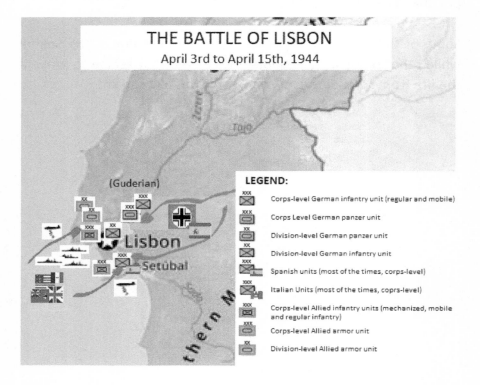

THE BATTLE OF LISBON
April 3rd to April 15th, 1944

(Guderian)

**LEGEND:**

Corps-level German infantry unit (regular and mobile)

Corps Level German panzer unit

Division-level German panzer unit

Division-level German infantry unit

Spanish units (most of the times, corps-level)

Italian Units (most of the times, coprs-level)

Corps-level Allied infantry units (mechanized, mobile and regular infantry)

Corps-level Allied armor unit

Division-level Allied armor unit

(...) I gave the order to start the engines to all my units when the sun fell over the horizon on the 2nd of April. As agreed with theater commander Von Rundstedt, we would advance at night to avoid the overbearing allied airstrikes. The titanic struggle that would follow would see intense battles and epic destruction.

The Allies had landed in force in the Lisbon and Oporto area, and it was decided to strongly counter-attack the landings in the Portuguese capital to throw it back to sea. The reports talked of a mighty deluge of fire from the Allies, completely swamping the German division defending the town. By the end of the 2nd, the unit was in shambles and retiring in confusion to the interior and evacuating the city's rubble. It could not hold as it was attacked from all sides, even from the rear with American paratroops having landed the day before.

General Atama, commander of the Spanish corps stationed 60km north of the Portuguese capital, also received orders to move during the night and attack the southern part of the enemy landings, while I would slam all the power of Army Group Badajoz on the northern forces that were reported to have the heaviest armored formations.

The night was beautiful, and the weather warm, as is usually the temperature in these latitudes. I remember feeling light about the coming fight. My mood would prove not to be adapted to what was coming to me since the fight the very next day became one of the battles where I faced the most potent concentration of enemy firepower in the whole war. First, there was, of course, the planes, but also the numerous and powerful ships that would shell my forces relentlessly over the next two days and make our positions impossible to hold.

The drive to the northern part of Lisbon was remarkably complicated since many units crossed path with the annoying pockets of paratroopers strewn about the countryside. It did seem to me then that the Allies had taken a page from our strategy used in England so sow confusion with the enemy when we landed there during Operation Sealion.

In the end, we simply could not become bogged down with un-important fights across the landscape, so I ordered all mobile units to drive by and ignore the pockets of paratroopers firing at them. After all, none of them had any heavy guns or ordnance that could hurt my panzers. We lost several Hannomag and a couple of Panzer IV to the annoying Canadian paras that had been able to mount a very serious ambush about ten kilometers from our objectives. Still, apart from that specific event, casualties were light. We all knew that having enemy soldiers in our rear would become a severe problem at one point, but there was no time to consider this on the first day of the landing as it needed to be counter-attacked with the utmost vigor.

After the first rays of light showed themselves on the 3rd of April, it did not take long for the 5th panzer division, leading the attack in front, to report rumble-like noises in the skies. It announced the dreadful arrival of Allied airplanes. Our fighter cover also was there just above our units, and we gratifyingly heard the low, thunder-like boom of our incredible ME 262 jet fighters. The looming and overwhelming dogfights were hard to miss since they happened above us, like some grotesque fireworks show. The only difference was the rain of bombs and debris dropping all around us exploding.

A minute or so into the air battle, large, overbearing whistling noises started to be heard coming from the west. Those were the battleship naval shells flying to us to create pandemonium within our midst. One cannot understand the sheer terror and dread that began a naval bombardment. There was, of course, the hell-like explosions and fire, but also the constant ground-shaking and the loud, thunderous noise.

As it happens, id ordered all the units under my command to join the battle as soon as humanly possible to avoid the naval guns that would not dare to fire if we were battling at close range with their side. This would also negate a certain part of the Allied air power.
The fight was joined pretty much all around the line at 10 AM. We had already taken many casualties because of the Allied bombs and shells, but I felt my units still strong enough to give the enemy ground forces a terrific beating.

I cannot discuss this campaign without omitting the remarkable arrival of the Tiger II on the battlefield. As mentioned earlier, I had at my disposal a super-heavy panzer battalion that contained 40 tiger II tanks, which I put in the lead elements along with the 5th panzer division. Not wanting to miss these incredible machines' actions, I drove to them at just about the time battle was joined with Allied Grant and Sherman tanks' forward unit. What followed was simply a fantastic display of power.

The opposing tanks formations met at a field in between two forests. Both units of armor rolled out of their respective wooden areas and started blazing at each other. The Americans moved forward, knowing from experience that they'd need to close the range fast to penetrate the German armor. But they'd never met the new Wehrmacht beasts of war yet. They blazed away at the panzers, being probably about three times more numerous. The Tiger commanders simply, calmly, stopped their tanks at the edge of the trees and started shooting, picking off one US tank after the other, making them a blazing, exploding wreck with each hit of the high-velocity 88mm gun.

All the while, it was simply incredible to witness the Allied shells bounces wildly (upward, horizontally...) on the thick 150mm armor. It even became dangerous for the troops behind the Tiger II, with so many wildly bounding armor-piercing shells that we lost two Panthers and two Hannomag units to ricochet hits.

The sharp and complete destruction of the American tank unit was followed by a mad dash back to the protection of the forest by our forces. I remember the battalion commander ordering the retreat back into the woods, hearing the coming of yet another powerful airstrike that must have been called on the scene by panicked enemy officers. Backing up in the trees did not protect our panzers effectively; however, the Allied tank-buster planes (Mustangs, Spitfire mark XII and others...) raining fire indiscernibly into the woods, hitting several Tigers II, destroying 5 of them from hits on the cupola or the backplates of the engines. I remember smiling that these were the only Tiger II casualties of the engagement, none having been destroyed by enemy tanks!

At the head of the attack and after the enemy planes flew away, our invincible Tigers crossed the field, followed by the rest of the 5th divisions' armor and myself, to a position wholly abandoned by the enemy. One look behind, as we lined up to go through the large road in the forest, and I remember seeing dirty black smoke, smoldering, fierce fires, and American tank wrecks. It was an excellent start to the day (...)

Heavy battalion commander Erich Walder was at the train station of the large Russian city of Orel. His unit had just completed the rail journey to the frontlines. They'd left the tank training yard of Munster five days ago, at the vanguard of the Panzer Lehr division. Theater commander Erich Von Manstein had asked to get the Tigers II units first. Walder was expecting the rest of the unit and its overall commander, Fritz Bayerlein, to arrive soon.

They'd been ordered to assemble near the city of Orel, which was positioned halfway between Moscow and Rostov and close to the frontlines. The fact of the matter was that it wasn't known yet where the Russians would decide to attack. General military-strategic analysis gave good odds for an attack on Rostov and Moscow, but it was just unknown were the inevitable Soviet offensive's main thrust would come from.

And so Manstein had decided to concentrate powerful armor formations in the center where it could intervene north or south. The Panzer Lehr, superbly equipped and considered a veteran division because of its cadre of experienced personnel, would be at the tip of the panzer group.

There were no questions about who held the initiative on the Eastern Front in 1944. The Soviets had wrested it from the Wehrmacht with their convincing and powerful offensive in the Caucasus.

It was due to simple mathematics. The Axis just didn't have the numbers needed to stop the incredible flood of men, tanks, and planes that the USSR was pouring out of its factories daily. With a staggering ratio of 1:5, the Germans and their allies were forced on the defensive, where it was at least possible to be more careful with casualties. What was lost for them was just not as replaceable as with the Red Army, which seemingly had an endless pool of manpower and machines. Even in the megalomaniac halls of Berlin, where most of the Nazi fanatics resided, Goering, Goebbels, and the SS leaders recognized the impossibility of being on the offensive for the time being, especially with the forces needed on the other fronts.

Walder, inspecting one of the vast and reinforced train rail cars that had been designed specifically to transport the super-heavy 70 tons Tigers II, was amazed at the sheer size of the panzer. He'd been inside one, driven one, fired one in the Munster training yards. He still could not believe how powerful that machine was. Unreliable drivetrain and engine, but definitely the tank you'd want in a scrap.
A bit further away, he looked at the giant crane, slowly lifting one of the beasts out of the railcar. Again, another thing that had had to be built to be adapted to the weight it would have to load and unload from the rail cars. It gently landed the Royal Tiger on the ground, which was immediately swarmed with techs, so they could move the panzer away for the next one to be dropped.

Already twelve of them were lined up just outside the train station in the large field that sported light, dirty snow. The winter and spring thaw were almost over, and with their departure would come the renewed fight.

## Calais Harbor
## Naval dockyards April 3rd, 1944

The long line of soldiers from the 124th German infantry division was unloading from the large troop transports on Calais Harbor's docks. The last time they had seen this area as a unit was in 1940, en-route to their stunning victory over the British. The men seemed high-spirited, busy as they were chanting the popular Wehrmacht marching song "Soldaten, Camaraden" with all their voices.

Dozens upon dozens of old captured French trucks awaited for them to board and be driven to the Calais train station. Their destination: The Eastern Front. They'd heard the horror stories and the hardships of the men there, especially of the Moscow debacle in the 42-43 winter. But they were also eager to fight the Communists hordes that threatened to engulf the whole world. As the Reich propaganda was glaring the dangers of world Communism and the potential fall of civilization, the common soldier could not help but feel compelled to do something about it.
Now, when they got to Russia a month later, their opinions of the high and mighty Reich and its civilized values dropped significantly, to almost nothingness. But in the meantime, they were convinced of their noble mission, and moral showed it.

The 124th was part of the thirteen divisions from the United Kingdom garrison that were being rushed to the Eastern Front as rapidly as the Reich's transport and logistical system could move them. The situation was dire against the Soviets. The OKW had decided that they would start contracting the Wehrmacht to have it more concentrated and evacuate areas that were considered

indefensible. Unfortunately, the decision was dictated by Germany's current predicament, the horrible ratio of forces against the Allies' combined forces. The United Kingdom was such an area, with its looming invasion. There was no doubt in any German leader's minds that they could stop or at least bog down the Western Allies attacks in the Islands. Still, to do so, they would have not only to leave the 13 divisions badly needed elsewhere but send reinforcements, in the form of more troops, tanks, and especially fighters, that right now were desperately needed in Russia and Southern Spain.

Already one motorized and one panzer divisions (the SS Leibstandarte Adolf Hitler) had been shipped to the marshaling yards in Orel, where Manstein was constituting an operational reserve to meet the enemy onslaught when it would be launched.
The trick was, for the OKW and the OKH, to be discreet about it. The longer the invasion of the UK could be delayed, the better. So, the division in charges of the northern defenses had been left in place, and the other one split into ten battalions' of 1000 men and spread across the British landscape to offer a delaying resistance. A division has also been left in Ireland, and the four others already evacuated.
The United Kingdom was ripe for its liberation, and there was nothing the Third Reich could do about it.

*Extracts of Heinz Guderian 1952 book, Panzer Leader*
**Pyrrhic victory, 15th of April 1944**

(...) Of our ground supremacy and definite victory, there could be no question. From out attack on the 3rd of April to the end of the 15th, we ruled the Portuguese land, destroying well over 700 Allied tanks, killing untold numbers of soldiers, taking thousands of prisoners, and had been able to confine the landing remnants in the north of Lisbon to a narrow strip of land by the coast about three kilometers long and one deep. The Allies were desperately dug in and resisted with all they had, supported by their mighty naval guns and numerous airstrikes.

But the overall situation, and the attrition to the forces under my command, did not give the same cause for rejoicing. First of all, to the south of Lisbon, the Spanish corps that had moved to the area to intercept the mainly British and Canadian divisions that landed there had had to retire on the 4th, after having lost about 25% of its numbers. The combination of naval shells, airstrikes, and the fact that the Spanish soldiers were not adequately equipped to fight (they mostly had either World War One equipment or surplus weapons from our arsenals) made for their un-avoidable defeat. They gave a good account of themselves in the first few days but eventually had to retire, as the fire volume was simply too much for these poor troops.

So, for all instances and purposes, this meant that my Badajoz Army Group, while very successful, would soon be threatened from the rear and of destruction. There were also the paratroopers, still scattered everywhere in the Portuguese countryside that made supplying my forces a complex operation at best. Furthermore, the Oporto landings, in the north, had met success.

The Spanish troops, and the German division that had been posted in the city for its defense, were retreating. In good order, at least, toward the country's interior and its mountains, to prepared defensives position that Rundstedt had done since March.

Since our strategic position was threatened and that we could be encircled if we kept the pressure on the Allied landings we had so thoroughly trashed, that our supply was low at best and finally that our attrition rate, because of ground combat and naval/air attacks, it was decided that we would retire at our best possible speed, during the night of the 15th, to our original Badajoz positions.

While I remember being fiercely disappointed by the turn of event, I must point out that I was quite proud and felt immense gratitude to the mighty and brave fighting troops under my command for so well a performance. Yes, we were retiring to Spain and the Portuguese mountains, but we had given the Allies something to remember. Without their big naval guns and their damned planes, they would have been swept from the map.

This respect for our fighting skills and our panzers' strength would stay with the Allies and their state of mind for the rest of the campaign. Never again would Montgomery and his lackeys advance or attack with the same abandonment as he did in these first few days of April.

It would serve us well for the difficult campaign that lay ahead, that was the battle for Spain and Gibraltar.

*Extracts from Von Manstein's 1958 book, LOST VICTORY*
**The strategic situation before the start of the Russian May offensive (to April 30ᵗʰ)**

(...) The Eastern Front's strategic situation was improving somewhat in these early days of spring 1944. After the severe hardships of the winter 43-44, where we repulsed – barely- a powerful Communist offensive near Moscow and won a significant tactical victory in the Don Ben near Rostov.

However, we had lost much ground to the Red Army, and I wasn't confident we could take them back, with our forces' current dispositions. All of the land in front of Moscow had been given up (not willingly) to the overbearing Russian Bagration offensive that had seen the fall of Yaroslavl (our northeast flank), Ryazan, just southeast of Moscow, and the central city of Voronezh to the south, near Orel.

The Caucasus was gone up to the Caucasian mountain foothills, Maikop and Groznyy, having fallen as well. Rostov was holding the entrance into Ukraine in the south, at the tip of the Azov Sea.

Numerically speaking, a great effort had been underway since the start of the 1944 year, and I felt confident than with the weekly arrival of new, fresh, and even experienced divisions (from the British Isles), the Wehrmacht would be able to organize some line of defense against the Soviet hordes.

Army Group South was well dug in trenches and well-stocked with infantry and some mobile units. Von Kleist was responsible for the Rostov-Belgorod-Kharkov area's defense and had four infantry corps (three Germans and one of mixed allies' divisions), representing twenty divisions.

In the center, the line was held by the Army Group Center, under my command. By far the strongest of the East's army groups, two of them armored with over seven corps, so more than forty divisions, with more arriving daily. I was also building a robust mobile reserve just south of Orel with, in the lead, the recently arrived Panzer Lehr elite (and superbly equipped) division, along with another panzer unit that came back from the UK.

In the north, general Von Kluge, recently named to the command position, closed the front north of Kalinin with three corps, or fifteen divisions plus one Finnish corps that held its border north Leningrad.

Facing us were an estimated 20 armies (each Russian army contained three corps, while one corps contained four divisions) spread out along the frontline. The crucible of the problem was to guess where the blow would fall when the weather campaigning season started.

I believed that it would be where we didn't expect it. OKW, Halder, and Model in the lead, thought that the Russians would capitalize on their Caucasus gains and try to pry open the southern front, while I was of the mind that they would attack from Voronezh.

Thus, we reached the compromise of putting the operational mobile reserves near Orel, which was nicely situated to intervene in both directions should the Soviets decide one or the other.

They ended up surprising us, again, with their point of attack, but in the end, it didn't change the fact that we were able to move our forces to meet the threat. 1944 would prove to be a very another challenging year.

## Naples Harbor, Southern Italy
## Naval dockyards, April 20th , 1944

In Southern Italy, the major harbor of Naples was one of the significant naval facilities in the country. It had grown in importance since the Axis middle eastern conquests. While some of the oil went thru trains to Iraq, thru Turkey, and then to Europe, most of it was transported by tankers. Several sailed from the Persian Gulf, thru the Red Sea, via the Suez Canal into the Mediterranean. Others were railed to the harbor of Suez to be loaded on other tankers. It was brought by an army of trucks (the Axis had requisitioned every conceivable truck they had found in the theater) from Persia to Suez to be then loaded on tankers or other smaller ships.

It was not an easy process, and while the Axis had conquered the Middle East, it hadn't mastered its resources. The oil itself was worthless for war. One needed to refine it to make it useable. Most of the refineries were in Germany, occupied France, and northern Italy, so the oil had to be transported there for refining.

Economically speaking, it was a wasteful process, one that would not give any profit to a company. But the Axis was at war, and it did not matter how much it cost to make the most precious liquid needed to fuel its machines with which to fight it.

So even with all the world's difficulties and the economic waste and expense to bring the oil to Europe, there was more than enough to go around. The Germans, Italians, and French had only so many refineries, after all. The rest was being hoarded in some truly gigantic tanks and crude oil depots in Southern Germany. By the end of 1944, even if losing the whole Middle East, the Third Reich would still have enough oil for years. So consequently, it would have enough to fight its wars for a long time.

The great majority of that oil was transiting thru Italian ports. Some tankers made the journey up the Adriatic to Venice, but most stopped in Naples. The harbor area had been significantly reinforced by the Italians who had put hundreds upon hundreds of their excellent anti-aircraft gun, the canone da 90/53 (90mm gun), built by the company Ansaldo. The Germans had also contributed by shipping two full regiments of 88mm anti-aircraft guns to the city. Three squadrons of Italian fighters, the Macchi C.205 Veltro, the newest of their fighter. It was excellent and had already shown its worth in the North African campaign, proving itself capable. It had been able to go head-to-head even against the excellent Mustang P-51. Also, the Germans had stationed two squadrons of the FW190 and one of BF-109 G. There were even talks of stationing a ME-262 jet squadron in the city as well, for its strategic importance was paramount to Rome and Berlin.

These assets were scrambling to get ready to meet the large bombing group that was approaching Naples. The early detection radar (Freya radar system) installed by the Germans in Sicily and at the Italian boot's tip had detected enemy bombers' flight. Hence, the Germano-Italian command knew it was coming.

The Allies, confident in their air superiority, had only a limited knowledge of what was happening in Naples. They knew that it was well defended and that it was the main oil terminal, but that was about the sum of their intelligence level. Nonetheless, the high command in Casablanca had decided upon a probing raid. And see what kind of hornet's nest it would prove to be.

For the last few weeks, it had been concentrating on trying to find the tankers at sea and sink them, but it proved more difficult than imagined. The Axis was aggressively patrolling the Central Mediterranean, and the ships were also well escorted. So now it would go for the head and try to shatter Naples.

But they would be disappointed. With perfect advance knowledge of their arrival because of the German radar system, all the fighters had been scrambled in the air, 350 in all, and were waiting. All the guns were operated and also fully stocked in ammo. Everyone was fresh and ready.

When the bombing raid (200 bombers, 250 fighters) was about 15 kilometers from the city, they were intercepted by the multitudes of Axis planes, and the ensuing fight destroyed many of the bombers. Then, two or three minutes later, the Axis fighters made themselves scarce. This meant that they had cleared the airspace for their anti-aircraft comrades to riddle the sky with their guns. From the Allied pilot's perspectives, the sky seemed to light up with explosions, and more planes started to fall off in flames or simply exploding in flight. By the time the raid got over Naples' harbor area to drop its bomb, about only 40 of them had not been shot down or turned back because of damage. Their fighter escort did not fare much better. They dropped their bomb load wildly and turned tail as fast as possible.

On their way back, they were re-intercepted again by the Axis fighters, and died too. What got back to the airports in Algeria and Tunisia was only a shadow of the force that had left that same morning. Twenty-five bombers made it home intact, 50 more were heavily damaged, and the rest lost with all hands. For the fighters, they fared a little better but came back with only 150 of them.

The raid itself had dropped most bombs in a wild pattern that hit nothing important, apart from one bomb that hit the harbor's docks. It would take some time before the Allies would decide to attack Naples again, especially when they received news that Me-262's had been shipped to the scene.

# Extracts of Heinz Guderian 1952 book, Panzer Leader
## Battle in the mountains of Portugal, 16th to 30th April, 1944

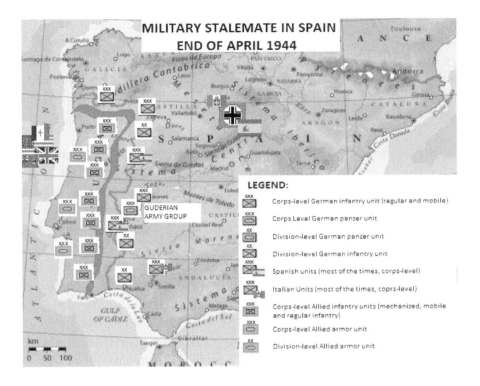

Two major invasion routes offered themselves to the Allies in their upcoming Iberian campaign. These routes were pretty much the same that Wellington's army used to battle the French in the Peninsular war of 1808-1811. Both main roads went through the Portuguese mountains, so it was an area suited for defense. Most certainly, there were other ways to enter Spain if one needed to. In reality, the two main entries into Spain, which were traversed by plains and flat terrain lodged between mountain and mountain passes, were the only real options for any modern army. They were the only routes that could support and entertain a modern military by the size and accessibility of their roads. So, the Oporto landings would go straight east toward Almeida in Spain, in a straight line into the mountains, to eventually burst into Spain.

And the Lisbon invasion forces would try to go where I was, on the Badajoz road. The city had been a major fortified area in the Middle Ages. Even in the Peninsular War, Wellington's army had had to assault the giant fortress before resuming its advance. For us Germans, the fight would not be in that city, but westward, where we had been able to anchor our defensive positions with the rugged and mountainous terrain. But it was a given that since we failed to push the enemy back into the sea, they would undoubtedly invade Spain through this traditional route.

On the morning of April 16th, after we had successfully disengaged from the Lisbon area's enemy, my troops retired in good order toward the Badajoz road. We dug in west of it, in the rugged mountains and regions, to block the road as best possible, and with the most cover (it was a wooden area).

The Allies, badly shaken by our counter-attack on their Lisbon landings, did not pursue but continued to consolidate their forces and land more troops in a few days afterward. And so, we were able to prepare sensible defensive positions, in the relative safety of the area, amidst constant allied air raids and overhead dogfights with our Luftwaffe. One could get a sense, at that time, that our air force was slowly retaking a part of its past glory. The ME-262 Jets, appearing in ever-growing numbers, were starting to impact the air campaign substantially. I didn't know it at the time, but OKW had prioritized the Spanish theater for the fighters, and the Reich (with Albert Speer in the lead) were scrambling to make more of them. Also, two strong Luftflotte of BF-109 and FW-190 arrived by the end of April, being flown in from the British Isles. Again, I did not know it at the time, but the supreme command was in the process of evacuating the United Kingdom to bolster our defenses on the continent.

So, for the first time in a long while, my forces were relatively safe from the constant, overbearing, and destructive action of Allied planes. By no means were they gone, but at least there was a sense that something was being done about them for us poor soldiers on the ground.

I even surprised myself in being reasonably confident of reaching some military stalemate if the Luftwaffe could continue its buildup and protective umbrella. The same kind of optimism was apparent in the theater commander, Rundstedt, on his visit to my Badajoz HQ (located in the old fortress) on April 20th. The Allies had started to advance again, but with the strength of our defenses and 88mm gunned panzers (Tigers, Tigers II), they were blocked on a somewhat straight frontline from north to south west of the old Portuguese border.

## New equipment
### Lisbon harbor, April 29<sup>th</sup>, 1944

US army engineers, working the recently repaired docks of the Lisbon harbor, did not give too much attention to the new tank unloaded from the transport ship on one of the large port facilities cranes.

They did realize that the machines slowly brought to the ground and aligned in a neat row near the boats had a very long gun of a type they'd never seen before. They'd seen, first hand, what the German panzers had done to the lightly armed and brittle Sherman tanks. Only their superior numbers had eventually won the day, but on a one-on-one basis, the Tigers, Panthers, and now the fearful Tiger II's, easily won the day in any given fight.

They'd worked around the clock to make the harbor operational and were still doing so. They were just too tired to take notice intellectually. So, they didn't care what they were unloading.

But the US army general standing beside the big transport ship looking at the scene was interested. Keen, curious, and eager. America's standard medium tank of World War Two, the M4 Sherman, had deficiencies in firepower and protection compared to the best German tank designs. A more powerful tank was in development in the USA called the Pershing, which was supposed to go head-to-head against the heaviest of the German panzers. But for the moment, the US army would have to do with the up-gunned version of the M4-Sherman tank lining up by the hundreds in Lisbon. The new version sported a 76mm high-velocity gun that was supposed to at least be able to penetrate the enemy armor given the right conditions. The new Sherman version had been called the Firefly.

Several more would be unloaded in the next two days, and most of the replacements on the very high losses they'd taken fighting the terrible German counter-attack would be with these new models.

General George Patton could not help but swear heavily to his staff officer. "Finally, we've got a damn chance of hitting the krauts with some firepower!". The staff officer just nodded. It didn't look like it, but the general was happy, and there was cause for it. He had seen his boys die because the stupid engineers and cowards state sides had not bothered to give them the relevant machines with which to fight the war. Patton had seen how far behind the Allies were in tank development. He'd sent more than one letter to high command about it. Hell, he'd even written to Roosevelt himself!

He'd also heard that the Brits were busy building a heavy tank called the Centurion and that the machine would also arrive in the European theater soon. He hoped to god that it would be soon. Because eventually, they would have to go thru and destroy all those damned Nazi Panzer divisions, if they ever wanted victory.

# La Fonda Inn
## Santa Fee, New Mexico, April 30th, 1944

The United States of America, along with scientists from all over the world, we're working on a bomb so powerful that it had war-ending capability. It was a far-flung project that had, ironically, started in German laboratories when scientists had proven the theoretical feasibility of nuclear fission. There were sites all across North America, none aware of the other. Some producing heavy water needed in the development process. Some other extracted the Uranium from Canadian mines.

And last but not least. Some others made the actual research and testing to make the bomb a reality. It was the most critical link in the whole project, and it was located near Albuquerque, in New Mexico. The small secret town was called Los Alamos, and it was up on one of the high mountain plateaux that was accessible via a winding and steep road.

Otto Skorzeny and his commando team knew all of this because of one man named Klaus Fuch, an expatriate German national that was spying for the Soviet Union. Unfortunately for the USSR and the Western Allies, the Germans had found some of the correspondence he sent to his Russian handlers in the demolished NKVD HQ ruins in Moscow. The building had been thoroughly smashed and blown up with an impressive amount of explosives. Still, the German Gestapo and Abwehr people sent to the site after the Reich conquest of the Russian capital had struck gold in one of the building's deep roots that had somehow survived the explosion.

Fuch was a staunch anti-Nazi that had moved to the USA before the war. He was a prominent scientist with some talent, so he was recruited into the project. The Allies didn't know it, but the man was a genuine Marxist and spied shamelessly for the USSR. Skorzeny thought it was pretty ironic that he was greatly, albeit unknowingly, helping the Reich. The spy had sent very detailed information on what the scientists were doing and where they were located in a very secret location up in New Mexico's mountains. Unfortunately, there wasn't much in the way of scientific data recovered, so it wouldn't help the Germans build their bomb, but it would greatly help the SS commando master to destroy what the Western Powers were doing.

For some reason, only seven of the original ten men commando that had landed with him in the Carolinas had made it to the rendezvous point in Oklahoma. They probably had either been killed or apprehended. He was not overly worried about the capture of these men as they only knew the meeting point, and yet still, none of them had all of the details of the mission. Officially they were on a mission to go to the West Coast to sabotage the military harbor of San Diego.

They'd then proceeded along Route 66 to New Mexico. Once there, it didn't take long for the Germans to gather enough information from the civilians about a place near the state's capital. Something was happening in the mountains, and for Skorzeny, it had been easy to connect the dots. It was all mysterious to non-military people but obvious to someone looking for a secret place like the SS officer and his men were.

They'd found a great place in the wilderness to make camp and hide. Skorzeny's plan was simple. They would climb the mountainside the Los Alamos town was on (it was located on a flat, top of the mountain plateau) and kill the scientists. It was well guarded by American standards, but the SS man thought it was laughable. He'd decided in his planning that it didn't matter if the town or facilities survived. They just needed to destroy the people doing the research. And they were numerous.

Santa Fee was the main town near Los Alamos, where the project got all its supplies and where the scientists went with their families once in a while, and sometimes (amazingly!) not even escorted by guards.

Located on East San Francisco Street, La Fonda Inn was the place that was a favorite watering hole for the scientists and their wives who ventured down from the Hill for a taste of civilization during the Manhattan Project. Fearing that they might loosen up too much and reveal the project's top-secret goal, covert government agents monitored Los Alamos residents as they unwound there in the inn's restaurant. Skorzeny stayed at the inn and played the part of a traveler. He'd been sitting in the inn alone and quiet (his men were still at their secret camp in the wilderness) and had identified all the US government agents. He had seen the procession of scientists to the place. Indeed, they loved it.

He didn't hear anything secret in the inn but could make a somewhat accurate picture of how many scientists were working in Los Alamos. Hundreds upon hundreds. As he was taking a sip from his whisky glass, he looked at the two agents that were now seemingly tasked to monitor him precisely. They'd been doing so for about a week, but that didn't matter. Otto didn't do anything suspicious. As he finished his drink to go back to his room, he decided that he had watched these people enough and that it was now time to act. And besides, he couldn't stay longer in the inn without risking being questioned by the authorities.

He hoped his men (the ones that spoke perfect American English) had been able to procure everything they would need on the black market. They would need a lot of ordnance and guns to kill so many people.

# CHAPTER 3

# Extracts from Von Manstein's 1958 book, LOST VICTORY
## Operation Kutuzov, the offensive on Kursk and Kharkov, May 1944

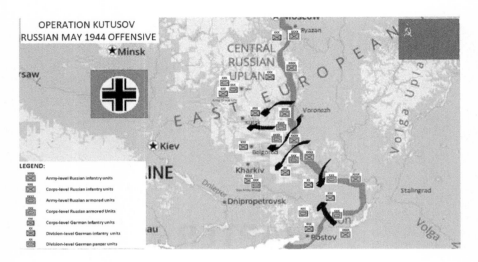

In this fine 1944 spring, the question was where the Soviet would choose to attack our positions? For after careful discussions and much debate with the Fuhrer at a conference at the Wolfsschanze on April 22nd, the Reich would launch no large-scale offensive in Russia for the campaigning season. Our forces were too scattered. We were attacked from too many sides to contemplate the concentration of troops necessary at that point in time to contend with the numerous Russian hordes in a meaningful manner.

We had and were still receiving a stream of reinforcements from the evacuation of most military units from the British Isles and the creating new, powerful units like the Panzer Lehr division. This helped plug the gaps in our lines, but most importantly, to form an operational reserve that would act as a counter-attacking element should the Russian breakthrough our lines. The resulting forces were promptly named after its strongest element, the Lehr Army

Group, which had an unusual number of armored units in its panzer ranks.

In the meantime, the German high command had finally elected to name a theater commander for the Eastern Front. Something that Hitler had always flatly refused to do because he loved to play soldier and be in control. After an initial interest and sometimes piece metal involvement from time to time in 1943 and the winter of 1944, Goering was not bothering enough with the real details of commanding a front to be involved as his predecessor was.

On April 27th, 1944, Halder, the chief of the general staff (commander of OKW), flew to my Smolensk HQ to announce that effective immediately, I was named field marshal and also in overall command of all forces on the Eastern Front.

For all instances and purposes, this meant that I was free, finally, to use all the assets available to the Wehrmacht in the USSR. Unfortunately, I did not have enough time ahead of me to do all of the troop's movements I wanted because of the imminence of a Soviet offensive, but several steps were taken.

First and foremost, I ordered the backward movement of the infantry corps (145th, 176th, and 61st infantry divisions) to move out of the Don Salient that had been where the front had fixed itself at the end of the winter. This area, located just north of Rostov, was in danger of being attacked and encircled from north and south by the Red Army.

Secondly, I ordered with immediate effect the evacuation of all "bridgeheads" that were kept on the Chir and the Don river, since Goering had wanted us to stay in place in March because he still entertained some hope of a renewed offensive. This would reinforce our defensives positions.

Third, any bulge in the front that could be exploited by the enemy was reduced to a manageable proportion. I sent a message to all army group commander (North: Kluge. South: Kleist, Center: Hoth, recently named after me) so they could give me their evacuating options. By April 28th, I'd approved all of them, and the German troops then moved to better pastures.

The goal of all this was that preserving the Wehrmacht's fighting capability in the East was our tantamount priority. The simple fact that the ratio of forces was much in our disfavor and that it was not looking to improve much in the near future forced us to adopt this stance. No longer were we able to roam, attack, and dictate the war's tempo to the Soviets.

In clear, the strategic initiative had tilted toward the Red Army, and from now on, if we wanted the Reich to survive, we would have to react to the enemy's moves.

By May 2nd, I felt happy enough about the short-term dispositions I had been able to implement as a theater commander and had a reasonable sense of hope that things would improve. Reinforcements were pouring in, and we were also receiving more and more new weapons of war like the Tiger II and the miraculous ME-262 fighters.

I went to bed that same day, asking myself what the Russians would do since all signs pointed toward a large-scale attack soon. I was of the mind that they would either seek a decision on the Moscow front or the southern front. I had consequently prepared the fighting troops for both eventualities but had to wait to see where the red Army would put its attack's weight.

I was answered that very same night at 4 AM when an orderly came to wake me up from my bunk bed at the bunker's HQ to report heavy artillery bombardments in the Rostov area, Moscow area, and Belgorod front.

Without a doubt, this was the unmistakable sign of a Soviet offensive, for the Russians always did so before they sent their men into the attack. They also bombarded two to three areas to keep us Germans on our toes concerning their real point of attack.

At dawn on May 3rd, the Russian hordes set forth in front of Rostov in a powerful frontal attack, with hundreds of Yaks and Tupolev bombers overhead. The Moscow area troops also reported a strong frontal attack in their sector facing south into the Ryazan direction.

But the most severe attack or what seemed to be the most in my mind was the reports of strong armored formations attacking with powerful numbers near Belgorod and potentially in the direction of Kharkov. The three attacks looked very serious, but my instinct and experience pointed me toward that specific offensive. For it was the most dangerous one in strategic terms. With a breakthrough at Belgorod and a storming of Kharkov, the Soviet forces would cut off the whole southern wing of the Army with a quick drive to the Black Sea. Since most of our troops were forward-positioned, this could be a disaster of epic proportions.

By 11 AM, the Lehr panzer group had orders to drive at best speed to intercept the offensive toward Belgorod. The German troops would then be able to attack the Red Army units on their northern flank.

The 1944 campaigning season had started.

# The Battle of Novgorod
## May 7th, 1944

Designed as a breakthrough tank for breaching enemy defenses, and allocated to a handful of special heavy tank battalions, the sixty-ton Tiger I seemed to have it all: firepower, armor, and for the mid 1940s, it was reasonably agile. With its square, castle-like shape, and long cannon, the Tiger I even *looked* deadly. But Hitler's generals and weapons designers were not satisfied. With Teutonic perfectionism, they complained that the Tiger I's KwK 36 gun was not the most powerful version of the 88-millimeter cannon (not that Allied tankers would have noticed the difference). But size and power were never enough for the late Fuhrer. Even before it was out of the assembly lines at Kassel, Hitler had ordered a bigger version designed and produced.

Enter the Tiger II, or Konigstiger (Royal Tiger). At seventy-five tons, it was a lot bigger than its predecessor. It's longer-barreled (and thus higher velocity) KwK 43 88-millimeter cannon could penetrate five inches of armor at a range of two kilometers (1.2 miles). With Sherman and T-34 crews having about two inches of frontal armor between them and eternity, no wonder a supersized Tiger must have seemed the devil on treads.

The Tiger II also featured numerous improvements over the Tiger I. The original Tiger had vertical armor, rather than the more effective sloped (effectively increasing armor thickness) found on the T-34 and the later German Panther. The Royal Tiger had well-sloped armor that was six inches thick on the front hull. Its turret could traverse 360 degrees in nineteen seconds, compared to sixty seconds for the Tiger I, a weakness which had theoretically allowed a fast-moving Sherman or T-34 to maneuver behind a Tiger I faster than the German tank's gun could track it.

It had also been designed in mind to face the dreaded KV1 and KV2, the Soviet Army monsters, that by 1944 had been replaced by the even more potent IS2 (Ioseph Stalin tanks) that sported 120mm frontal armor (to the King Tigers 160mm armor) and powerful 120mm rifled gun. The German designers and leaders had been eager to see how both tanks would do against each other.

Well, now they would be served, as the first battle between the two behemoths had just concluded. Tank commander Erich Walder, commander of the Panzer Lehr division heavy panzer battalion, surveyed the smoldering mass of tank hulks in the field facing his units. Victory was sweet, but not without cost. They'd destroyed the unit of IS-2 that was attacking them, not just because their Tiger II were incredible marvels of engineering, but because they had been more experienced. The 88mm high-velocity KwK 43 gun had opened the Is-2 like tin cans, but the opposite had been, unfortunately, true as well. The gigantic 120mm canon of the Russian tank had penetrated the frontal armor of the Royal Tiger with as much impunity as the 88mm gun. Only their slower rate of fire and low ammunition capability had assured their ultimate destruction.

His rapid analysis of the blackened, smoking, and afire tank ruins told him that they'd destroyed at least 50 IS-2 tanks. But the panzer unit had lost, for its trouble, 12 units, dropping the Tiger II complement of the heavy battalion to 28 working tanks. Two would be back soon in the fight because they only had their tracks destroyed. Still, the rest was just as smoldering and ablaze as their Soviet counterparts. Many had glancing hits that had created holes or light damage on their external armor.

The sun was slowly setting on the horizon, making the view of the endless fields of the Russian land stand out against the black smoke climbing high in the air. The last two days had been outstanding. The unit had finally joined battle with the Yvan's on the morning of the 5th of May, encountering an ill-fated T-34 tank brigade, destroying the whole lot in an hour for no losses.

Then the same day, later just before dark, they'd done the same to another T-34 unit. After that, on the 6th, as their brothers also advanced victoriously behind them, they together (with the panthers, Tiger I, Jagdtigers anti-tank unit) destroyed an entire tank division and shattered a mobile riffle division. And then they'd encountered the IS-2 tank units that were lying in front of Walder in ruins.

All that time over their head, the Luftwaffe and the Soviet air force had battled intensely to control the air. The German fighters to protect their brothers on the ground, the Soviets to have a chance of dropping bomb unto them. Theater commander Von Manstein had assured the Lehr Army Group commander, Werner Kempf, of constant friendly air cover. Walder and his comrades in the heavy battalion had marveled at the magnificent jet fighters, with their low rumble, thunder-like noises, and white contrails slashing thru the poor and slower Russian fighters.

The battalion would see more challenges , as the Russians were reported to have broken thru cleanly south of Belgorod, while the city itself had also been stormed and occupied by several Soviet rifle divisions. The battle for the city would be the affair of the infantry that was coming soon behind them. Walder expected that by next morning at the latest, the division (and his battalion) would receive an order to drive around the enemy infantry position and attack due south toward the Russian armored units moving full speed toward Kharkov.

## Rehclin-Larz Airfield
### Main Luftwaffe aircraft testing facility, May 8th, 1944

Able to reach a speed of 870 kilometers per hour, the Arado Ar-234 Blitz was the fastest operational combat aircraft in the world, slightly faster even than its cousin, the Messerschmitt Me-262 jet.

It was the world's first operational jet bomber and, in many ways, the most advanced of the Third Reich's secret weapons. It was important enough that Goering referred to it several times in staff meetings with his military leaders. Goering was annoyed that Britain's De Havilland Mosquito reconnaissance aircraft, constructed mostly of wood, was speedy enough to zoom over Germany's forces with near-total impunity. The Führer often boasted to his staff that the Ar-234 jet was even faster than the prop-driven Mosquito and that it would sweep it from the skies. And it would do a lot more. The Allies would probably not even be able to intercept it when on a bombing mission.

It was a wonderful day of May at the Rehclin-Larz airfield, located in Mecklenburg, Western Pomerania. As with the ME-262 testing, there were a plethora of high officials from the Reich. First and foremost, a proud Herman Goering, magnificent-looking (he'd lost weight recently) in his white Luftwaffe uniform, that always liked to defer his glory to his beloved air force. A new toy with which he could bolster his prestige.

The Arado bomber lifted off the runway with the help of the specially designed take-off trolley. The pilot pushed the gas to the maximum and raised in the skies in the blink of an eye, and in a thunder-like boom. It was an awe-inspiring sight.

"Mein Fuhrer," said a proud and happy Albert Speer just beside Goering. "The Arado company will be able to build them at the new Luftwaffe aircraft factory at Alt Lönnewitz in Saxony." The Reich's leader just nodded, busy as he was mesmerized by the plane's incredible performances. "We expect that they will be able to make 25 per week, indeed as fast as we can get the BMW 003 jet engines. By year's end, we will have a very potent, powerful, and most importantly high-speed bomber force", finished Speer to a still silent Goering, head jerked up at the skies.

The bomber flew overhead and then climbed again with powerful speed and noise. The Allies were in for a surprise. It was the only way for Germany, which was over-produced in every category, to have a chance of winning the war. Have better weapons, and in enough quantities to make a difference. The bomber forces had significantly been affected by this unfavorable ratio of forces since it could hardly go on mission un-escorted. Indeed, the Reich had not been able to conduct any important bombing raid in over a year.

In contrast, the Western Allies had near-complete mastery of the air. The beleaguered Luftwaffe fighters were already pretty busy just trying to fend off the hordes of planes attacking the Wehrmacht ground forces as it was. So there just weren't enough o escort bombers. The solution was to field planes fast enough that could not be intercepted by the enemy.

Without the resources of a vast empire and the plentiful oil of the Middle East, the jet project would have proved a fool's errand. But since the Reich had the capability and the means to make a lot of them with their large industrial might (and keep them flying with gas), they could tilt the balance of power in the air in favor of the Third Reich.

Goering still looked at the sky, but this time with a large smile on his face. His Luftwaffe, as he had always envisioned, would win the war for the Fatherland.

## Alma, Province of Quebec, Canada
### New powers LTD factory, May 1st 1944

Frank Whittle, former CEO and primary inventor of Powers LTD, a British aviation business that had been developing jet engines before the fall of the UK, was walking the ground of his new company in the sector of Isle-Maligne, Province of Quebec. It was located near what was to date the biggest electric dam in the world.

The empty, large alloy-clad building was swarming with the very efficient and super lovely local French-speaking people. Isle Maligne was located north of Quebec City, a train ride away. The whole sector was dotted with paper pulp companies and also had the largest aluminum complex in the world (Arvida). And to top it all, an army of skilled workers. The area was the perfect place to build a new factory: available space and unlimited energy with the dam's proximity. And most importantly, no one would come to bother his work again. The was the Atlantic Ocean to guarantee it.

He has been very close to a breakthrough in 1940 when he'd agreed with Rolls Royce for them to make the particular parts he'd needed, but then the damned Krauts had come and invaded the Kingdom, and everyone that mattered had to flee to North America.

Ever since then, Frank had been quite busy trying to get Churchill's government to notice him and his project. But the Empire was quite busy just surviving and organizing the return to Europe then. But something significant had changed. Dramatically, in fact. The Germans had come up with the first operational jet fighter in the world. With superior speed, the Reich's pilot had maneuvered around the Allied pilot and outran them. They'd also been able to target the bombers with almost near impunity. It was pretty bad.

The Allies did not have a plane that closely resembled the level of technology that the Nazis had. The results had been a disaster for the brave Allied pilots. The first attack by the ME-262 as it was called, had occurred at the end of February in Spain. At first, they had been present in small numbers, and while they were incredible, they'd been still few.

Then they started to appear in ever greater numbers, to a point where they became more than just a nuisance, but a genuine worry.

The forces tasked with protecting the landings in Portugal and bomb the Axis troops were getting trounced. They still mastered the air because they had the numbers, but their casualty ratios against the enemy were simply unsustainable. The writing was on the wall. If the Axis could field enough of the miraculous planes, they would win back the skies.

On the 5th of March, Whittle had been called for an audience with Prime Minister Churchill in his Chateau Frontenac Quebec city castle. The old bulldog had been quite amiable to him and had also apologized for the "shortness of views" of some of his underlings (that had ignored him), and simply asked Frank a one phrase question: "What do you need to make me some jets, M. Whittle?", in between two puffs of his cigars. He'd given the man a list. A list he believed was just the stuff of dreams for crazy scientists. After all, he was a ruined industrialist, having lost everything in the Nazi invasion of the homeland.

To his pleasant and relieved surprise, he'd gotten whatever he wanted—even the most extravagant demands. An extension of the mega aluminum complex built in Alma had been added in haste, and he received an army of engineers, scientists, and qualified workers.

Many were Americans, as the USA was also building a mirror factory in Virginia to make their jets when they would be ready. He also received unlimited funds. Whatever he needed.

Initially, if he'd been allowed to continue with his project unabated in the United Kingdom, Whittle had at the time believed that he would come up with a viable and operational aircraft between 1944 and 1945.

Now that he had to start from scratch, he was not sure, but with the incredible impetus of the staff, scientists, engineers, and American money, he believed he could make a miracle happen within the year. After all, he still had his plans. He also had Boeing's full cooperation, the excellent American aviation company that had built the B-17 and the B-29's.

The Allies would need the planes for the Germans were about to swap the skies with their jets.

The 88mm KWK 43 high-velocity gun barked again, and another empty shell fell with a loud clang on the floor. The tracer could be seen as a flash going toward its target, some Soviet fortified position that harbored an anti-tank gun. The explosion it created made the sandbags that were protecting the place scatter in all directions, followed by dirt, shredded body parts, and pieces of the enemy gun. What was left was just a smoldering fire and lingering greyish smoke.

The Soviet had been able to lodge two rounds into the frontal armor of Walder's Royal Tiger, bouncing off wildly, one vertically shooting up in the air to disappear in the sky, the other bouncing as well, but arcing up, spinning wildly on itself to fall in the dirt not far to churn it wildly before exploding.

This latest destroyed gun was the signal for the panzer grenadiers of the Panzer Lehr to advance. They'd disgorged out of their numerous Hannomag armored transport vehicles and were running toward the ragged Russian trenches. Walder ordered his gunner to target one of the visible machine gun nest that was protruding on top of the small, non-descript grassy hill in front of them. The machine gun could do nothing against the powerful panzer's armor, but it would be able to kill a lot of soldiers if it wasn't destroyed. There were no visible threats to their tanks, so they switched to infantry-support mode.

They'd been fighting pretty much non-stop for six days now, consuming Pervitin pills like they were candies, sleeping for mere minutes whenever they could. The powerful counter-attack by Army Group Lehr had been wildly successful in Belgorod; the division retook the town in a storm of fire and blood. But they didn't have time to rejoice, for the Red Army immediately counter-attacked with a full riffle army and three tank divisions. For days now, the army group had been bogged down fighting off the enemy, that were taking horrendous losses. The Tiger II they had were now down to 21 units, and the rest of the division pretty much a loss ratio of 25%. They were not fit for parade ground review.

But the same, even ten times over, could be said for the Russian casualties. They'd thrown units after units in the German line of fire. Every time getting them destroyed. But at the same time, inexorably inflicting casualties that the German forces could ill afford.

Walder believed that the knife fight with the damned Soviets would continue for a long while and wondered if the high-command would eventually order a retreat since they could not sustain that level of losses. He wondered what was happening on the rest of the front.

If he'd known, he would have been horrified. The overall situation wasn't much more brilliant than their petering out counter-offensive. The Reds were throwing units after fresh units in the gap they opened between Rostov and Belgorod, all aimed at Kharkov. To the point that the situation was untenable for all the Wehrmacht forces east of Kharkov, so that Marshall Von Manstein, Eastern Front theater commander, had ordered the troops defending Rostov to breakout and fight their way west to Mariupol on the Black Sea, with the ultimate objective of retreating to the Dnieper, that Manstein was feverishly preparing as an ultimate defensive line in South Russia.

For if Walder had known that his forces were now fighting hard and bitterly only to cover the general backward move that Manstein had ordered at the Dnieper line, he would have been appalled. So many battles were left to be fought...

It was a significant retreat and one that had not been taken into consideration lightly. But the importance of the Soviet attack, and the overwhelming nature of it had made it an obligation.

The goal of the German strategic retreat was the Dnieper, but that was months away, Manstein wanting to be at that line ideally only at the end of the campaigning season. The brilliant commander-in-chief had no intention of merely retreating. Instead, he wanted to retire, counter-attack, retire again, surprise the enemy. All in the name of conserving the forces he had at his command while inflicting the maximum damage to his enemy. In short, the Soviets would pay for every inch of ground that they would want to liberate in their country.

## *Extracts of Heinz Guderian 1952 book, Panzer leader*
## Stalemate and defense, May 1944

To this day, I remember the Portuguese campaign with a particular fondness. At that point we'd reached a sense that we had finally been able to master the Allied advance, after all these months of fight and retreat, first in French North Africa and now in the Iberian Peninsula.

The ME-262 jet fighters had finally brought about a certain safety for our troops since the Allied planes did not always venture over our lines anymore but only came when they attacked our ground forces. Before the advent of the 262's, life was a constant watch over the skies for the damned Allied planes. We couldn't move troops in the open during the day for fear of having them attacked and destroyed.

Consequently, now that we had some sense of peace from the scourge above, we were able to solidly anchor ourselves into the Portuguese mountains on formidable defensives positions.

The Allies themselves seemed content to fight local battles, gaining a small patch of lands every time. But there was no big offensive for the whole month of May across the Iberian peninsula. The Western Powers were stuck and now condemned to a slow crawl of a battle.

This restored sense that we had finally mastered, for a time, the enemy advance was also very positive for the troops, that received a much-needed rest. For they knew too well that the initiative was in the Allies' hands and so they would choose the moment they would attack again. The German fighting troops were, in my opinion, a superb instrument on the offense, but also was the same in defense. The toughness of the common soldier is something that

I am still proud to talk about today. We also had excellent equipment. Only their plane could have a significant impact on our panzers, and now that we had sufficient air cover, they could no more merely shell us from the air.

Theater commander general Rundstedt also had been quite busy bringing up some serious artillery in the form of two K-51 railguns that were, in any case, idling about in some German military depot. The canons, safely protected in special bunkers in the rear on their dedicated rail line, fired about ten times a day, and every time they did so, we heard the low, powerful whistling sounds of its large shells, passing over our lines to go crashing in a mighty explosion within the Allied positions.

All the while, more and more reinforcements came in Lisbon and Oporto on the enemy side, so we knew that this state of affairs would not be permanent since we received but a trickle of new forces (everything was earmarked for the Russian front). But the pause and the relative security of our troops was a godsend to all of us. The difficult months ahead after May 1944 would attest to that.
In the meantime, I went about planning, improving defensive positions upon defensive positions, and toured the frontlines, where I saw many a soldier that was determined to fight for the fatherland.

One cannot forget to mention the Spanish and Italian troops that were numerous in the theater. If not as well equipped as our forces, they did not lack bravery and skills. The Ariete and Folgore divisions, for example, were two superb examples of excellent Italian fighting divisions that had also been with me for most of the crucial campaigns of North Africa. And then the Spanish soldiers, intent on defending their homeland, did not lack in motivation.

Both forces were always supplemented with German forces, not because I did not believe in their fighting spirit, but because they needed some heavy equipment support if we wanted them to stand up to the Allied usual deluge of fire. The Wehrmacht divisions, with their excellent Pak43 anti-tank guns, 88mm guns, Tigers, Panthers, and more, could provide all of that. And they did.

Suppose we had been adequately reinforced and supplied at that moment. In that case, I believe that we would have been able to throw the Allies back into the sea and would have been able to force a military stalemate in the West. Still, as the urgency of the situation on the Eastern Front did not permit it, we were forced to a defensive stance that could only lead to more retreats and the ultimate finality of the war's end. But, it could not be helped; the Reich was stretched thin all over the map. Our job, as Rundstedt aptly put it in one of our many discussions in these months of the campaign: "Heinz, we just need to hold as long as possible..."

# Extracts from Von Manstein's 1958 book, LOST VICTORY
## War of maneuvers and mobile defense , May 1944

The Soviet High command had made their choice. They sought decision for the whole Eastern Front on the southern wing of the German army. In choosing so, they did well, for this was where the great plains of Ukraine resided, and where a war of maneuvers was possible everywhere. Not many forests or natural obstacle to block mobile forces from moving around.

They came with their usual incredible quantitative advantage and sought to swarm over the Reich's defenses. They confronted us into a battle of attrition that we could only lose. And so, we did not oblige them.

While the objective of war, in political terms, is to control a country, an area of land, or bring about the enemy's surrender, in military terms, it is quite different. Controlling territory has no impact on the most critical objective: You have to defeat your opponent's capability to make war to bring about its defeat.

By their large offensive, the Russian high command wanted just that; To destroy the Wehrmacht's whole southern wing in Russia. If we'd decided that our objective was to control territory, thus keeping control over our frontline from Belgorod to Rostov, they would have probably reached their goals, since even if we'd been able to repulse them. Our attrition rate would have been so horrendous that our army would have been too severely worn down for the next Russian offensive.

From the very start of the Soviet attack in the Belgorod-Kharkov-Rostov sector, I had no intention of doing such a thing. While Goering and Speer would complain about losing the vital, resource-rich, and factory heavy Donets basin, my goal was to preserve my forces' fighting power while inflicting the utmost damage to the enemy.

The next few months were consequently dedicated to a war of maneuver worthy of making history books. Under my control, the German fighting machine would fight, retreat, defend, counter-attack, move back, stand firm, but all in the same overall objective. Inflict casualties, retire when obvious that our attacks were bogging down and continue to fight smartly.

At the end of this campaign of movement and mobile defense, the ultimate line of defense would be the Dnieper river, the large body of water that ran continuously from the Black Sea to the Pripet Marshes. From early April, I had had the Reich's war ministry send me hordes of the Todt organization's men, war prisoners and materials to buildup the fortified line that would anchor the southern defense of the Russian land. The line would be solidified by major cities like Dnepropetrovsk and Kiev, amongst others. Once the 1944 summer campaign concluded, I envisioned that that defense line would be the rock on which the Russian waves would come and break themselves.

So, in the meantime, the forces in the South had to meet the Russian onslaught without being destroyed. The 44th infantry corps (145th, 176th, and 61st infantry divisions) succeeded in its fighting retreat West in the Don Bend without being encircled, thanks to our command's quick decision to move them backward.

The Rostov forces also moved northward (to cover the 44th corps retreat) and westward; several divisions pulled out. At the same time, I tasked the 12th Italian division to man the trenches with the 4th German para brigade within the city. Their job was to delay the

EASTERN FRONT SITUATION
MAY 15-30TH, 1944

LEGEND:
- Army-level Russian Infantry units
- Corps-level Russian Infantry units
- Army-level Russian armored units
- Corps-level Russian armored Units
- Corps-level German Infantry units
- Division-level German Infantry units
- Division-level German panzer units

enemy as long as possible, and then we would try to evacuate them by sea.

In Belgorod, the Lehr Army Group had succeeded in re-conquering the city briefly occupied by the Russians. But by May 12th, it was facing attacks so strong that I ordered them to retire westward, with the cover of the city in the center. Its job was, however, done. For the most part, it had checked the powerful thrust toward Kharkov, giving time for the rest of the troops to get organized.

On May 18th, the battle was also joined in Mariupol, west of Rostov on the Black Sea coast. Our forces would be able to make a stand there for five days , inflicting high losses to the Soviets for little of ours, safely in the city and in our defensive position. Only on the 23rd when the position was flanked from the north by Russian armor elements, that they retired westward again.

Of course, the Don bend was entirely occupied by the Soviets, and Rostov was holding, barely, and the Italian Navy was evacuating the leftover troops. Belgorod was well behind the frontline now, with the Lehr Army Group executing a brilliant fighting retreat toward

Kharkov, where I intended to make a decisive stand before continuing our backward strategic move.

On the 20th, it seemed like Kharkov would again be the scene of a major battle, as three Russian armies (around 350 000 men, in one riffle and two armored) clashed in the center of the big city with the Lehr Army Group and an additional corp. The horrific battle of attrition that I had wanted to avoid was unfortunately joined because the forward troops got engaged too deeply in the fight. While it could not be helped and created many more casualties than I intended, it gave more time for the rest of the front to retire and for my Dnieper defensive line to be completed.

By the 27th of May, both sides were exhausted, and the Russians paused for several days in Kharkov's rubble. Several other areas of the front showed signs of the Soviet offensive slowing down somewhat.

On the 29th, the last men of the 4th para brigade were evacuated by the Italian Navy's sailors. Rostov was in Russian hands. The fierce battle that had also been raging since the 21st of May in Kursk slowed significantly, Russian pressure lifting on the 28th.

The campaign was far from over, but apparently, the Red Army needed a breather. Unknown to us at the time, their casualty rate had caused them to stop for reinforcements and refit.

## Stavka meeting
### *Kuibyshev, Siberia, May 27th*

"Comrades," said Stalin in his most menacing voice to the assembled generals of the Red Army. "We must continue the attack," he said, trying to stay calm on the outside. Inwardly, he was fuming. The offensive that was supposed to destroy the southern wing of the German army was petering out, like all the others before them. This could not be permitted. His victory had waited long enough.

He kept the silence hanging for several seconds, calmly looking at all the generals in the face. He would have liked nothing better than to send a bunch of them to the firing squad. But he had learned from bitter experience when in 1942 he had done just that in the middle of fighting operations. The results had been catastrophic. So, he would still have to be gentle. But Stalin had a long memory and a very lovely little notebook on which he kept a list of people "needing to disappear."

He inhaled deeply, stood up, put his hands behind his back, and walked toward the big conference room window that was overlooking the industrial area of Kuibyshev. The city was his new, temporary capital. The generals were now looking at his back.

"Zhukov, my dear general," he said in his most flowery voice. "what do you need to resume the attack?" A collective, silent, and almost perceptible relief washed thru the conference room audience. Zhukov was only too happy to oblige his master with an answer he had hoped to be permitted to give. "Comrade First Secretary," he paused, opening a file that was in front of him. "The Army needs but a week or ten days of pause to bring replacements forward to replenish the depleted units. I also have here the suggested move of units that are right now posted to other sectors"; he paused again. "12th Guard Riffle army, 67th tank corps, and 147 Riffle Corps could be taken out of the line on the Moscow attack to be brought south".

To this, Stalin turned back, facing the general with his always un-readable expression. He sat down again and fidgeted with his pipe. That was a good sign, though Zhukov. Stalin still took his pipe out when he wanted to think and was in a calmer state of mind. "The Hitlerite's will also undoubtedly bring more reinforcements and probably follow our Moscow troop movement with some of their own, but I believe that they will move away divisions and maybe a corps, while we will move three times those numbers, thus greatly helping our numerical superiority in the south," he finished expectantly, hoping for a positive reaction from his unpredictable master. "Please do so, general," said Stalin as he lit his pipe, puffing a couple of times. "And as for the rest of you..." he slowly pointed with his free hand while the other was holding the pipe. "You'd better give me results, or by Lenin himself, I will have you removed from the army." His warning sent, he could tell that everyone present (maybe except Zhukov that always seemed unimpressed by his tirades) were cowed. They all nodded.

Stalin then went back to his imposed silence for the rest of the meeting, with Zhukov and other high command officials issuing orders and discussing the next moves that should be done. Everyone knew of the First Secretary's wish to liberate Kharkov and Kursk first and foremost, so most of the discussions happened within the boundaries to achieve that goal.

Stalin also thought it interesting that Zhukov was predicting that by the end of the campaigning season, the Red Army would be at Kiev and Dnepropetrovsk's gates. He was confident that Manstein, at one point, would simply retire behind the large Dnieper river. He laughed inwardly. If Zhukov could pull THAT out, he would make him a marshal of the Soviet Union, and maybe even some others, as well. Once in a while, his underlings needed some carrots. He didn't like it one bit, but it was necessary to keep the best ones happy. As for other generals, they would simply go on Beria's list. He didn't know which one yet, as this would depend wildly on their combat results. He reveled in the unpredictability of it all. Some of these men didn't know it yet, but they were already dead. The real funny part was that Stalin didn't even know which one either. He would soon happily find out.

## A lull in the fighting
### Southern Russia, Kharkov's outskirts, June 2nd

Heavy panzer battalion commander Erich Walder was happy. He looked at ten pristine Tiger II rolling by, new paint no scratch, and everything in perfect working order. These machines came directly from the Kassel factory and were representing much-needed replacements that brought his force back to 30 units in the battalion.

Several tank crews from previously demolished Royal Tigers had gotten new rides and were all smiles while driving in front of their unit commander. Gratefully, the fighting had stopped or slowed to a crawl on the 27th of May. They were now on their 6th day of quiet. The logistical train had been busily bringing up the necessary supplies for the continuation of the battle. Walder had been thus impressed; He did not remember such bountifulness in supply since the early days of the French campaign. The fighting troops were receiving replacements during a battle phase, which was rare. Two more Uk garrison divisions had also arrived from the city's railhead, not two days before. It was simply amazing.

For Walder, there was a real sense that things were improving in the general sense. Yes, the Reich was retreating on every front, but it seemed more potent, with more supplies and better weapons.

Which was not just an impression, but a growing fact. The Reich was losing ground, yes, but the core of the country and its allies were unscathed. Germany's industrial base was free to churn out as much stuff as they wanted without invaders destroying the factories or bombing them from above. And they had ad much gas as they wanted.

And as it was contracting ever deeper on itself, its communication lines were shortening. The Russian rail system had been finally brought to European standard since his last visit in 1943. It had been a lot of work to widen the gauge of all rails laid down in the German-occupied USSR. More trains meant better supplies for the fighting troops.

He wrote as such to his dear Ingrid in almost every one of the daily letters he sent her to her Berlin address. He had promised as such, that is to write every day when possible. Both were very much in love, and Walder longed for her presence. Ingrid also seemed to be more positive in her letters, as the food situation for civilians and civil army workers had somewhat improved. The harvest from the conquered territories was finally affecting the German war economy.

Still daydreaming, he gave a mechanical-looking Nazi salute to the two Tigers II proudly rolling by his command tent. They went to their forward positions under the batch of tree and camouflage nets where the rest of the battalion was parked to avoid the Soviet air force's curious eyes.

He could see the central part of Kharkov, full of large, black, and sky-climbing smoke clouds in the distance. While the Russian advance was stalled for now (everyone was sure it was temporary), the static fighting on the frontline themselves was still going on. His unit had been exempted from that fighting as urban warfare wasn't suited well for the hefty 75 tons lumbering giants, that were the Royal Tigers. In most instances, they could not even advance thru streets that were simply too narrow.

A flight of ME-262 jets passed overhead, going straight for the center of Kharkov, in a thunder-like noise and white contrails.

Another dogfight, thought the battalion commander. There was also the constant sound of whistling artillery shells over his head. German artillery giving their daily welcome to the Yvan's. But the men had long stopped to notice such trivial noises as they were part of their everyday life since 1939. The only time they found it bothersome to the extreme was when the enemy was lobbing shell at them.

## A new line of defense
### In between France and Spain, Pyrenes Mountains, June 3rd

General Rundstedt was walking along the half-completed reinforced concrete bunker. He was standing in the first part of the construction, while several meters to his right, the engineers were busy dropping concrete into the mold to complete the gun emplacement it would be. The sun was slowly setting on the horizon, giving a beautiful view of the mountains. The German defensive positions were being built in the thick of the wooden area on top of the old range of peaks that had always separated France and Spain. A flight of crows passed overhead, complaining loudly about all the commotion the workers were making. Looking south, he could see the plains of Spain. Looking north, more plains, but French. His view stretched to the horizon in both directions. The area was untouched by war.

He'd walked up to the position on foot, wanting to do the relaxed little trek up the French side of the mountain on an old Roman road that was still intact. The route started in the small town of Ceret, at the base of the mountains. The city was south of the old medieval fortress city of Carcassonne.

The old general hoped to god that things would not come to having to battle here, but there was no choice in the matter; he needed to plan for the worst, given the crushing Allied material superiority. They held them at bay in Portugal, and things showed signs of improvements in the air war. But there was no telling how long this state of affairs would hold.

He had asked OKW and OKH for funds and men allocated to this project. At first, it had not been easy to convince the Fuhrer and the Reich's foreign office, as this move would be viewed very badly by the Spanish government. It gave Franco the signal that the Wehrmacht would eventually abandon his country to its fate.

Which is a sense was true, but what could be done about that? If their defeat was complete in Spain because they resisted to the last bullet and with too forward a positioning, the Allies would be able to roam free into France, and then the war would indeed be over.

As it stood, the Gothic line, the grand name the propaganda ministry was planning to give to it, was the ultimate defense for Fortress Europa, Germany's Europe. With these high mountains and a robust and manned defense, it was believed they could hold the Allies at bay 'til the end of times.

Ribbentrop had been flown to Madrid, and Franco had been promised asylum in Germany with the full extent of a government in exile until the war was over and won by the Axis. Franco had not been happy and had told the old general himself in a visit a day after the Ribbentrop meeting, but he was a realist. He had seen the Allied power for himself and read the reports from his troops on the frontlines. There was no exaggeration in thinking that it was possible that Spain would be wholly occupied.

The work here would take months to be completed, but when done, the Gothic line would indeed be a sight to behold, and the Allies were in for the fight of their lives if they wanted to pierce it. In the meantime, Rundstedt would do everything in his power to keep them at bay and confine them to Portugal. He also had a big fight for Gibraltar and the Mediterranean entrance and had no intention of leaving it to the enemy without a real bloody battle.

# The Battle of Kharkov
## Renewed fighting in Southern Russia, June 12th

The large flight of Katyusha rockets was coming for Walder's position. He could hear Stalin's organ's high whistling sound, the most feared rocket artillery the Soviet employed in every fight there was to be had in Russia. Cheap to produce and mounted on simple trucks, it was highly mobile. Not remarkably accurate, it was a design flaw that the Yvan's had solved in the typical Russian way. With enough quantity firing that they were bound to hit something.

He closed the hatch of the Tiger II. He was not overly worried about his security or any other tankers in the heavy battalion. Apart from a fortunate hit that could destroy a track or find its way in the tiny holes of the engines (not impossible, he had seen it happen), the panzer's armor would be able to withstand the withering fire.

He was a little more concerned about the men in the Hannomag troop transports or busy cowering in the trenches in between his Panzers. They could be shredded with the barrage. The numerous rockets whistled closer and closer and then started to hit the ground about 200 meters in front of their positions. A loud, overpowering rumble ignited the sound waves and made the ground itself shake with frightening tremors. It grew to a deafening boom as it got over the position. Then all hell broke loose.

The tank was rocked by a couple of direct hits on the front armor and showered by shrapnel and dirt. The men of the Panzer Lehr division were experiencing what was called a rolling barrage. Walder knew from experience fighting the Yvan's for years that soon, the bastards would send their mixed tanks and riffle formations. Planes roared overhead in their multitude, and another sound could be heard over it all, if faintly—soviet regular artillery firing in the rear of the frontline positions.

It indeed was a frightening sight, and not many troops in the world could withstand that barrage but the Germans, in well-prepared positions. The soldiers had a nickname for it. They dubbed it the Russian steamroller. It was simple in its Slavic effectiveness. Concentrate firing power, troops numbers, and overwhelming artillery shelling. Then advance. Then swarm over. Not worry about losses.

After a dreadful span of time, he estimated around ten minutes, it stopped as abruptly as it had started. He risked opening the hatch to see the damage around the positions. At a glance, it seemed appalling. The dirt, which was already pitch black from earlier ground churning explosions, seemed even blacker. The ground was smoking, and little, short-spanned fires were scattered around. An inexperienced soldier would have decided, here and then, that nothing could have survived the onslaught.

But some seconds later, the ground around the Tigers seemed to move. For the most part, the brave grenadiers were alive and well, so moved out of the accumulated dirt and debris that had showered over them. Several seemed shell-shocked, being helped out by their comrades with Pervitin pills. Walder saw at least ten of them dropping a tablet into a comrade's mouth. One needed to be sharp and quickly out his daze because the enemy was coming, and fast. There was no time for dizziness. There was nothing better than those pills that every real fighting soldier on the Eastern Front was or would consume at one point against the overwhelming masses of the Red Army. At least it gave them the short-term boost they would need to fight the overwhelming odds.

The Panzer Lehr Division was positioned in the center of the city, where it had been possible for the big tanks, like Panthers, Tigers, and most especially the Tiger II's, to deploy in the large, modern streets.

They'd been sent there two days ago in a desperate counter-attack, ordered by their unit commander, Fritz Bayerlein. The Soviets had broken thru in the sector, and there was nothing heavy enough to stop the IS-2 tanks and T-34 in their enormous quantities to outflank many units of Army Group Lehr fighting in the city.

The battle for Kharkov had started four days ago by an intense Russian artillery barrage, airstrikes, and the full weight of two of their armies (over 180 000 men, in armored and riffle units) was making itself felt. The German infantry corps (30 000 men) entrenched in the city had rapidly been in grave danger of being swarmed over, so German theater command (Von Manstein) had rushed the army group (90 000 strong) into the fray. Since then, the Yvan's had sent more troops, not having enough men to overwhelm the Wehrmacht in the town. The Germans had obliged by also sending more men into the furnace, and the battle had then taken truly epic proportions.

Belgorod was well behind now. The Panzer Lehr had attacked and won there, but had had to retire, since the Russian had flowed around them like a spilling river. And now it was the same, but in Kharkov. There were so many enemies it was mind boggling.

The city that had somewhat been standing before that spring was now a wholly jumbled up pile of rubble, dead, broken machines of war and blood. Several years after the war, the battle would still be remembered as one of the Eastern Front's bloodiest fights. The Russians were advancing in their multitude, and Manstein had decided to make his stand there.

The rest of the Wehrmacht's southern wing was also buckling under pressure from the Russians. Mariupol(on the Black Sea) that had been somewhat holding after the intense Rostov battles had the day before been ordered evacuated, the troops moving backward, yet again. It would fall officially soon.

North of Kharkov, the city of Kursk, was also falling to the Russian hordes. Their numbers' simple weight was too much for the five or so divisions that had been cobbled up together for its defenses. The Axis forces were retreating in good order, but retreating nonetheless.

Walder had been privy to the general situation because of Bayerlein's visit to the frontline the very same day. The general had also predicted that the order to pull back would arrive within a day or two at the most as soon as either Kursk or Mariupol fell, in fact (or both).

Every since the start of the Kutuzov offensive, the Axis had been retreating. Rostov was now well behind the lines, as well as Voronezh, Belgorod. Kharkov, Kursk and the Black Sea coast all the way to the Crimea's entrance were now the fighting frontline. Furthermore, it did not seem like the Russian offensive was loosing any steam. The Germans, Walder included, would have to continue fighting and retreating.

# Gun duel in the Marshall Islands
## Kwajalein Atoll, June 16th, 1944

The Marshall Islands, located about 4000 kilometers southwest of the Hawaiian Islands, had been, until the outbreak of World War One, occupied by imperial Germany. The Japanese that had joined the Entente in 1915 had gleefully occupied the small islands and atoll chain, as well as many others all over the Pacific, like the Marianas or the Carolinas. In the 1930s, Japan had, of course, fortified most of them into bases, building defenses, port facilities, and airfields.

The areas were essential to the Japanese concept of perimeter defense for its empire. Every island was to be fortified and defended, thus supposedly making the American advance difficult and bloody thru the Pacific(in the complex idea of Japanese naval layered defenses). As complicated as this was to implement for the imperial high command, it nonetheless was a fact that the Americans would eventually need to saddle themselves to the task of clearing out a path into the Pacific to win the war. For the road to the Japanese home islands did not lay on the Midway-Wake Island axis since the distances were too great. The USA would need to approach closer to Japan before attacking it.

Ever since their reconquest of Hawaii in 1943, the US had been busy repairing it's base and supply logistics. After its victory at the Battle of Midway and having cleared Oahu's flanks (liberating Wake, Johnson, and Midway), they started to send significant reinforcements to Australia and New Guinea. The Marshall Islands also represented a ripe target for the USA, but their intelligence information on the area was not substantial. Admiral Nimitz had consequently decided to send an armed reconnaissance task force to test the islands defenses. The fleet was lead by aircraft carrier Saratoga, flanked by two powerful battleships, the West Virginia and the French battleship Lorraine, plus three cruisers, the

Pensacola, Portland, and Raleigh. Several destroyers screened the force from further away to ward off submarines.

Japanese strategist and admiral, Isoroku Yamamoto, had retired to Japan and planned the next phase of the war that would still prioritize defense (after the Midway setback). He'd ordered a large segment of the Imperial fleet to be sent to Truk Atoll, in the Carolina Islands, since the main American fleet had also been reported sailing into Australian waters so would soon be probing Japan's bases in New Britain and the Solomon Islands. He also sent a small (but mighty)task force to the Marshall Islands to be assigned to the area's defense, including none other than the super battleship Yamato. Another battleship, the Yamashiro, flanked it. Simultaneously, their air cover would be taken care of by the light carrier Junyo (plus the island's airfields), and cruisers Nachi, Furataka, and Myoko plus the usual screening of destroyers.

So, the stage was set for yet another battle in the Pacific. The American task force, sailing close to the small atoll of Wotje at the Marshall Island chains entrance, quickly attacked the small airfield and Japanese fortifications there. Vice-admiral Miyazato Shutoku, Yamato's commanding officer and also in charge of the Japanese tack force based in Kwajalein atoll, did not take long to react when he'd heard of the US navy approach to the area he was tasked with defending.

By the middle of the 16th of June, the Saratoga's fighters had already warded off several airstrikes from the Island's airfield. It also had shore-bombarded Wotje to ruins. Shutoku, steamed full ahead with his battleships, intended to fight it off with the US Navy's big guns. The Japanese made it to the island's vicinity by dusk, spotting the Americans with the radar from Yamato. The American fleet commander, also possessing radar, spotted the enemy and decided to fight. He might have hesitated if he'd known the extent of Japanese proficiency for naval fighting at night (they'd trained hard on that aspect) and the fact that Yamato was with the enemy task force.

As the light fell off the horizon, giving the sky an orange glow and the sea a mirror-like state, the big guns from the battleships on both sides lit up with powerful explosions. The Japanese fired first since Yamato could fire from further away because of its main guns sporting 460mm of pure power, compared to the 406 mm of the US battleships, and 340mm Lorraine. The Japanese managed to have one shot hitting the French Lorraine's superstructure before the Allies closed the range to fire their salvos.

By then, it was utterly dark, and both fleets continued to approach each other, firing away as they went. By 2 AM, the Japanese ships had closed the distance to short-range, flanked by a small non-descript atoll, and then the Yamato indeed showed its power. It found the outline of the battleship West Virginia against the moon, not two kilometers away. To the spotters on the ship, it almost seemed like the enemy appeared out of thin air. Such was the vagaries of night fighting at sea, as they had learned in their relentless training. One always had to be ready for action and to recognize the sign that a ship was nearby (sound, outline, small lights, or moon's reflections on steel, for example).

Firing its full three triple turrets salvo, it hit the American ship with the full force of its guns, creating a spectacular explosion that lit the night – and both fleet- for a long instant. All vessels from both sides then suddenly opened fire with all guns blazing. The gun exchange was spectacular, from a distance, full of flashes, tracers, large sprouts of water, explosions, awesome sound. Each side poured as much metal as they could into the other.

But this type of heavy firing could not be sustained for long. West Virginia, already stricken by the Yamato's first salvo, loudly exploded, splitting in two to sink in mere minutes. The Yamashiro, dueling with the French Lorraine, also bested its opponent, silencing it with several well-placed salvos. The Japanese cruisers were also able to straddle their opposing US numbers with many hits as well.

By 3 AM, none of the Battleship commanders responding to radio calls, the Saratoga commander ordered the full retreat south, only flanked by the destroyers. The rest of the small American task forces were also silent.

For the small cost of damage on the battleship Yamashiro (one of the main gun turrets had been destroyed by the Lorraine) and on the cruisers, the Japanese had killed two Allied battlewagons that were already sitting at the bottom of the sea by 6 AM. Of the American cruisers, only the Pensacola was able to retire, damaged but alive. The Portland and the Raleigh also were destroyed.

On surveying the extend of the disaster the next day in Hawaii, Nimitz vowed to come back to the Marshall's, but this time with overwhelming numbers.

## Berlin Chancellery
### Meeting of the OKW, June 20th, 1944

"The current situation in the East is very unsettling," said Von Paulus. He was hanging over the large map of the Russian Front that stretched the whole large table. Beside him, Halder, chief of the General Staff. Just beside, Walter Model, and in front the Fuhrer of Germany, Hermann Goering. All four men were in full military uniforms. Goering was in resplendent white, and the other three in finely cut Wehrmacht military uniforms.

They were standing in a sizeable white-painted room, adorned with the Third Reich's multiple flags on the wall. An expensive black carpet was also covering most of the floor. There were two large doors, in front of which were standing SS guards in an immobile, impassive position. A giant chandelier hung over the scene.

It was an amazingly furnished room with nice chairs in the corners and lining up the walls. There was also a coffee tray with treats and drinks on it. But none of the men seemed to notice, absorbed as they were in their meeting.

"I agree with you, general Paulus", said Halder, giving a glance at Goering, that was facing them. "But the situation seems to be improving, contrary to what we've seen operationally to this point", he finished. Model nodded silently and then spoke in is always calm manner: "The Soviet offensive is powerful, but Von Manstein has the forces to face it, and the Dnieper defensive line he wants to retire to should be able to withstand whatever the Yvan's will want to throw at it".

"Generals", said Goering in his gravest voice. "I fail to see the positiveness you are talking about. Since the start of the year, we have been reeling back from large swaths of conquered territories, been chased out of all of the North Caucasus, lost Stalingrad, Rostov, Kursk, and now Kharkov", he paused, looking at the three men with a dark face. "Please tell me how it is a good thing that we've lost all of that petroleum and the all-important Donets basin", he finished menacingly. Goering was no Hitler, meaning it was not a butcher like his former master but was known to be reckless when needed to be, as he had shown it on multiple occasions since his taking over Nazi Germany.

Before answering, Halder took a deep breath. He had some convincing to do. "Mein Fuhrer", he started in his most respectful voice, "I agree with you that our loss of territory is very problematic to the war industry..." He was interrupted by Goering: "And to the Reich's prestige!!!" He slammed his fist on the table". "You military types do not understand the political ramifications of losing so much and showing ourselves to be weak!" The Fuhrer was raging, almost foaming at the mouth. He had tried to explain to these minions that while their line of communications and troops concentrations were now better and gave them fewer headaches, the political realm suffered dearly. He continued his tirade:

"Turkey, Bulgaria, Hungary, even the Iraqi nationals, for god sake, are wavering! Don't you understand that! As you know, Franco would also leave our alliance if he was the only one to decide!", he slammed his fist again on the table. The three generals facing him were utterly silent. They knew better than to interrupt the man while he was in a fit of rage.

And Goering was right. The Turkish prime minister, Inonu that had already been against the war in the first place when pressure from within made him sign the tripartite pact of the Axis, was now said to have opened secret negotiations with the Allies. If Turkey left Germany, it would be an utter disaster, as it would not be possible to use the Baghdad to Berlin rail line to bring the oil if Ankara left the Reich. Only the naval route would be left for the Axis to get the precious substance. And that was also in jeopardy with the possible loss of Spain and Gibraltar.

Now, they had quietly pressured Frankish Spain into staying with the alliance for the simple reason that it had a robust military presence in the Iberian Peninsula. This was not the case for Turkey, which was pretty much empty of troops, and none could be sent with the state of affairs in Russia and the west. It was more the opposite. Germany needed the Turkish forces all over the map.

The Turkish had even petitioned Goering himself to remove all of the Eastern Front units, except from the Caucasus. This could simply not be permitted. So, Inonu had been flatly refused, but he would force the issue again if more defeats were inflicted on Germany.

"Gentlemen," repeated Goering icily, this is where you will stop the enemy, and there will be no more retreat or strategic withdrawal permitted!" He put his fat finger on the Dnieper river. And then he moved it to the entrance of the Crimea. "This will also be held at all costs", he said with a dark smile. "But mein Fuhrer", started Halder cautiously. "While I understand the political needs for such a move, the Crimea will be tough to hold as it will be cut off from the mainland link with the Reich, and thus will only be able to be supplied by sea", he finished, lowering his voice seeing Goering about to explode. "I. DON'T. CARE.", said the leader of Germany, with a tone dripping with acid. "You find solutions to this problem, and I keep Turkey in the war", finished Goering. The three men nodded, looking at each other, seemingly for support that they didn't find.

"And also tell that supposed genius commander of yours (...Manstein...) that he is not allowed one inch of retreating in Moscow and Leningrad. We almost faced disaster with his little mobile show last year, and I will not permit this again." The Reich's dictator was in an angry mood, and the generals knew better than to continue the discussion. They changed the subject to milder matters, like new weapon developments or Guderian's defensive successes in the Portuguese mountains.

All the while, Goering, listening to their babbling, surprised himself to think about a good shot of morphine to calm his nerves. He had gotten rid of the stuff with great pains, but the longing always came back, especially when he was stressed and pressured. And the Reich, of which he was its most supreme citizen, was attacked on all sides and showed clear signs of braking down.

He didn't know how long he would last in keeping the dreaded but blissful substance away...

Skorzeny signaled four of his men to go up the steep ridge they'd been climbing on. They could barely see him in the pitch-dark, moonless night. They'd approached the tall mountain plateau that the small, secret town of Los Alamos was built on. Fuch, the German-Jewish-Marxist-lover-spy of the USSR, had said in his papers that it was the most guarded US secret. Well, not anymore, he thought with a thin smile. He'd found the place, thanks to the spy, very detailed letters and instructions that were supposed to be for his Russian handlers.

He thought it incredibly ironic that the man, a notorious anti-Nazi, had helped the fatherland with his spying, albeit unknowingly. He pulled on the climbing rope that was stirring below him. One of his men climbed over, and he tapped him on the shoulder. Brave Sturm! he thought briefly. And then the next men were up. Ten meters to his left, the other group of four men had also climbed the side of the plateau.

The whole commando was loaded with guns and explosives, so it had been a tough climb from the mountain's base. They'd even had to kill a patrol of American soldiers that had been walking down the narrow path they were on before the final climb. They were in a hurry since they didn't know if this would raise the alarm only in the morning or soon. They'd done what they could to hide them from the path, but they would eventually be missed and then someone was bound to raise an alarm about it.

They'd made plans with the crude sketches describing the camp that Fuch had sent to his NKVD contacts. From there, they'd determined that most of the scientists slept in their own houses. So, he'd tasked six of his men to quietly transit from house to house and to kill everyone in them. Families included. No one could be permitted to raise the alarm. The rest he kept for him and Sturm, and the other remaining man. They were to destroy the large laboratory sitting roughly in the middle of the little secret town. They'd brought large quantities of the explosives acquired on the black market from stupid American criminals that didn't know it would be used against their country. Skorzeny thought a moment about it. No spy would have ever been able to do the same in Germany. First and foremost, the gestapo was surveying and watching everything, but also because the state controlled the weapons. American seemed full of guns and ordnance, to his great amazement. It was simply amazing that the enemy country had made it so easy for him to acquire the means with which to do his mission.

With a subtle glance and a small, perceptible head gesture, he signaled all the men to fan out in their designated areas of the town. It was time for them to kill some white-robed scientists. Skorzeny felt a little remorse about having to kill the wife's and kids, but after thinking long and hard about it, it just couldn't be helped. It would not be possible just to kill a scientist in front of his women and hope she would stay still while the men to other houses to kill more people. He would lose a lot of sleep over it in the next few years. In fact, while he would be praised as a hero of the Fatherland in Germany for his daring raid in Los Alamos, he would be considered a war criminal by the Allies because of his deeds today.

He tapped Sturm on the shoulder again, receiving a nervous smile from the big man. "Let's go," he said, gesturing to Sturm and the other men, that followed with determination on their face. All the while, the unsuspecting American scientists and the soldiers tasked to defend them slept or dozed in their usual blessed state of secureness. Mainland America had not yet been attacked in this war, and there was no way for them to feel threatened in any way. For they were in the middle of the USA, in the desert, and the most secret location in the whole North American continent. Or so they thought.

Because evil, silhouetted men advanced with care to their sleeping quarters. Los Alamos had been compromised, and the best daredevil of the Second World War was upon them. It would be the biggest catastrophes for the Allies to date in the war. Not only would they lose the critical laboratory, equipment, and stocked uranium to date, but most of the scientists tasked with the project were killed or seriously injured.

When Otto Skorzeny started his descent back from a burning, alarm-blaring Los Alamos plateau, he left 7 of his men dead, most of the Allied atomic program scientists also dead, and the Allies several years out of an Atomic Bomb.

## Washington D.C.
### Pentagon, supreme Allied headquarter, June 21st , 1944

For the first time in all his meetings with Winston Churchill, U.S. President Franklin Delano Roosevelt had never seen the man as speechless as at that moment. The mouth was open, the famous cigar hanging loosely, about to fall on his expensive tailored suit— empty eyes.

Along with French leader Charles de Gaulle's, the two men had been sitting down in the oval office on the plush couches, discussing the upcoming Scottish and Irish twin invasions. Looking around, it did seem like everyone was totally, utterly shocked. Admiral King, General Marshall, the British and French generals, even the aides. A fly could have been heard. King was standing erect, looking in the distance, his coffee in hand, immobile.

Roosevelt had just been handed a communication from New Mexico. From the most secret project the Allies had at the time. The project which the scientists claimed would produce a bomb so powerful it had a war-winning capability. Truckloads of monies had been sunk into the project. Scientists from all over the world had been involved, with over a hundred sites in North America also contributing.

There had been a raid on the place. No, not a raid. A massacre. Almost all of the scientists were dead, including Oppenheimer and General Leslie Groves, the man responsible for the Los Alamos project. The laboratory and equipment... Gone as well, or damaged beyond repair. The families, even the kids... It was terrible.

"How..." apparently Churchill was regaining some of his composure and then stopped. "Get me more information on this, general," pointed Roosevelt at Marshall, that quickly acknowledged, turning tail to head off to get the info his boss wanted.

Roosevelt dropped the communication's paper on the small table facing the couches and took out a cigarette from his holder. No one was yet talking, and he knew he had to try to regain his composure. He concentrated on the menial task of lighting the cigarette, then took a long puff of smoke, and let himself relax on the furniture.

After several seconds, he finally talked. "Well, gentlemen," he said, pausing and seeing that everyone now looked at him with expectant eyes, even the most famous bulldog of the British Empire, Winston Churchill. "It looks like we won't have any miracle solution, after all," he said, inhaling his cigarette again.

"You know what Franklin," said Churchill, straightening his jacket and also taking a bit of his cigar, "You are right. If we lost our home country, the United Kingdom, nothing could be worse than that. We will just have to fight the Nazis with our good old guns", he finished with typical Churchillian stolidness. The old war dog seemed to gain his energy back.

The rest of the group finally, in the following minutes, found their motivation and determination back. They'd all hoped that the Atomic bomb project would be the end of the war, but now that it wouldn't, they saddled to the task at hand.

And they talked and planned. They discussed the upcoming invasion of Ireland, of the fleet in the Atlantic sailing toward it. They spoke of the forthcoming "must happen" naval showdown with the Kriegsmarine as a prelude to northern Scotland's landings. They discussed the difficulties in Spain and how they would break the deadlock. They discussed new tank designs, of more bombers to destroy German industry, of the jet fighter project being setup in Alma, Quebec. These fighters were badly needed for they needed now that the Reich had super-fast planes.

Whatever the Reich did, the men of the free world would never relent until the evil Reich were erased from the face of the earth. No missing "biggest bomb ever seen" would impede them from their objective. They would just build smaller bombs in their thousands. Then they would bury their enemy in it.

# CHAPTER 4

## Blohm and Voss shipyards
### Maiden voyage, June 21st , 1944

The last German dreadnought battleship to ever be built silently slid out of the Blohm and Voss shipyard and into the open sea. It was the last of the H-Class design battlewagon to be completed because the Third Reich was hard-pressed on all sides, and it just didn't have the resources to spare to continue the luxury of warship buildup. Without Hitler to fuel it with his naval enthusiasm, Plan Z, the grandiose Nazi maritime shipbuilding program, had lost impetus. And besides, the reality of Germany's dire situation had caught up with it. No more steel could be allocated to anything that floated, except maybe submarines.

At the beginning of 1944, it had been decided to cancel any new naval construction, but to finish what was almost done. And the monstrous battleship that was now taking to sea was the result. And what a result it was. A true king of the waters, designed to bury its opponent in power. It could slug it out against the mighty Japanese warships Yamato and Musashi or the American Montana. It displaced 63 000 tons and sported eight large guns of 420mm caliber. Ringed with anti-aircraft guns and some awesome armor, it was designed to withstand battleship fire as much as aircraft bombs. Also added was an additional armor belt below the water for more protection against torpedoes.

The ship had been grandly christened as the battleship Hitler, to honor the late Fuhrer. Some in the Reich political hierarchy had been worried about giving such a name to a ship since it could be sunk. This could negatively affect the country's prestige. Especially since the high sea fleet was just about to face its final confrontation with the Allies. But in the end, Goering had ruled out any objections, as he had wanted to honor his dear, and unfortunately dead, master. The Hitler would soon join its brothers off Wilhelmshaven harbor and sail directly for the Orkney islands and the new naval base of Scapa Flow.

The mission was simple, if probably unfeasible. Stop the for-sure-to-happen-soon Allied landings. Admiral Lutjen, commander in chief of the fleet, had received very clear order. Engage with the fleet and either come back victorious or sink beneath the waves. For all instance and purpose, this meant that the Reich leadership, Goering at the head, had decided that the instrument they had in hand, namely the Kriegsmarine high sea fleet, would be used to try to block the landings in the United Kingdom. In his usual unfounded enthusiasm, the new Fuhrer believed that the fleet, along with his beloved Luftwaffe, would destroy the Allies and send them all to the bottom.

Since the Reich had pretty much evacuated the Isles, it was the only option it had. The high-command had bolstered the air complement in Scapa Flow and other airfields in northern Scotland, so it was hoped that with that and the powerful ship they had at hand, the Kriegsmarine would somehow prevail over the numerous allied hordes.

The impending fight would be an unequal one. The Allies had three naval nations behind them: the USA, the United Kingdom, and the French. Even the damned Canadians had started to make ships and even christened a battleship (Canada) to date!

So, the powerful Hitler, that sailed toward the blue horizon on this fine day of June 1944 went to war on what was it's first, and probably last, voyage.

## Battle in Southern Russia
### Donets Basin and Kharkov fronts, June 15th to June 30th

The Russian army's offensive had been irresistible from the start in May. First by storming over Rostov making the 44th infantry corps (145th, 176th, and 61st infantry divisions) retreat in haste from the Don Bend just above Rostov.

All the while, a powerful attack was executed by no less than three Russian armies on Belgorod (toward Kharkov), which rapidly fell on the first few days of the offensive. The Lehr Army Group, with the powerful Panzer Lehr German panzer division (and with the remarkable contribution of the Tiger II panzers), succeeded in retaking it in the same week, only to have to retire again in the face of overwhelming Soviet forces attacking from all sides.

Just north of that epic battle advanced more Russian forces with Kursk as a target. Again, the German troops retreated in good order. The commander in chief of the eastern theater for the Wehrmacht, Erich Von Manstein, had predicted this Russian offensive and had reacted to it is the only possible way for the Reich. Give ground, counter-attack where possible, win time, and delay the enemy as much as possible.

All the while, the Todt organization (and tens of thousands of Russian prisoners of war) were again hard at work to make a new line of fortification on the shores of the mighty Dnieper River. The German high command had decided to make their stand there because it represented a formidable natural obstacle. Forces were also being gathered at the built strong points along the line, and Manstein, all the while, won more time with a war of manoeuvrer in the area between the Rostov-Voronezh line to the Kiev-Dnepropetrovsk line.

By mid-may, Kharkov and Kursk were being besieged by enormous Soviet forces. Similarly, in the extreme south, the German and Axis forces fought desperate battles after desperate battles in the Mariupol area on the Black Sea's shores.

Heavy fighting broke out in the center of Kharkov amidst the gigantic factory buildings that made, before the German conquest, tanks upon tanks for the Red Army. Eventually, by the end of May, the German forces lead by the Panzer Lehr division had to retire, either by simple attrition of forces or by the fact that the Yvan's had so many troops that they were outflanking them from north and south.

Kursk then fell by the end of May / beginning of June. By mid-June, the Russians were in sight of the Crimea entrance in the south, facing Dnepropetrovsk on the Dnieper, but there they were stopped cold by a barrage of well-prepared Axis artillery. Some mobile warfare still happened south of that near the town of Melitopol.

Halfway between liberated Kharkov and German-occupied Kiev lay Poltava, where a significant tank battle was fought on the 20th of June. The Germans fielded 1200 tanks against at least 2500 Russians tanks. The major fight, mobile and confused, lasted for days on end, ending with the Wehrmacht retiring to defensive positions in the city of Poltava itself, but not before leaving a field of ruins in their wake. Superior German machines and tactics again made their marks on the Soviets. But numbers being numbers, the Red Army still rolled on over their enemy.

North of the Poltava front, more Russian forces advanced on a direct line toward Kiev, but still blocked by hard-fighting Axis troops. From the middle of June to the end of the month, confused battles happened across the frontlines.

And, eventually, there were the unmistakable signs of the Russian offensive running out of steam, after gaining from 350 to 700 kilometers of ground depending on the sectors. The fighting units needed a pause, their attrition levels terrible. The logistical train, long out of reach from the frontlines, was also required to deliver the needed war supplies for the continuation of the fight. The Soviet high-command was not done, however. Their plan for the rest of the campaigning season (until the October rains) was to take Kiev and cross the Dnieper in force. No one was keeping count in the USSR governmental instances, but it has been estimated, after the war, that the Red Army lost over 250 000 dead and 200 000 wounded in that offensive by the end of June. They would continue to bleed out more casualties in the renewed fighting several weeks later.

The respite, for the Axis, was, simply said, a godsend. If the Russians felt battered and worn down, at least they were advancing and victorious. The Axis armies, always retreating, fighting what seemed endless hordes of enemies, had been about to break. Already three Romanian divisions had been annihilated, and the Yugoslav eastern expeditionary force had all but been wiped out in the Kharkov Maelstrom. The Turkish government had recalled several divisions to the home front, which could only be interpreted by Berlin as signs of Turkey wanting out of the conflict. For themselves, the Germans had seen five of their divisions wholly destroyed and received over 100 000 casualties and the same numbers in wounded.

For the rest of the Summer of 1944, the Reich concentrated on sending all available reinforcements to that beleaguered front, while much-needed troops would also have been needed in Portugal and Spain. But there simply weren't enough. The Reich prayed to the high heavens for Manstein's defensive dispositions to work, for if the Red Army broke out of that Dnieper line, there would be much trouble for Germany.

# The battle of the North part 1
## The gathering storm, June 30$^{st}$ , 1944

The powerful Allied armada, centered on the carriers Furious, Ark Royal, Audacity, Bonaventure, the small American Langley, and the escort carrier Sangamon, plowed the cold-water waves north of Scotland. It was mighty in its own right. With over 250 planes, it could challenge any naval force in the world. It also had a large air covering force of 300 P-51 aircraft that flew from the Faroe Islands and a host of 250 bombers configured for naval action.

The flanking force for the flattops was also imposing, with battlecruisers Renown, battleships Prince of Wales (recently repaired), Ramillies, Valiant. The Canadians were again coming with some muscles, with the newly minted battleship Canada, escorted by three mint cruisers built in the Maritimes shipyards and five destroyers from the British Columbia shipyards. The USA also had provided the recently made battleship, Indiana, with its 35 000 tons of steel and three triples 16-inch gun turrets. They had finally sent the refitted battleships New Mexico, Mississippi, and Idaho.

The fleet under Admiral Spruance that normally operated near Spain had joined the northern fleet to ensure the Allies would have total superiority in naval ships. Several of its ships had been sailed back to North America after Gibraltar's disastrous battle, where most of the battlewagons had received substantial damage. All were now repaired and ready for action, except for the French Jean Bart, that had been sunk by the German shells at the Gibraltar battle. It was composed of: The British carriers Argus, Eagle, Hermes, adding another 150 planes to the mighty northern fleet. The flanking force (surface guns) was also very powerful. The French fielded the battleships Bretagne and Courbet. They also had brought the cruisers Jeanne D'arc, Cœur Vaillant, and ten destroyers. The British had brought battlewagons Malaya, Duke of

York, and Centurion with cruiser Berwick, Kent, Cornwall, five light cruisers, and ten destroyers. Finally, the American Battleships Colorado, the 9th cruiser division (2 cruisers), and 22 destroyers completed the enormous task force.

The overall commander for the Allied fleets was Admiral John Tovey, a smart and aggressive admiral. The British had more ships for the coming fight, so they would command. The right flank was assured by French Admiral Darlan and his vessels, while the left would be under the American Spruance and British Ramsay.

Sailing just south of the Orkney Islands, the German High Sea Fleet was also looking for a fight. All the ships that the Reich could muster had been marshaled for this vital battle. The Islands were almost devoid of defenses, with only three full fighting divisions and militia-type units. So, it would be the job of the fleet to fend off the Allies. Nothing could be done about the reported landings in Ireland, but admiral Lutjen, commanding the German forces, had the full intention of plunging his fleet into the thick of the fight for Scotland.

The fleet was centered around the Reich's three Aircraft carriers, the Graf Zeppelin, Europa, and Seidlitz. The German battleships were led by the Hitler, sporting its 63 000 tons and 420mm guns. More battlewagons followed, namely the Moritz, Hindenburg Frederick Der Grobe, and Lion (former English). One more battleship had been completed, the 6th H-Class battleship (the 4th had been sunk in an earlier battle), called the Blucher, a 42 000 tons monster with 400mm guns. They were flanked by the mighty Bismarck-class ships, the Bismarck itself and the Tirpitz, and finally the former French battleship Alsace. The fleet was finally complemented by 18 destroyers, six light cruisers, six heavy cruisers and had 50 U-Boats just in front of it and in the vicinity.

The battle that was about to be joined would be one epic event. The Allies needed to stay close to the landing fleet (five divisions), so they would have to duke it out with the Axis fleet coming up to challenge them. Both commanders had a pretty good idea of where the enemy was since the area where the battle was being fought (North Sea and North Atlantic) was not as large as the Pacific, so a fleet could hardly hide if someone searched seriously enough for it. And both fleets had put great effort into detecting each other.

So, the fight would first be in the air, for the fleet that could gain mastery of the skies could sink the ships of the other. But this was highly doubtful, for the sheer number of planes involved on both sides made it impossible for total air superiority. The Allies had their numerous planes (with multiple P-51's, Spitfires, Seafires, Hellcats) while the Germans had brought their BF-109, FW-190, and several squadrons of the dreaded ME-262 jet fighters.

If the Axis fleet could close the range with the Allies without being destroyed from the air (which was highly probable), there would be a duel of battlewagons to remember. And finally, while not numerous in the area, the Germans submarines could still have a severe impact if they also joined the battle.

# The battle of the North order of battle

| | |
|---|---|
| CV Graf Zeppelin | CV Furious |
| CV Seydlitz | CV Ark Royal |
| CV Europa | CV Audacity |
| BB Hindenburg | CV Bonaventure |
| BB Moritz | CV Hermes |
| BB Fredrick Der Grobe | CVL Langley |
| BB Bismarck | CV Argus |
| BB Tirpitz | CV Eagle |
| BB Hitler | BC Renown |
| BB Blucher | BB Price Of Wales |
| BB Alsace | BB Valiant |
| BB Lion | BB Ramillies |
| 15 Cruisers | BB Mississippi |
| 22 Destroyers | BB Idaho |
| 50 U-Boats | BB Idaho |
| 200 naval planes | BB Canada |
| 600 ground-based planes | BB Malaya |
| | BB Duke of York |
| | BB Centurion |
| | BB Colorado |
| | BB Courbet |
| | BB Bretagne |
| | 35 Cruisers / Light Cruisers |
| | 55 Destroyers |
| | 15 Submarines |
| | 400 naval planes |
| | 1000 Ground-based planes |
| | |

## Operation Leprechaun
### *Lublin and Dublin, June 30ˢᵗ, 1944*

THE ALLIED LANDINGS OF IRELAND
JUNE 30TH, 1944

Ireland and Northern Ireland (former British territory) had been invaded by the victorious Axis in 1940 and 1941. The rationale behind the attack was not because the Reich wanted more territory, but because it tried to deny Ireland to the Allies that could use it as a springboard to invade the United Kingdom.

But in the end, grand strategy planning had not made any difference. The whole  British Islands  and Ireland could not be held in  force  by the Axis that had  had  to recall most of  the troops that had been previously occupying the area. At the height of Ireland's occupation, the Axis had entertained five infantry divisions and several armored regiments of older types of panzers. Important fortifications had also been built in Dublin and Lublin and on the West coast at various smaller towns.

But in the end, there were just not enough troops to staff them all. The Island's overall commander, lieutenant-general Sturmmer, had only been left with a second-rate division to keep the peace in the country and fend off an Allied landing. There were many partisan problems, especially in the northern part of Ireland, where many active and numerous cells were powerful enough to control several areas.

The division Sturmmer had been left with was a reorganized one since the four divisions that left also picked up most of the best men. He was left with low strength, lightly equipped units. All the panzer had also been disengaged from Ireland for other fronts. He decided that he could not defend the whole country and concentrated on Dublin and Lublin, splitting his division into two brigades.

The Germans awaited the Allied invasion with resigned feelings. They could simply not stop the enemy from taking over. For their part, the Allies were not aware of the full extent of the Axis forces weakness in the islands, although they had a good idea of it. They had many spies in Ireland because of the many ties its citizens entertained with their brethren's multitudes that had emigrated to the United States.

The only issue they had to juggle with was where to land and how low they could keep their casualties. First of all, they wisely split the landing forces into two groups. In the northern landings, in former British-Irish territory, the English would land, and there were reasonable hopes that the local population would welcome them.

In Dublin, it had been smartly decided to send in only American troops, as the hate between Irish and British ran deep. General Marshall also took great care to have the three divisions landing in or near Dublin with substantial Irish roots soldiers.

As the Allies had coordinated their attack in Ireland and Scotland, the landing troops were ashore in both cities on the early morning of June's 30th, the same day the battle of the north happened. No extensive naval bombardment was executed in the attack, the Allies wanting the local population's support.

In the end, the six divisions that landed faced light opposition, and general Sturmmer rapidly issued a surrender order for his two brigades on the same day. There was no point in putting up too much resistance; he had been put there to be sacrificed and deter the Allies from landing in Ireland as long as possible. His mission over, he ordered his men to wave the white flag everywhere.

Mopping up operations would last for a couple more weeks, as German military and Irish militia collaborator units had to be rooted out and rounded up to be sent to large prisoner camps.

But in a general sense, by the 1st of July, Ireland was free again.

# Extracts of Heinz Guderian 1952 book, Panzer Leader
## Portuguese battle, June 29th- July 4th

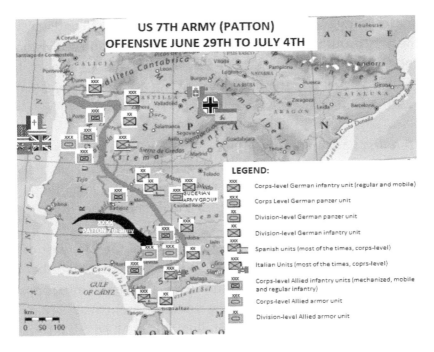

One thing could be said about Patton. He could direct an offensive. On the early morning of the 29th of June, after one amazingly powerful artillery bombardment (the American artillery complement was more than excellent), several US armor divisions, under Patton's impetus's, cleanly broke thru our dazed lines of defenses. Amidst heavy air attacks, many a German unit was lost or heavily damaged to the irresistible attack.

It was as if the enemy lunged desperately forward to breakout, in one last gathering of the will. The US forces, pushed by the strong personality and energy of their general, leading from the front like the best generals amongst us in the Wehrmacht, shattered the forward positions of infantry units holding the line just east of Badajoz on the main road to the Spanish plains.

I ordered the evacuation of the city of Badajoz and surrounding defensives positions in haste for the enemy breakthrough was very serious just south of the city. We were already not receiving any news from two of the divisions posted on the frontlines, the Spanish 17th infantry, and the 25th German infantry divisions. I learned later that, entirely stunned by artillery and air attacks, they were overwhelmed in the first hours of the attack, and by 9 Am on the 29th, their command post had simply surrendered.

For the first time in months after establishing the military stalemate in Portugal, my command faced a severe crisis. Most of the Axis forces retreated in good order, for those who didn't merely get bypassed were destined to surrender a few days in the future.

Soon, by the end of the 30th, the major city of Merida, east of our Badajoz defensive position, also fell, after a brief but sharp battle. I did not push too hard to defend the city as I gathered my troops for a counter-attack when an opening would present itself. That was the only way, in my opinion, for fending off the Allied breakthrough. For if Patton had an intrinsic quality in the offense, all these types of generals were the same, including me. There was a time when it was the right moment to stop attacking and consolidate. But this rarely happened before the panzer commander got a bloody nose or ran into some significant problem because he advanced too hard, too fast.

And so, our lines bent, and the Americans advanced. They even overran the Seville HQ, the old command post of general Rundstedt. It rapidly became apparent that the enemy's objective was further south, namely Gibraltar, since I retreated the bulk of my mobile forces north and Patton didn't follow, instead plunging toward Andalusia.

After three days of bad news, dire casualties and defeat reports, we finally started to get some good things going our way. The 4th Spanish corps, under general Blanco, helped by the heavy panzer battalion I had despatched to the area, and the 5th panzer (Panthers and Tigers II), had been able to stop the US forces in front of Cadiz, one of the last possible defensible position before the Rock of Gibraltar.

Patton's attack petered out in the broken terrain 70 kilometers west of Malaga. The Italian forces were able to stem the tide finally, again helped by some of our elite troops to achieve that goal.

On this, I must take a minute to talk about the Italian and Spanish forces under my command. While many historians have been hard and judgemental on both countries' war achievements, nothing negative can be said about the fighting soldiers themselves. I was privy to many instances where the bravery, proficiency, and overall quality of the troops helped wrest many a victorious decision from the Allies.

If only these troops had been better led, with proper officers, or equipped with the latest equipment, they could have done the same kind of achievements as the Germans. And, last but not least, most of these troops were utterly immobile in terms of modern war. There was not much motorization in the Spanish and Italian armies, their countries not producing the means to do so (trucks, tanks, and such). Consequently, many a unit was simply overwhelmed with speed by the enemy, encircled and eventually destroyed, out of supply.

Once in a while, when conditions were met and enough support from substantial troops with proper equipment, they could hold and contribute significantly to the war effort. In the case of Patton June-July offensive, this was the case. For without the vital contribution from the Spanish and Italian armies, we would have been soundly defeated.

By the 4th of July, Patton's 7th army advance had ground to a halt. However, it had created a large bulge in the front that had increased the length of the frontlines by at least 300 milometers, and we simply did not have the troops to cover it all. The Allies were bound to find ways around our defensive positions, for, in many instances, there was almost nothing defending the empty spaces between the strong positions we'd established.

For this very reason, general Rundstedt and I concluded, at a conference in the evening of the 4th at my mobile HQ, that a counter-offensive had to be mounted, at the earliest time possible. This attack was brought out of necessity, for there was no hope of holding southern Spain with traditional defenses lines. The troops just weren't there. So, we needed to attack and push back the Allies west to shorten our front.

For this, no reinforcements would be available, as the terrible news of the twin landings in Portugal and the United Kingdom, plus the large, looming Soviet offensive in the east, made the OKW busy with too many fronts. We would be left to fend for ourselves with the troops we had at our disposal, depleted as they were.

# The Battle of the North part 2
## The wolfpack menace, June 30$^{st}$, 1944

If there were any chance that the seriously outnumbered Kriegsmarine could win the upcoming epic naval battle, something would need to happen. After all, the Allies enjoyed an almost three to one superiority in aircraft carriers, and the battleship ratio favored them heavily with 15 against the German's 9. Again, three to one superiority for the Allies in auxiliary ships, and finally the worst ratio of all, a two to one advantage in planes, which meant for all instances and purpose that the Allies would have air superiority for most of the battle.

But there was one area where the Reich had the edge, the numbers, and the experience. The U-Boats. As it was, Grand Admiral Raeder had tasked his second in command, Admiral Doenitz, to gather all the submarines that could be there for the upcoming battle. The U-boats had done more than their part for the war effort ever since the start of the Second World War. They'd been active in the Atlantic and near the American coasts, sinking merchant ships or anything that could float and not retaliate. Everything that was a light cruiser and bigger usually did not have depth charges so could fall prey to the Germans. They'd kept the Allies merchant marines quite busy, and most destroyers (more than 200 hundred) were plowing the merchant ship lines to detect, root out and destroy the damned U-Boats.

All across the wind-battered waves, the Allies had noticed, recently, that the number of attacks and sinking's had significantly dropped. That was because the Kriegsmarine had ordered its U-Boats to gather in one gigantic wolfpack that would accompany the high sea fleet to what many believed in Germany as its last battle.

From all corners of the Atlantic, they came. All the U-Boats aces had been brought for this moment. Otto Kretchmer (260 000 tons sunk), Wolfgang Lüth (225 000 tons sunk), Erich Topp (195 000 tons sunk), Heinrich Liebe (175 000 tons sunk), and all of the other surviving thirty "100+ club" commanders. Some of them had even sunk battleships, aircraft carriers. Many had brushed deaths many times.

It had been challenging to get all of them to work together, as they were all lone wolfs, used to their fighting alone in small "wolfpacks." But in the end, they'd all relented to admiral Doenitz orders and adhered to the plan that the best of them all, Otto Kretchmer, had sketched. It would be a straightforward matter, after all. They would lay in wait on the enemy fleet's probable path to Northern Scotland, scattered large to make sure they'd detect the fleet as it sailed south. Once they'd detected the fleet, they would all be radioed (to hell with radio silence) to gather on the opposing fleet and would attack with one mighty attack. The trick was to attack simultaneously, and the targets would be capital ships (battleships and aircraft carriers).

And that is precisely what Kretchmer was about to do from his own submarine. He just watched one more time thru the periscope. It was just below the surface, ready to fire. He'd radioed to all of his colleagues to gather on this point on the sea. They let the screen of destroyers and lightships go over them to find themselves inside the protective ring of anti-submarines equipped ships. He'd given them a specific moment to fire, estimating the time it would take for the Allied armada to get to the gathering point he'd radioed.

He'd spotted a fat battleship, looming large and inviting in front of the U-boat. "Fire." He gave the order with his always quiet-like voice; looking again thru his periscope, he could see that one ship had already been hit, another U-boat captain already having fired.

It would now be a race for survival. They fired a total of 4 torpedoes at the enemy fleet before diving as deep as they could, for the Allied destroyers and anti-submarine planes would soon be on them and gather for the kill.

28 German submarines had been able to get to the meeting point for the attack. Torpedo wakes raced to their targets, and it did not take long for the Allied sailors to spot the engines of death coming for their ships. From all sides, ships started to dodge wildly in every direction. The armada was spread over a large space of water, so they had the room to do so. Many ships avoided torpedoes, but in the end, some were bound to get hit.

The battleships Malaya, Duke of York, Centurion, and Idaho, took severe damage from multiple torpedoes. The British aircraft carrier Hermes took three torpedoes amidship and caught fire immediately, listing heavily to port. And then all hell broke loose for the German attackers, as in minutes, Allied destroyers, planes, and other auxiliary ships pumped hundreds upon hundreds of anti-depth charges into the water. Sonar pinged in every direction, and it did not take long for the vengeful sailors to find targets. An hour later, over 15 U-boats had been either destroyed or forced to surface, in which case they were rapidly gunned down by the multitude of canons that were eagerly looking for targets.

For most of the day of the 30th and the 1st of July, the U-boat menace would appear and disappear. They didn't do as much damage as the German naval high command had hoped, but they evened the odds somewhat.

## The Battle of the North order of battle
## (after Kretchmer wolfpack attack)

| | |
|---|---|
| CV Graf Zeppelin | CV Furious |
| CV Seydlitz | CV Ark Royal |
| CV Europa | CV Audacity light torpedo damage |
| BB Hindenburg | CV Bonaventure |
| BB Moritz | CV Hermes severely damaged by torpedoes, scuttled on July 1st |
| BB Fredrick Der Grobe | CVL Langley |
| BB Bismarck | CV Argus |
| BB Tirpitz | CV Eagle |
| BB Hitler | BC Renown light torpedo damage |
| BB Blucher | BB Price Of Wales |
| BB Alsace | BB Valiant |
| BB Lion | BB Ramillies light torpedo damage |
| 15 Cruisers | BB Mississippi |
| 22 Destroyers | BB Idaho severe torpedo damage did not participate in gun duel |
| 50 U-Boats 15 losses after Kretchmer attack | BB Idaho moderate torpedo damage |
| 200 naval planes | BB Canada |
| 600 ground-based planes | BB Malaya severe torpedo damage |
| | BB Duke of York torpedo damage |
| | BB Centurion |
| | BB Colorado |
| | BB Courbet |
| | BB Bretagne |
| | BB West Virginia |
| | 35 Cruisers / Light Cruisers 3 sunk by submarines |
| | 55 Destroyers |
| | 15 Submarines |
| | 400 naval planes |
| | 1200 Ground-based planes |

# Extracts from Von Manstein's 1958 book, LOST VICTORY
## The central and northern Russian front, July 1st situation

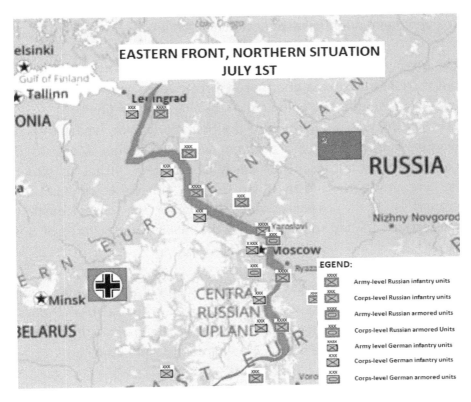

**EASTERN FRONT, NORTHERN SITUATION**
**JULY 1ST**

LEGEND:

- Army-level Russian infantry units
- Corps-level Russian infantry units
- Army-level Russian armored units
- Corps-level Russian armored Units
- Army level German infantry units
- Corps-level German infantry units
- Corps-level German armored units

While the situation worsened everywhere else, the front and, consequently, our position was remarkably stable during the first part of 1944 in central and northern Russia. The Soviet high command had made their choice and sought a decision in the south. While many in our ranks believed that the Russians had inexhaustible resources, the relative quietness of the frontlines from north of Voronezh to Leningrad proved to the contrary. So, there was hope, after all.

It was not like the Red Army was not attacking our troops in the area, as fierce street to street fighting raged for most of 1944 in

Moscow and other localities, but it lacked the very major elements that would enable it to breakthrough: Namely armor, air units and artillery in the usually significant quantities needed by the Soviets to overwhelm our qualitatively superior forces.

The enemy was still numerous, and one could not lower his guard, but the fact that no major armored forces were present gave us the edge in preventing the enemy from seeping thru our lines.

The fighting was reminiscent of the first World War, where trench warfare and artillery bombardment were the norms. Moscow, in particular, was the scene of much bloodletting. Street to street fighting amidst the mostly destroyed city, but we could hold our ground with a casualty rate so important that constant reinforcements had to be sent into the maelstrom for most of the year.

Being on the defense in this large a sector helped me transfer troops to the south, as we were always at a tremendous quantitative disadvantage there. Most of the mobile units were thus sent south, where the decisive battle of 1944 happened.

For the rest, all the forces in the central and northern sectors continued to be busy with strengthening our defensive lines and position, and the supply situation improved considerably. Gone were the days of 1942, where the troops barely got what they needed to survive. Numerous rail lines and supply depots had been established, and the troops operated in relative comfort. We'd been occupying the area for over two years, after all, so that had given the Wehrmacht's logistical arm the time it needed to support our fighting forces properly.

In 1944, I believe that our "eastern logistical limit," as it has been called by many a historian and military analyst after the war, was no more. The Wehrmacht could then have been logistically capable of reaching the Ural mountains, having as a base the central hub of Moscow and Smolensk.

But we were no longer in 1942 and 1943. The Third Reich simply did not have the strategic initiative anymore. While local offensive could still be entertained, it was no longer possible to launch any kind of Barbarossa-style campaigns or 1940 world conquest-like advances. The Allies had caught up to our troop numbers and then greatly surpassed them. Nothing was a pushover anymore.

The simple matter was that we were being overwhelmed by masses upon masses of men and materiel, so Germany's only chance to secure some kind of positive outcome for the country was to be on the defense and bring the war to some sort of stalemate so the Allies could be brought to the negotiating table.

As we reached some form of stalemate in the central and northern sectors in 1944, I hoped that I would be able to do the same with the Dnieper defensive line to secure the southern sector. Total victory was no longer attainable, but I still thought we could eventually force the Allies to the negotiating table.

## Missile attack
### The first Fritz X missile attack, June 30th, 1944

The flight of 5 Dornier Do 217 bombers flew as level as possible, escorted by a host of FW-190 fighters. They approached the Allied fleet with the bombers' full speed, which wasn't much compared to fighters. The Dornier's had been configured for anti-ship operations months before to accommodate a new kind of weapon. It was called the *Fritz X*, and it was one of the first missiles to be fired in anger in any form of combat operation. Not only that, but it was the world's first precision-guided weapon.

Back in 1938, in their Spanish Civil War involvement (with the famed Condor Legion), the Kriegsmarine and Luftwaffe had both recognized the difficulty of hitting moving ships. And so, from then on, the Reich had started to finance the necessary research projects to create something that could be guided to its target at sea.

What came out of it was a missile that could be fired from bombers, which was radio-controlled by line of sight. The Fritz X, in particular, was guided by a Kehl-Strasbourg radio control link (German manual command line-of-sight). It was far from easy to operate and had several flaws. First, when the bomber fired the missile, which was very slow even to the day's standards, it had to slow down even more to stay behind or above the Fritz X missile. To guide it, one needed to see it and pilot it to its target. A tail flare was installed in the rocket to assist the bomber's operator in tracking the weapon. It also had to be fired five kilometers from the ship it wanted to hit and had to hold a course on a level heading, not able to dodge away against fighters, or anti-aircraft. Finally, as the Allies would discover later, it was very susceptible to radio jamming, which could prevent the operator from guiding it to its target.

The second in as many days, this raid was to be the first recorded flight and hit on ships for a guided missile. The Allies had unknowingly destroyed the first strike the day before, so they didn't even know what it had tried to do. The other flight of Dornier had acted in a weird way to the Allied fighter pilots, staying level even when fired upon, so when the large P-51 fighters interceptor flight had scattered the FW-190 escorts, they'd been able to shoot down all of the five bombers. They'd been weird reports of some sort of glider racing to the battleship Prince of Wales, but the anti-aircraft flak guns had promptly destroyed it.

So, without any fuss, Gaston Lamirande, his mate August McIntyre and other Bonaventure squadrons fighters approached the particular flight of Dornier and FW-190 fighters. They didn't feel anything different, except that they had even numbers with which to fight the enemy, a rare occurrence these days, as the Allies had the quantities in the air war.

Gaston pushed his plane to full gas to approach the first fighter in his line of sight. Both planes closed the range in seconds, and both pilots could see the other's line of tracer shells arcing wildly toward their fighter. Again, the French-Canadian pilot got lucky and hit the German plane first, bursting his enemy's left-wing into fragments. Hence, the FW-190 immediately tailed down, spinning wildly to hit the water in a fiery, but brief crash.

The fight was pretty much even, two Dornier bombers even being shot down, but at one point, Gaston could have sworn that he saw what seemed to be a smaller plane or some type of glider rocket-out of the German's bomber bays.

On a hunch, he veered his plane toward one of the weird-looking gliders. The … he didn't know how to call what he saw… flew level, at speed lower than his fighter, so he had no problem catching up to it. By then, he and the "glider" were getting very close to the ship. Gaston had one of them in his line of sight and fired a burst of his canon. It didn't even dodge of veer away, so it was hit and disintegrated in flight.

As Lamirande was retaking altitude to potentially try to spot the other "gliders" on a course for the fleet, he noticed that the flak guns on the ships bunched up around the Bonaventure started to lit the sky with tracer shells. Again, the weird flying machine didn't dodge but kept flying straight. They seemed, to Gaston, on a collision course for the ships. By that time, only two of the Fritz X missiles were left, and both went thru the anti-aircraft barrage unscathed.

What followed was a fantastic display of destruction. At full speed, the Fritz X was designed to pierce 130 mm of armor (5.1 inches). The guiding pilots on the Dornier Bombers, which were also getting close to the fleet, guided them everywhere except on the 12 inches thick armor belt of the battleship Valiant superstructure it was aiming at. The missile hit one of the main gun turrets in a loud and destructive explosion, sending a large plume of smoke and debris in the air and surrounding sea. The other guided missile had been aiming at the carrier Bonaventure. Still, for some reason, the operator on the Dornier bomber re-directed it to the poor American Cruiser Vincennes that was gallantly trying to shoot it down. The Fritz X hit the ship with so much force that it merely splintered in all directions, igniting its main magazines and destroying the cruiser outright.

Their terrible deed done, the two remaining Dornier's veered back home, toward their Scottish airbase. Above them, the dogfight continued for some time, and the stunned allied pilots and sailors could only finish the fight with the FW-190 in impotent rage at what had been done to their fleet comrades.

The Fritz X would be produced in great numbers for the rest of the war, the Germans being able, this way, to cope with their inferiority in surface and aircraft carrier ships. They would even be integrated in coastal defenses when the time came for the Allies to try and return to the European mainland on the French beaches.

They would inflict much death and destruction on the Allied naval fleet and personnel at the end of the engagement. Gaston flew back to the carrier, followed by a somber mood. No one would party tonight in the officer's mess.

# The Battle of the North part 3
## The Kriegsmarine last charge, June 30$^{st}$ to July 1st, 1944

With a large air umbrella covering it for all its sailing journey, the German High Sea Fleet steamed full speed toward the last reported enemy fleet position. Above it, fierce air battles ensued from the moment it reached Aberdeen on the eastern coast of Scotland on the morning of the 30th of June. Admiral Lutjen, the overall German fleet commander, wanted to close the range with the enemy. Several German ships received bombs and torpedoes. On the way to engagement range, they lost two cruisers and had three battleships damaged by enemy planes. The Seydlitz aircraft carrier received two bombs on its runway, making its plane rebase in the airfield near the coast of Scotland. The ship would sail back to Germany in the afternoon since it could no longer participate in the fight.

The damage was surprisingly not crucial to the fleet because the Luftwaffe concentrated all the jet planes available in the theater (150) to the fleet's covering. Being very close to their airfield, they taxied from fleet to runway to refuel in record times. The Allies throwing planes after planes at the German ships would lose many pilots that day, trying to get across the Axis air umbrella.

Another reason for the slight damage was the fact that the Allies also had to cover their ships from the other German attacks, first from the damned U-Boats threat, then the Fritz X missile and other naval-attack planes (Dornier 217, JU88, for example) that threw themselves at the horde of ships coming for Scotland.

While the air battle would undoubtedly be a significant factor in the day's final results, the surface battle that was about to be joined would be the deciding factor. Also steaming full south, Allied overall combined fleet commander John Tovey boasted what was probably the most powerful fleet gathered for one battle to date in history. Himself on the bridge of battleships prince of wales, he led three columns with each five of the big gun's ships. Fifteen awesome tools of war slid effortlessly on the turbulent northern waters. During the morning and early afternoon, they fended off large U-Boat attacks and also Luftwaffe air attacks. They'd even had to endure a new weapon, guided naval air missiles. While the fleet had sustained some important damage, it was still a lot more powerful and its enemy, by an order of magnitude.

Tovey had had to order a speed reduction for all his ships to accommodate the slowest units that had lost much momentum with the torpedoes and bombs they received. Valiant, Ramillies, Idaho, Duke of York, Malaya, and finally, Bretagne had either been hit or damaged by the subs or the Fritz X, so had consequently been affected in their overall knots speed. Nonetheless, this did not matter much to the Allied admiral since the Germans sought battle, so speed was not the most important factor on that day, but many guns. And he had a serious edge.

In the middle of the afternoon, the Germans finally opened the battle, with the mighty battleship Hitler, brimming with its 420mm guns, able to fire from extreme range. Simultaneously, every other gunship in either fleet would have to wait another twenty minutes or so before being in range. Large sprouts of water rose and fell in the Allied fleet midst, the Hitler blazing away with all it got. Even with radar operators and spotting planes, it was difficult to hit a moving target from that far away. For 15 minutes, the Allies held their breath, with every near misses of Hitler's. But eventually, the Germans, with their excellent radar, gun-range finder, and experienced sailors, found their mark.

Four of the gigantic 420mm shells (there was no other caliber of that size in the Atlantic) finally hit an Allied ship. The unlucky receiving end was the American battleship, Colorado. A gigantic explosion shrouded the mighty ship in an instant. A great flash was seen by the vessel in the vicinity. While that flash still blinded everyone, a second, larger explosion blazed loud, and an enormous plume of dark smoke and debris skyrocketed in the air and horizontally on the Colorado port side. A minute later, when the smoke cleared, not much could be seen. The after-action reports talked of some sailors seeing the American ships' rear decks disappearing into the water. But whatever happened, for most present near Colorado, the vessel was simply gone, replaced by a large debris field, and an oily, floating mass.

For a time, everyone in the fleet that saw the event (mostly the command bridges of the other battleships and surface ships) were transfixed. But the Hitler's shells loud, whistling sounds brought everyone out of their trance. More shells landed right where Colorado had been, churning the darkish, mushy, fiery patch of debris even more.

The two groups of opposing ships were all in range by 14h30 in the afternoon. On both sides, the sight was mindboggling. The German coordinated a powerful gun broadside, ships all in a single file. The gun faced in the enemy's direction, and rippled the sea in front of them, creating a godly flash. At the same time, the noise of it could be heard as much as 60 kilometers away in Scotland's hinterland.

The Allied response was even more impressive. Never again in history would 14 battleships fire together in that large a broadside. That loud boom was heard even further away, as much as 75 km! The sea in front of the ships seemed to boil. In fact, it was. Vapor rose like misty vapor in front of the battleships after their first combined mighty shot.

And then on both sides, the shells started to land, a moment from each other. The Allied fleet took severe damage, the Renown being straddled with three shells of the Blucher, while the Mississippi saw two of its main gun turret destroyed. Ramillies, Valiant, Centurion, Courbet, West Virginia, and Canada also got hit but were able to shrug off the hits with their armor belt, losing only secondary guns, speed, or other. Only the Malaya, already weakened by severe torpedo damage, was the worst for it, being hit by lucky shot from the Bismarck. Receiving five shells, two of them on the conning tower, it seemed to be a floating island of fire and didn't shoot back after being hit. But no one had the time to pay any attention to that little a detail in the maelstrom.

If the German guns had done some critical damage, it was nothing compared to the storm of steel that the Allies had thrown at the Kriegsmarine's ships. Over 125 battleship shells landed in the first fired broadside, and it created hell for the poor Nazi sailors. The battleship Moritz was straddled with no less than eight shots from the Valiant, Mississippi, and Courbet. The hits that rocked the beleaguered ship stunned its crew and created damage beyond comprehension for any average person. The ship was already almost out of the battle; only two of its gun turret would fire back after. Alsace and Lion also got the brunt of the enemy's wrath, hit multiple times on their decks, armor belt, and conning tower. Both ships would remain in the fight, but with much-diminished firepower and an almost non-existent speed. The ship could still fire but would be doomed, as it would not move out of the area after the battle. The Bismarck, Tirpitz, Hitler, and Hindenburg also got hit several times, but mostly shrugged it off and continuing the struggle.

And then the ships fired when ready, making for a cacophony of fire and sounds, in the un-coordinated shelling. All the while, the

smaller ships, cruisers, destroyers, and the likes steamed full speed to close the range. They would join in the fight about 20 minutes into the long-range gun duel.

By 15h30 (an hour into the mighty naval battle), the losses were terrible on both sides. On the Allied side, the Bretagne, Mississippi, Ramillies, Valiant, and Duke of York, were either blown up and now flaming hulks or sinking to the sea's bottom. The Germans had lost the H-class battleships Hindenburg, Moritz, and Fedrick Der Grobe. The Bismarck and Tirpitz were by 15h25 blazing hulks that would no longer fight that day. The Alsace and Blucher were sinking, listing heavily, but still fighting. Only the Hitler, being hit multiple times, had been able to shrug off the hits, retaining all its powerful gun turrets, but blackened by dozens of hits on its armor belt and superstructure.

Both sides were in bad shape, and things got even worse for the Kriegsmarine. The Allies launched the most significant air raid of the day by 16h00 on the task force centered around the two aircraft carriers left to Admiral Lutjen (that hovered some distance south of the primary battle, sending waves after waves of planes). The German 75 ME-262 (the other 75 were over the battleships force further north) and 150 FW-190 fighters got badly swarmed by over 700 Allied aircrafts, fighters, and bombers alike. The German airmen extracted a terrible toll on the enemy, but there were too many to cope with, and dozens upon dozens of the naval bombers were able to drop their bombs or launch their torpedoes.

By 16h15, all two carriers were severely stricken. They were on fire, listing to port or starboard, the Europa even sinking rapidly. By 17h45, all hands were evacuated from the ships, and the cruiser Breslau, Goeben, and Hohenzollern scuttled the flaming, sinking hulls.
At that point, it was every man for himself for the Kriegsmarine. Admiral Lutjen was dead, having been killed in one of the fiery explosions that rocked the Bismarck. Not many high-level German commanders were left either alive or intact, functioning ships.

Admiral Theodore Krancke, commander of the mighty Hitler, took over command by 19h00. As night approached, the skies cleared of planes, and both sides, exhausted from the heavy fighting of the day, fired more sporadically, both fleets trying to retire a little out of range. For admiral John Tovey, commander of the Allied fleet, it was to lick the wounds and prepare to fight the next day. For Krancke, it was not the same. His fleet was almost destroyed, and what was left still floating was crippled or heavily damaged at best. Ordering a large smokescreen to be laid across its front, he called the turn-around of the whole High Seas Fleet, or what was left of it. It would first limp back to London harbor, but only for quick repairs on its many damaged and stricken ships.

The German Kriegsmarine had been defeated, and now nothing was standing in the way of the Allies reconquest of the United Kingdom.

For the first time in the war, the Allies had won a clear, resounding victory over the Axis.

# The Battle of the North final results and casualties

| | |
|---|---|
| CV Graf Zeppelin crippled by air raid, scuttled by 17h45 | CV Furious |
| CV Seydlitz crippled by air raid, returned to Germany, did not participate in fight | CV Ark Royal, heavily damaged by Fritz X on July 1st |
| CV Europa crippled by air raid, scuttled by 17h45 | CV Audacity light torpedo damage |
| BB Hindenburg, sunk by Duke of York, 15h19 | CV Bonaventure |
| BB Moritz, heavy damage from 3 BB, sunk by Canada at 15h27 | CV Hermes severely damaged by torpedoes, scuttled on July 1st |
| BB Fredrick Der Grobe, sunk by Malaya and Renown at 15h15 | CVL Langley, sunk by German airstrike on July 1st |
| BB Bismarck crippled by Centurion and Courbet, no longer fighting, 15h25, scuttled by U-Boats at 20h00 | CV Argus deck damaged by Fritz X bomb |
| BB Tirpitz crippled by Price of Wales and West Virginia by 15h19, scuttled by U-Boats at 1h00 AM on July first | CV Eagle |
| BB Hitler moderate shell damage | BC Renown light torpedo damage, moderate shell damage |
| BB Blucher 2 gun turret destroyed, sinking by 15h30 | BB Price Of Wales, moderate shell damage |
| BB Alsace Slowly sinking by 15h30, but still fighting (heavy list to port), scuttled at 8 AM on July 1st | BB Valiant 1 main gun turret destroyed by Fritz X (sunk by Fedrick Der Grobe at 15h30) |
| BB Lion, moderate damage, conning tower hit | BB Ramillies light torpedo damage, sunk by Hindenburg (15h14) |
| 15 Cruisers -2 to plane attacks 10 cruisers sunk by gunfire | BB Mississippi, sunk by Bismarck on 15h15 |
| 22 Destroyers 12 sunk | BB Idaho severe torpedo damage did not participate in gun duel |
| 50 U-Boats 15 losses after Kretchmer attack, 1o more losses on the 30th and 1st of July. | BB Canada, moderate damage |
| 200 naval planes. 167 lost | BB Malaya severe torpedo damage |
| 600 ground-based planes 367 lost | BB Duke of York torpedo damage (sunk at 15h20 by Hitler) |
| | BB Centurion, heavy damage, still afloat |
| | BB Colorado sunk by BB Hitler |
| | BB Courbet, heavy damage |
| | BB Bretagne 2 Fritz X bomb hits, light damage, sunk by 15h07 (by Tirpitz) |
| | BB West Virginia, moderate damage |

| | |
|---|---|
| | 35 Cruisers / Light Cruisers 3 sunk by submarines 1 sunk by Fritz X missile, 10 sunk during the gun duel |
| | 55 Destroyers, 8 lost |
| | 15 Submarines, 5 lost |
| | 400 naval planes, 250 lost |
| | 1200 Ground-based planes, 650 lost |

# The landings
## Northern Scottish shores, July 2nd , 1944

With the German High Sea Fleet's virtual destruction, the Allied landings' results were a foregone conclusion. Added to that fact was that they were mostly un-opposed. The Germans had kept very meager forces in the United Kingdom. Two weak infantry and not very mobile divisions. Not even assembled in one place to fight, but scattered all over the major cities, for the British populace was in a restless mood.

In fact, things had never quieted down after the conquest in 1940 and 1941. Tons of partisan groups had taken to the hills and forest all over the place and had harassed the German authorities. More than one operation had been executed against them, but as with Russia, the problem just grew bigger every passing day and with every additional reprisal that the German gave to the partisans and local towns. The more the Germany Nazi and Gestapo brutalized the populace in retaliation, the more the brave British citizens took arms.

So, the commander in England, General Heinrich Zeitler, had chosen the best of all his bad options. He scattered his forces all over the country to slow the Allies down in their conquest of the land. He did post a battalion (1 German division= 12 battalions) of infantry in Inverness, in the northern wastes, and another in Aberdeen.

He'd ordered them to entrench and slow down the enemy as best they could. They'd been supplied with a sizeable number of anti-tank weapons, like the PAK 1943 anti-tank gun or the excellent 88mm flak guns.

After the battle of the North, Zeitler had expected that his forces would  have another two to three days to prepare for the unavoidable assault. But one of the things that the Germans didn't plan for, or couldn't have done anything about anyway because they just didn't have the capability, was a paratrooper attack.

The Allies had taken notes of the Wehrmacht incredible successes in 1940 and 1941 with their Fallshirmjagers operations in London, Low countries, Malta and Tabriz. They had proven that parachuted forces could overwhelm unprepared or numerically inferior forces and rapidly take cities. They'd also taken more notes on the failed operation that the Germans did in Cyprus, where carefully prepared defenses and numerous troops massacred the German soldiers.

And they'd done their homework, sending hundreds of raids and reconnaissance flights, in addition to the information the numerous partisans gave them. What came out of it was that the Germans were not in force in the north, and so that paratroopers could be dropped with a reasonable chance of success.

After the para forces were sent to Portugal in the recent landings, two Americans, one Canadian and one British division, were still available. They were gathered in the Faroe Islands at the end of May. On July 2nd, in the early morning light, the four units were dropped in Inverness, Fort William, Aberdeen, and Dundee, about 50 kilometers from Edinburgh.

By 10 Am the morning, all four objective cities were taken, and all German troops in their vicinity had surrendered. All the while, an additional six divisions of Allied troops (3 Canadians, 2 British, and 1 American) landed in the extreme Scottish north, with no real opposition apart from scattered fighting. On the falling light of the July 2nd skies, the Allied commanders on all sectors reported complete success all across the line. The Allies were back in the United Kingdom.

# BBC Radio address
## Churchill to the people of the Empire and of the free world, July 3rd , 1944

(...) In a thousand years, the world will still talk about this very moment. The moment when liberty began its march toward final victory. All the United Kingdom people, either be Scottish, Welsh, English, can now see the beacon of freedom coming to them. For the forces of good are on the winning side everywhere. Not only that, their boots are speeding in Northern Scotland, in North Africa, and Portugal. The whole world sees the light seeping thru the cracks of the crumbling wall of steel that had emerged, not four years in the past(...)

(...) For the forces of evil, namely the disgusting Nazi regime, should beware. The free men of the world are at their door. They should beware because we will smash their armies, their will to fight. We will smash their cities as they smashed ours. We will disintegrate their capability to make war for this folly never to happen again in a thousand years (...)

(...) Soon, mother vengeance will be upon Germany, and we, the free people of the British Empire and of the world, will make sure that the maelstrom of war burns them down until they are no more. People, of London. People of Edinburgh. People of Manchester. People of the whole Kingdom. Rise and undo the shackles of oppression. Rise and thrown back the invader across the sea(...)

(...) You ask, what is our goal? I can say: It is to wage war, by sea, land, and air, with all our might and with all the strength that God can give us; to wage war against a monstrous tyranny, never surpassed in the dark, lamentable catalog of human crime. That is our goal(...)

# President Roosevelt to the Congress
## Roosevelt's address to the nation, July 3rd , 1944

My Fellow Americans.

Last night, when I spoke with you about the fall of Rome, I knew at that moment that troops of the United States and our Allies were crossing the Atlantic in another and greater operation. It has come to pass with success thus far. We have beaten the forces of evil on land, in the air, and at sea.

And so, in this poignant hour, I ask you to join with me in prayer: Almighty God: Our sons, pride of our nation, this day have set upon a mighty endeavor, a struggle to preserve our Republic, our religion, and our civilization and to set free a suffering humanity. Lead them straight and true; give strength to their arms, stoutness to their hearts, steadfastness in their faith.

They will need Thy blessings. Their road will be long and hard. For the enemy is strong. He may hurl back our forces. Success may not come with rushing speed, but we shall return again and again; and we know that by Thy grace, and by the righteousness of our cause, our sons will triumph.

They will be sore tried, by night and by day, without rest -- until the victory is won. The darkness will be banished by noise and flame. Men's souls will be shaken with the violence's of war.

For these men are lately drawn from the ways of peace. They fight not for the lust of conquest. They fight to end conquest. They fight to liberate. They fight to let justice arise and tolerance and goodwill among all Thy people. They yearn but for the end of battle, for their return to the haven of home.

Some will never return. Embrace these, Father, and receive them, Thy heroic servants, into Thy United Kingdom. And for us at home -- fathers, mothers, children, wives, sisters, and brothers of brave men overseas, whose thoughts and prayers are ever with them -- help us, Almighty God, to rededicate ourselves in renewed faith in Thee in this hour of great sacrifice.

Many people have urged that I call the nation into a single day of special prayer. But because the road is long and the desire is great, I ask that our people devote themselves in a continuance of prayer. As we rise to each new day, and again when each day is spent, let words of prayer be on our lips, invoking Thy help to our efforts.

Give us strength, too -- strength in our daily tasks, to redouble the contributions we make in the physical and the material support of our armed forces.

And let our hearts be stout, to wait out the long travail, to bear sorrows that may come, to impart our courage unto our sons wheresoever they may be.

And, O Lord, give us faith. Give us faith in Thee; faith in our sons; faith in each other; faith in our united crusade. Let not the keenness of our spirit ever be dulled. Let not the impacts of temporary events, of temporal matters of but fleeting moment -- let not these deter us in our unconquerable purpose.

With Thy blessing, we shall prevail over the unholy forces of our enemy. Help us to conquer the apostles of greed and racial arrogances. Lead us to saving our country and with our sister Nations into a world unity that will spell a sure peace -- a peace invulnerable to the scheming's of unworthy men. And a peace that will let all of men live in freedom, reaping the just rewards of their honest toil.

Thy will be done, Almighty God.
Amen.

President Franklin D. Roosevelt – July 3rd, 1944,

On the eve of a renewed Red Army offensive in the south, of which we could see the signs with increased patrols, artillery bombardment, and Soviet air presence, I remember feeling quite right about the overall situation if the Axis forces on the southern wing. I had the full intention of frustrating the Stavka's plans for the south.

After receiving several new divisions, amongst other a couple of SS panzer divisions that were newly created (two Hitlerjungen units, or Hitler's youth units), I reviewed the disposition of our forces that were still east of the Dnieper. The Poltava and Melitopol fronts were holding steady but would need to be retired rapidly over the river once the fighting started in earnest.

I also was confident that while the Soviet forces would bypass the Crimea entrance and thus isolate it from a land connection, we could still hold our control over the region with the Perekop Isthmus, which was not five km across and so very easy to defend and fortify. We'd entrenched two veteran divisions there, along with three Italian and one Turkish supporting division and much heavy artillery that had been left there ever since the siege of Sebastopol. Supplies would be taken care of by the Axis navies (Turkish, Bulgarian and Italian).

The Todt organization had worked well, along with the thousands upon thousands of Russian prisoners of war that we'd put to work on the defensive positions. The Dnepropetrovsk and Kiev areas would be very hard-to-take areas. All along the large Dnieper, trenches, artillery, troops, bunkers had been dug, built, and manned. All was ready to receive the Russian hordes, of which I felt confident that we would stop cold.

What was left was to make sure the war of maneuvers that would be executed soon when the enemy started to attack would inflict as many casualties to the Yvan's as possible, but not to hold the territory. The Panzer Lehr Army Group that had been melded into the new, overall army group that I re-named as Army Group Dnieper would be ordered to retire and fight as they moved west, but not to engage the Russian hordes completely. The trick would be to attack just enough not to get entangled in a furious fight that would inflict needless losses for a territory that I already planned on giving away to the Soviets.

All the less-mobile divisions had already been moved across west to their defensive positions. What held the front in Poltava and Melitopol were mobile and mechanized forces, beefed up with armored elements. The Panzer Lehr Division had been kept on the front to feint the Russians into thinking that we would leave the bulk of our forces on the eastern bank of the Dnieper.

The only gray area left was the fact that OKW had removed three air fleets out of the four I had for the southern front. At the same time, they did the same in the north, leaving only a meager total of two Luftflotte (or just over 800 planes) for the whole Russian Front, which was insufficient. Of course, one had to think of the overall strategic situation. These planes were needed in the face of the vast problems the Western Allies were creating with their powerful offensives in Spain and the United Kingdom's vicinity. Nonetheless, I could not help but feel helpless and naked in the face of what would surely be a Russian onslaught from the air. In the next few weeks, it would prove to be just as problematic as I had envisioned in my most negative perspective, unfortunately.

While we bolstered our anti-aircraft defenses significantly in the defensive works that Todt's people and POW built, It would not be enough to fend off the hordes of Yak bomber planes that would swoop down on our brave forces when the Stavka launched their powerful attacks.

But overall, the Axis forces in the southern part of the Russian front were ready for the next phase of the campaign.

# Extracts of Heinz Guderian 1952 book, Panzer Leader
## Counter-offensive, July 12ⁿᵈ- July 15ᵗʰ

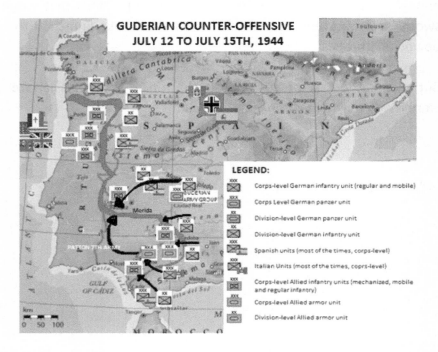

Six years after my successful Badajoz counter-offensive, and long after the war, I was to share several drinks in Berlin with former Field-Marshal (named to the distinction in 1944) Rundstedt at a Wehrmacht officers reunion event. While sitting at the same table during the evening, we happened to discuss the events of 1944. The Field-Marshal told me that he had never understood how I managed to carry out his orders to advance on Badajoz so quickly. I was able, belatedly enough, to give him the explanation. As a result of its operational role, the Panzer Group was able to see the situation from the same perspective as that of the Army Group and thus reach the same conclusions. We had hit the Ami's where they'd expected it the least (in a manner of speaking), I explained to the old war leader in great details, and over many drinks.

(...)By July 5th, the fighting along the southern Spanish frontlines had died down to fixed battles right up to July 11th. The US was not known to be fond of high attrition battles (their tendency to avoid casualties was a well-known fact thru the war), so kept well away on their side of the no man's land between our respective trenches, waiting for their proverbial material superiority to be restored to a point where they would be comfortable to attack again. By the 8th, there were apparent signs of a renewed offensive, as the US 7th army received a steady stream of supplies and replacements. At the same time, our logistical train suffered greatly because the Allies were slowly getting the upper hand in the air. Consequently, air raids against rail lines, trucks convoys, and the likes were frequent, as the Luftwaffe made itself scarcer and scarcer with each passing day.

On July 10th, after receiving, finally, the supplies that would be needed for the advance and attack southwest, I was cabled the final go-ahead order from general Rundstedt. My orders were clear. Cut across the front and take back Badajoz. In this way, it was hoped by high command that we could crumble the southern offensive toward the very strategic Gibraltar rock. I did not believe that we had the forces necessary to destroy the enemy in the Peninsula and certainly not in my sector, with the mighty US 7th just south of my starting point for the counter-offensive. But with a quick advance to Badajoz, we could cut the enemy's supplies in such a way that they would need to retreat and double back to the Portuguese border.

On the early morning hours of the 12th, before the sun was up, I paid a short visit to the front and had a word with the reconnaissance battalion leaders that had just come back from a foray into enemy lines. They'd been able to acquire a pretty accurate description of the situation facing us. It was thanks to their tireless efforts that we had had such superb intelligence of the enemy. Among the best of those officers was Lieutenant Von

Bunau, who was later to lose his life in Germany's service, near Merida. So, my army group was facing, more or less, a full mechanized corps, spread over an impressive stretch of the frontline. It seemed that the US did not believe that we could launch an attack, for the units facing us behaved as a screening force.

I would prove the American commanders wrong in their assessment that we'd reach the "bottom of the barrel" as they certainly thought we had. Contrary to their misleading beliefs, we retained a powerful punch with our ground and armored forces. I had several SS panzer divisions, like the Death's head, which was a superb instrument of war, regardless of their political views and pretensions of racial superiority. Also, at the very tip of our advance would be the by now famous (or infamous if you were on the wrong side of their gun nozzles) Tiger II's, of which we received enough to bring back the 4th heavy panzer battalion up to strength (nominal of 40 units).

At 6 AM, after a powerful two hours artillery barrage from our brave forces (we'd been able to husband enough ammunitions to have a very efficient shelling before the attack), we set off in the first rays of light of the coming Spanish day.

The Americans were shocked or appeared to be, judging by their reaction to our sudden attack. By about 1 PM, we'd sliced thru an entire US division (the 87th), leaving most of it behind for the infantry to deal with. By the end of the same day, we were back at Merida, and I even dined with the commander of the 87th, general Stillwell that had been freshly captured. He was still stunned by what happened, but my staff and I tried to remain civil and courteous to him and his men. They'd been captured by one of our fast-moving motorcycle battalion (again Lieutenant Von Bunau), trying to retire in confusion, with a broken-down Studebaker truck on the side of the road.

On the 13th, some of my units were hit on their southern flank by a severe armored American attack, and I drove to the area (south of Merida) to lead the fight. The numerous Sherman tanks would have overwhelmed us, but for the timely arrival of the 4th heavy panzer battalion on the scene, that made short work of the Ami's little foray into our flanks.

Then for the whole day of the 14th, we drove, fought, and clawed our way relentlessly toward Badajoz, which was reached in the early hours of the 15th. Not even one German soldier and commander avoided some good Amphetamines pills (Pervitin). Since the start of the offensive, we hadn't slept so constant were the battles, air raids above our heads, and American counter-attacks.

And then the reports that Patton's lead armored elements were in sight south of Badajoz arrived at my mobile HQ. The damned enemy also attacked with a new type of tanks that could, with the right angles and with well-placed hits, destroy even the Tiger II with their shells. The Sherman's gun-upgraded firefly models. We were lucky that they were still in low numbers during that powerful attack compared to their shorter canon brothers. But this did not bode well for the future, knowing the enormous prodigiousness of the American industry.

Nonetheless, the fight with Patton 7th was very intense for most of the day and reached a crescendo by nightfall. According to air reconnaissance flights sent over the US positions, the American general had brought everything back and abandoned his offensive on Gibraltar. Thus, it was a foregone conclusion for both sides that the battle must be won by material superiority, as we were hit by powerful ground forces and innumerable bombers from the air. During the night of the 15th and 16th, I asked and received permission to retire north.

Rundstedt was satisfied. With my stunning advance to Badajoz, the US offensive on Gibraltar was broken, and everyone was back to square one. We'd destroyed three US divisions, taken 20 000 prisoners, and captured incredible quantities of material. In this, my men and I were impressed by the level of luxury with which the USA fought its war. The Badajoz supply depot we'd captured almost intact had, of course, gasoline, ammunition and other everyday necessities of war, but also chocolate bars, cigarettes, and all sorts of things that were only a souvenir for us poor Germans. How could any country in the world win against such material superiority, I remember thinking darkly. For if they'd taken the time to transport such useless items to war, that was because they had had the space or capability to do so. As I tasted these delicacies, I could not help but also feel daunted by the task laid before the Third Reich and worried very much about the ultimate conclusion of the world conflict, because we faced such an industrial juggernaut.

# One last Dnieper crossing
## Yevheniya Bosh Bridge, Kiev July 27th, 1944

(Yevheniya Bosh Bridge, before the war in the 1930's)

Walder and his units would be one of the last to be across the Dnieper bridge, near Kiev. The date was July 27th 1944, and the Wehrmacht was on the run everywhere. For more than two weeks, since July 16th, the newly named "Army Group Dnieper" had been moving backward, defending, fighting, and even sometimes counter-attacking, without respite. And Erich, being in command of one of the strongest army units in the vicinity (a Tiger II heavy panzer battalion), had been in the thick of it.

The division commander, general Fritz Bayerlein, had visited the unit in person, the day before, to ask one more battle of Walder and is weary, tired men. He needed to hold the eastern bank of the Dnieper, in front of the Yevheniya Bosh Bridge, near Kiev to enable the rest of the retreating units to cross, and also for the army pioneers (military engineers) to prepare the charges that would blow up the bridge, for it could not be left to the Russians to use.

He'd been told that he, his units, and another battalion of Panther tanks were probably some of the last panzer east of the great river but very much needed to help out their brothers cross to safety, as well as a couple of Hungarian divisions.

The bridge was one of the last intact ones for hundreds of kilometers. The high-command had everything that could be used for a crossing blown up, from the Black Sea to the Pripet Marshes.

"just one more hour!" crackled general Bayerlein over the radio. Walder could see the mass of men and materiel streaming in haste on the bridge, harassed by a horde of enemy planes. The pylons were on fire from soviet attacks since the damned Reds had also been raining Katyushas after Katyushas rockets not only on Walder and the other panzers but also on the bridge and near it.

"Another hour of this fury?" Said his tank driver in an almost crazy voice, laughing loudly. "An hour of Katyushas?" He represented the mood of the crew quite well. Everyone was close to breaking point. The rockets, saw Walder looking through his field glasses, were mounted on tracked carriers which had labored over the small ridge, belching exhaust. After days of being attacked by these damned machines, they could finally see them, and they were close enough to be destroyed by their 88mm guns. Thru his tired vision, Erich radioed everyone in the unit to fire when ready.

The enemy vehicles carried sets of launcher racks loaded with finned rockets, aiming them crudely by pointing the truck's noses down the slope at the German panzers protecting the bridge and then angling the rack up and down by hand. As the Red Army soldiers did this, Walder's excellent gunner fired on them, and tracer shells tore into a pair of these machines. All the other tanks across the line did the same, creating maelstrom in the Russian ranks. Their rockets detonated on the truck racks, and colossal fireballs blew up over the vehicles that were hit, obliterating them and their teams. The fire expanded, coiling into many spirals that flexed, rose, and fell as it spread, causing the surrounding trucks to scatter frantically out of the way.

The Russians set off smoke flares to conceal their by now very motivated retreat backward behind the ridge's protection, so the area was shrouded with a cloud of thick, brown smoke. The Pak anti-tank guns, well protected on the other side of the Dnieper in their prepared defensive bunkers, fired into the smoke and over the heads of the brave panzer men holding the bridge open so gallantly. Walder didn't see if they hit anything, but flares and flashes of fire could be seen sporadically in the dust and smoke, giving the dark view a flickering dirty orange color. It was some strange fire.

"Scheisse," said his driver, that also was looking up at the ridge. He continued his swearing into a quick explanation. "Gasoline Jelly"! gasoline and diesel in viscous form, mixed with tire rubber", he said without emotion this time. "It will stick to anything, and will burn for hours." Walder was about to tell his own swear word in response when the first of the Katyusha projectiles came screaming down the hillside toward them. Spectacularly, they shot out of the dark-brown smoke in salvos of a dozen for each truck, making for a swarm of missiles, as if the panzer had never destroyed any of them seconds before.

The smoke formed into horizontal tornados in their slipstream, filled with the sparks that flew from the base of the long, dart-shaped weapons themselves. The missiles flew wide at first, shooting way off into the water and on the western bank, exploding there in a wall of coiling fire that grew to engulf a small church tower, covering the area with smoke and debris. The observers were quick to correct this, and the next salvo pointed at the tanks. All the while, the German poured tracers upon tracers rounds into the large smoke cloud that also burned and exploded. They indeed hit some Russians, but the damned Yvan's were numerous, so there were still more firing their rockets.

Luckily for Walder's crew, the rockets flew over their own panzer, but they all heard one hitting the tank just beside them. Others caught a panther on the group's outer edges, and the whole tank was consumed in a ball of boiling flames. Death for that crew would be slow and painful, and by roasting of all things, as the blazing, sticking liquid would drip down into the hull through any vent or crack it could find.

And then a minute into it, it was over. The Soviets were probably bringing more rockets, having expanded their supplies, for now. The PAK anti tanks and most panzers were still firing into the fiery midst, and Walder took the respite as an opportunity to peak out of his turret. The burning panther that had been hit earlier was a dim outline in its pillar of flames. Most of the other tanks were standing firm, but several Katyushas had landed amongst the Hungarians division trying to cross. An undefinable carnage was too much for Erich to look at.

As the smoke slowly dissipated, shapes appeared within it, and the low, squat outlines of IS-2 tanks (Stalin tanks) lumbered down the slope, toward the bridge and the German panzer defending it. Ten first appeared, then twenty, then fifty, at which point the brave panzer men stopped to count and opened fire. Another battle where they would be heavily outnumbered. The numerous tracer shells started to hit the lead enemy tanks, fired from the Tiger's, the panthers, and the Pak guns on the other side of the river. It shrouded them in furious explosions, while the Russians also returned fire with all their might. Tanks started to explode and die in both camps. The German tanks were potent, but the Stalin model was a match for anything the Reich could field.

Walder's tanks got rocked by several shells, but the frontal armor shrugged it off, the Soviet rounds wiping wildly in the air. But many panthers were hit, and even a Tiger II got damaged in their tracks or guns turret.

There didn't seem to be any hope, and he knew the order to retire over the bridge would soon come. But then, for one rare moment, the Luftwaffe saved the day, like in the good old 1942 days. From the west came many new Stuka anti-tank models, the one with the mounted cannons (Ju87-G).

Thirty-five magnificent planes, each with a pair of long cannons slung under its wings, came swooping down, seemingly floating in the air, to attack the Soviet tank formation from the sides. In moments, they were over the rumbling Yvan's moving mass and began firing their guns. The Stukas were able to fire down on the damned enemy beasts, on to the hull and roof, and above all into the engine decks to hit the thinly shielded vents over the power plant.

They all floated down, with the tracer rounds firing in bursts, which were short but intense. When the tracer hit the turret walls, they deflected in corkscrew patterns, but where they punched thru the upper surface of the grilles, they penetrated with the tell-tale puff of metal fragments as the shell entered the vehicle.

The whole impetus of the Soviet advance simply died right there and then, in the maelstrom of fire that the Stukas had brought. To make matters worse for the Yvan's, the bombers had arrived at the greatest of timing while there were no enemy fighters above in the skies.

All the while, Walder's units and the panther tanks beside them continued to pour rounds upon rounds into the front of the Soviet machines. They finally saw the enemy retreat in disarray behind the low ridge to join their Katyusha brothers on the safety of cover.

An hour and a half later, the last of the Tiger II of the Panzer Lehr heavy panzer battalion crossed the bridge without even a riffle shot thrown at the German defenders. The Reds had had enough for the day.

Another half-hour after that, while Walder was atop his turret looking worn and tired and his tank driving to the rear of the frontlines for some well-deserved rest, the German pioneers blew the long bridge in a spectacular display of demolition skills.

In the early darkness of the evening, the impressive explosion did not even prompt the tankers to turn around and look. They'd had enough fighting for a while.

## OKW meeting
### Masurian Woods, July 31st, 1944

Things did not look good. Not good at all, thought Frantz Halder, the chief of staff of the Oberkommando der Wehrmacht (OKW). The Reich was retreating on every front. It was being overwhelmed by masses upon masses of enemies. The loss of Ireland and the United Kingdom, already a foregone conclusion even if the Allies had not reached Southern England yet. It hurt the general, just thinking about it, considering all the energy and German blood poured into conquering the UK.

In Spain, while Guderian had won the Reich a reprieve with his brilliant counter-offensive in the southern part of the peninsula, there was no real doubt as to the ultimate finality in that theater. The high-command could send almost no reinforcements to the frontlines. Gibraltar would eventually fall, and probably in 1944, unfortunately. In Africa, the frontline was static, as they had had this one piece of good news on stopping the Allies dead on the rebuilt Mareth line.

And then there was Russia. The epic proportion fighting that was taking place there had seen the Wehrmacht and its allies reel back from battles to battles. They'd lost a lot of ground, first on the Volga and then the whole Caucasus up to the mountains. There was one last significant obstacle where they could stop the Soviet hordes, and that place was the great Dnieper river. Eastern theater commander Erich Von Manstein had devised a brilliant fighting retreat operation. In contrast, the Reich had feverishly built as many defensives positions as possible on the river's western bank.

The Russians were even starting to make probing attacks in Persia and Turkey's direction, which did not bode well for the Axis there since all of their oil-producing centers were located in that theater.

Halder did not believe that the war could be won by making the enemy surrender to German arms. But he felt, as many of his colleagues did, in creating a military stalemate, where they would force the Allies come to the negotiating table. But to do that, they would have to stop the enemy from advancing and giving them so many casualties that they were bound to think about peace.

He'd prepared his meeting as best he could, with the help of his two colleagues, Paulus and Model. They'd also been much helped by Albert Speer, that had provided excellent news on production figures from 1944 to 1946 and beyond, where it was hoped they'd produce enough fighters, tanks, and other means of war that they could bring some sense of parity against the numerous Allies. More miracle weapons were also on the way.

He believed in his plan. But an increasingly nervous and desperate Fuhrer needed to be reassured, and some hard decisions would need to be taken. Goering was not going to like the concept of evacuating the Iberian Peninsula when things would look lost, which would further weaken the Reich's political stance against the rest of the Axis alliance members. Among others, Turkey was the most critical partner in the group, and it was shaking to its foundation. It wouldn't take much for Ankara to sue for peace with the Allies. If that happened, it would un-hinge the whole Axis strategic position in the Middle East, significantly jeopardizing the precious oil production that was so vital to the war effort. The Balkan states, very nervous about the disaster on the southern Russian front, would also bailout if more serious military reverses happened.

He slapped his face hard, killing the damned fly that had been harassing him for several minutes and hindering his concentration.

The oppressive heat was also almost unbearable. Because of it, Goering had decided to hold the meeting outside the bunker (the ventilation system was broken) in one of the wooden buildings in the Wolf's Lair center. His undershirt was already soaked with sweat, and he could also see that his colleagues were suffering the same predicament.

And so, they were all mostly silent, awaiting Goering, that had been apparently busy with something more important than being on time for a meeting with all his top people. Gathered for the occasion were the aforementioned generals, Albert Speer, Grand Admiral Raeder of the recently defeated Kriegsmarine, and Heydrich of the SS.

After some more waiting, four black-clad SS guardsmen entered the room, walking stiffly and looking alert, riffle on their shoulders. They were followed a couple of seconds later by Hermann Goering, the leader of Germany. Wearing his usual resplendent white Luftwaffe uniform, he was fat and looked bewildered, even tired to the extreme. The rumors were that he had again fallen under the dreadful spell of morphine. Not many a man in the room admired Goering, and most longed for the time when Hitler was in command. They'd come to miss what was in their nostalgic opinion a great man and were slowly forgetting that with his demise had come a freedom of action that had enabled them to arrive at this point in the war.

Whatever were the faults of Goering, he really had nothing to do with the Reich's predicament. The actual dire situation had more to do with the simple fact that the Axis had decided to take on the rest of the World in a globe-spanning war. They could fight like demons, plan like geniuses, and lead their troops like Napoleon; nothing could change the fact that the Allies drowned the Reich in an overwhelming quantitative superiority.

The Fuhrer walked down the great table, quickly nodding to most men as he went past them all, to install himself in a large leather chair at the head of the throng of men gathered around the large table map.

He gestured lazily, in his characteristic move of the hand to Halder to start the meeting. "Thank you, mein Fuhrer," said the general in a serious tone. Halder was dead-set on the plan he'd wanted to propose and hoped that the Fuhrer would approve of it.

Putting his finger on the map at the Kiev location, he started to talk. "Gentlemen. As we all know, the overall situation doesn't give a lot of room for optimism". Most in the room, including the groggy Goering, though it was an understatement. "I think that everyone in this room no longer believes that the Reich can win a military victory against the Allies." He paused to let that simple fact sink in. It was, rather shockingly, the first time it had been said aloud in front of everyone. Halder had expected some arguing, protest, even outrage. But no one spoke, except for Goering, that now seemed to be listening with a lot more intensity. "Go on," said the Fuhrer in a somewhat acid tone. The smart look in his eyes was back.

Halder picked up his courage to continue talking. "But the OKW is unanimous on the possibility of arriving at a military stalemate. In this, we also have consulted with the main theater commanders, Rundstedt and Manstein, and the likes of Rommel and Guderian. They are all unanimous. The casualty ratio that we have thanks to our experienced troop quality and our technological edge is excellent". The general paused to see if anyone was not in agreement. Silence. He continued. "Now, ever since we have resolutely switched to the defensive on all fronts, that positive ratio has increased significantly. Not because we are inflicting a lot more damage to the enemy, but because we are receiving less. By being in defensive positions and prepared fortifications, we have been able, for the first time since 1941, to catch up with replacements in the casualties we have received." A collective and perceptibly positive gasp went into the room. Goering was intrigued. "What do you mean, general? Are we now winning the war?" he said with a quick laugh that everyone present in the room followed. "I will let Minister Speer talk on this." He gestured to Albert Speer, the Minister of Armament and Reich production, the 4th member of the OKW high command body.

Speer rose from his chair near the table and started to distribute folders to everyone. "I have prepared production figures for 1944, as well as predictions for the 45 and 46 years. I am also pleased to say, mein Fuhrer, that, as Halder claimed, production has finally caught up with losses. We are finally able to send replacement parts to the frontlines, most divisions receive a steady stream of recruits and new forces, and most importantly, most panzer III and IV's have been phased out of the armed forces to be replaced by Tigers, Tigers II, Panthers, and other auto-tracked anti-tank guns." Most of the audience had opened the folders and was leafing thru them. Halder saw many a smile. The Minister continued:

"The Fuhrer will also be pleased to hear that the ME-262 jet fighter has reached a new peak in production of 1000 per month, now making it the most numerous planes in the fighter arm of the Reich. What is slowing us down in increasing the size of the Luftwaffe interceptor forces is pilot training". Goering beamed with pride at this news. He would always be a Luftwaffe man. "We have even been able to test flight and produce several long-range 4-engined heavy bombers, to strike at America and beyond the Urals. Most of our anti-tank capability has been updated to have excellent PAK 43 guns, and over 2000 88mm anti-aircraft guns have also been shipped to the new defensive positions on the frontlines. Cheap to make, and now very useful in static defense warfare, we will keep up making more." Speer stopped and nodded to Halder that he was pretty much finished.

"So, we can now plan on expanding the Wehrmacht and maybe finally hope some sort of parity with the enemy over the course of the next year." He paused again to gesture at the Pyrenees, the Channel Coast, the Middle East, the Mediterranean, and Russia's frontline. "The Key, gentlemen, is to hold the fronts we have now. As long as we keep our resources and our production capability intact, and that we increase our fighting forces, we believe it is possible to hold the Allies at bay for long enough to bring them to the negotiating table".

"A bold and interesting plan, general," said Goering, now listening intently. "Can this be done?" he said, looking around the room, first at Heydrich, then at Model and Raeder. They all nodded silently. Most were already privy to the general aspect of the meeting, if not the details. Von Paulus, one of the three generals of OKW and the man behind the details of the planning and decisions on where to make a stand for the Reich, chimed in at that moment: "Mein Fuhrer, it is OKW's opinion and also the one of the leading generals in the field that under the right conditions, so rightly described by the Minister of Armament and Production, we can achieve a military stalemate. I say this because the only reason the Allies have been driving us back and defeating us to this point is because of their huge material superiority. If we can make them bleed enough, while we continue to buildup our forces because on the defensive, we believe it can be achieved", Paulus finished.

"Well, then, my dear generals and Ministers, make it happen," said an enthusiastic Goering. They all had a good laugh again, and then the meeting continued for a while to discuss the details.

## Allied leader's meeting
### Pentagon, Washington D.C., August 2nd, 1944

(...) "The front now extends from Northern Portugal to Cadiz, and Guderian's forces are again showing clear signs of disengaging their units north.", said one of the presenting officers on the situation in Southern Spain. After a humiliating defeat, the Allies had again regained the initiative in the Iberian Peninsula. "And we expect to be nearing Gibraltar within the next 2 to 3 weeks", finished the man.

Not feeling very well on that bright morning of August 2nd, 1944, Roosevelt was somewhat encouraged by theses news. Would they finally be able to unlock the Mediterranean and enter it to un-hinge the whole Axis position in that theater? His line of thoughts was again interrupted by a pain in his chest and also a great weariness. He hadn't been feeling well for a while now. His doctors were anxious about the state of his health and had told him he'd need to rest. But how could he? He was the Allied alliance leader, and while Churchill was quite capable of handling many things in the leadership role, he was the leader of a junior alliance member. For the United States were the only, and by far, senior partner in this whole venture. They provided most of the oil, now that the rest of the World's reserves were in Axis hands and most of the resources, manufacturing capability, and finances.

So, the American President needed to lead. Roosevelt didn't know, however, how long he would still be able to do so. The temporary feeling of weakness and dizziness finally ebbed away, enabling him to put his attention back to the meeting. Another staff officer had started talking. It was now the turn of one of General Eisenhower's men to talk. The general was the commander-in-chief of all Allied northern land and air forces in the North Atlantic and the United Kingdom.

(...) "The 57th US division has been reported well south of Birmingham yesterday, while Liverpool, Leeds, Manchester, Glasgow and everything in between are also liberated. The campaign is going well, and general Eisenhower estimates that he will be in London within a week or two. By the end of September, all of the United Kingdom and Ireland will be free of the Nazis", finished the officer. Even in his weak and half-feverish state, the President could feel the enthusiasm in the room.

Churchill was simply beaming with pride and was gently puffing on his cigar, while General de Gaulle's was smiling. Admiral King and many other officers showed large smiles on their faces. It was a grand time for the Allies. If only Roosevelt could feel well. He kind of dozed off for a while, eyes open but mind-wandering elsewhere. Churchill was now speaking, and Roosevelt did his best to listen to the British war leader. Winston was talking about his planned return to London. He would leave for Europe on a plane within the week to be at the forefront of the troops and be one of the first to enter the capital.

For a while on the matter of the United Kingdom, the talks went on what the Allies would do to finalize the liberation, what they would do after it, and how they would use the country to continue their attack on the Third Reich. The President, still mostly quiet, listened to the men talking about the British industrial base's reconstruction. They spoke of also organizing great air raids on German cities and industries. A host of bombers had been built in Canada and the USA in the last two years and the strategic bombing campaign that had been planned accordingly would finally become a reality.

By that time, most in the room had noticed Roosevelt's weird, silent attitude. "Is everything alright, my friend?" asked Churchill in his most friendly voice. The President snapped out of his daydreaming, composed himself as best he could, and quickly responded that everything was all right. "I am just listening today, Winston," finished Roosevelt in a low voice. The British leader knew better. "Perhaps, gentlemen, we should reconvene a little later today or tomorrow." This was not a suggestion but a Churchill-type order.

Seeing the President's apparent tiredness, everyone didn't make a fuss about it, and the meeting was over in five minutes. The rest of the discussions, mainly the Spanish campaign and the proposed lend-lease (supply) help to the Russians, would be discussed later. Everyone in the Allied ranks left the meeting room with the distinct impression that the leader of the free World was not eternal.

## Great Hall of the Kuibyshev Palace
### Dead of night, August 1st, 1944

The great leader of the Soviet Union, or the "little father of the people" as he liked to be called, walked alone in his Kuibyshev palace's great hall. It was the dead of night, and Stalin had just finished working. Once in a while, he liked to walk down the great room, basking in its Tsarist magnificence. The Romanov, former masters of Russia, had built this place into a luxurious palace, and all of its rooms were furnished with every finery that could have been built at the time.

While Stalin did not much care for personal wealth (he had, after all, the entire wealth of the mighty USSR at his disposal), he liked to come to this place to think. He thought it fitting to walk down the wall of opulence to think about his enemies and how he would destroy them. For the decadent West was about to be swamped by his fighting hordes.

He'd been worried, in the dark depths of the Axis 1942 and 1943 offensives, that his country would collapse. But it had endured. And the Hitlerite's had faltered. They were retreating. He wondered if the great offensive that had seen the Red Army drive from Stalingrad to the Dnieper would continue over the great river. He was not confident.

Already, numerous reports of failed crossings and attacks were coming back to HQ. For once, he didn't feel like it was any of his general's fault. Miraculously indeed, none of them would be either executed or sent to the gulags in the following weeks. The dictator understood that the offensive might simply have run out of steam. He was also fully aware of the enormity of the victory for the Soviets. They had the Axis on the run, and if not for the large Dnieper river, they would have been able to continue pushing right up to the Balkans.

With a cigar in hand, he stopped walking to look at one of the lavish Tsarist painting that was adorning the wall. Some depictions of Tsar Alexander the First, victor over Napoleon in the war of 1812. There another western invader had been destroyed by Russian might, stalwartness and strength. He drew a big puff of the cigar, inhaling it deeply. Maybe he would also go down in history as the great victor over the Nazi hordes. He certainly planned it to be so. Were there not a picture of him in almost every building, dwelling, or most insignificant house in the USSR? After the war, there would be statues of him in every city that mattered, he vowed inwardly.

He thought a moment on the continuation of the fight. Maybe he would need to talk to Zhukov about a bit of a change of strategy. If his armies were stopped on the Dnieper, he would tell his great general to start planning the campaign to liberate the North. He craved for Moscow to be free of the dirty Hitlerite hands.

He walked a little further. He stopped in front of another painting. This one of Catherine the Great, Tsarina in the 18th century. The mighty conqueror of the Crimea and the Caucasus reaches. Another model to follow. Stalin hoped to be just beside her on this wall for posterity. He felt pretty good that evening. The warm air of July was making his walk pretty pleasant, and the recent good military news swamped him with enthusiasm. Turning around, he decided to go back to his house for a quick nap before the essential matters of the morning caught up to him. He had an unavoidable meeting with his chief man Beria over breakfast in the Tsar palace. Many traitors had been uprooted with the recent large territorial liberations. A long, very long list of Nazi collaborators waited for his decision to see if they would die or else be deported to the ends of the earth in deep Siberia.

## New Mexico Wilderness
### 30 kilometers south of Albuquerque, August 3rd,1944

After days upon days of walking in the southern American wastelands, Otto Skorzeny and his team, or rather what was left of his team, finally gazed at what their map was telling them was the nominal border between Mexico and the United States. Nominal because there was no clear demarcation line between the two countries since it was not needed. There was no need to quarrel over one foot more or less of the desert.

Sturm, the one surviving member of Skorzeny's team, put a hand on the SS daredevil's shoulders. "Well, sir, we're here." Otto didn't respond but picked up his binoculars from his side pocket by his ankle to recon the area ahead of them. They'd lost everyone else on the many skirmishes with the damned Yankees after their very successful attack in Los Alamos. On the fourth night after the raid and as they were walking toward Mexico, they'd been discovered, by chance, by one US Army patrol that had been scouring the land to find them. The ensuing firefight had eliminated all of the surviving men except these two very hard to kill men.

They walked only at night, on dwindling supplies, helped by some of the small caches of water they'd laid about south of Albuquerque. Their feet were blistered, their face burnt, but they still had the look of elite soldiers. Men that never gave up. And they'd been rewarded. Beyond the border lay Mexico, where a submarine was waiting for them in the Gulf bearing the same name.

Once in the other country, they would be able to stay a little more in the open, the US Army could not reach them into this sovereign country. Sure, the Mexicans were in the Allie's camp, but the level of corruption and inefficiency harbored in these lands made it very receptive to the gold coins that the two SS men were carrying with them.

Skorzeny hoped to buy a small truck, horses, or anything that could make them move faster to their rendezvous. The U-Boat was supposed to make for the coast at a particular point in the Gulf of Mexico in ten days and would stay there hidden with men on the shores to await the SS commandos for another ten days. After which they would leave back for the safety of the Atlantic Ocean.

Otto hoped that the war was still going well for the Reich. He'd certainly done his part by destroying the research facilities and, most importantly, killing the scientists within. He had been quite unsettled at the level of advancement of the project. While they'd been able to destroy most of it, it also showed the certainty of the Allies developing this mega bomb at one point. Skorzeny would make sure to include this fact into his report once he got back to Axis-occupied territory. The German and their allies were on a clock race for which, in the end, they wouldn't be able to win unless they developed their bomb or brought the war to a positive conclusion before it could be dropped on the Wehrmacht heads and the magnificent cities of Germany.

Lost in thoughts, he noticed that Sturm had already started toward the whatever border, trudging along in dust and the rocky, sandy ground. He followed him, turning back only once to look again at the USA. He smiled at nothing in particular and turned back toward Mexico and his escape.

# CHAPTER 5

# The Liberation of the United Kingdom
## Churchill address to the nation, August 25th, 1944

Winston Churchill was back in London. He'd flown over to just recently liberated Heathrow airport, from Northern Scotland, where his first plane had landed, and the high command had been operating during the liberation of all the Home Islands. Once on the ground, he was put in an armored car and driven to the BBC radio station, that had been kept mostly intact by the Nazi occupiers since they'd used it for their propaganda purpose. Once he sat down, the radioman gave him the signal, and he nodded. He dropped the piece of paper on the desk in front of him in the small radio studio. He took his most solemn air and started talking.

After years of hard fights, sorrow, defeats, and retreats, but also of preparation, victories, and battles, he had delivered on his promise to come back. The British people, rejoicing on that day, took to their radio set to hear the great war leader make one of the most rousing speeches in the war's history.

(...)Yesterday at 2:41 a.m. at Headquarters, General Stahler, the German command representative in the United Kingdom, signed the act of unconditional surrender of all German land, sea, and air forces in the British Islands and Ireland to the Allied Expeditionary Force.

General Eisenhower, Commander in Chief of the Allied Expeditionary Force, and General Francois De Lattre Tassigny signed the document on behalf of the Allied nations at war with the Third Reich.

Hostilities will end officially at one minute after midnight to-night (Tuesday, August 26th, 1944). Still, in the interests of saving lives, the "ceasefire" began yesterday to be sounded all along the front, and our dear islands will soon all be free.

Today, perhaps, we shall think mostly of ourselves. Tomorrow we shall pay a particular tribute to our European comrades, whose countries are still occupied by the vile enemy forces.

The German occupation of the British Islands is therefore at an end. After years of intense preparation, we have come back, as promised, to our lands and lit the shining beacon of liberty once more. Never again shall we lower our guard as much as we did in the face of Nazi aggression and war machine.

Our deal ally, gallant France, is still struck down, and we, today, make a promise. We shall not rest until their people are free of Axis occupation. We will use all the Allied alliance's overwhelming power and resources to bring them down, aye.

Finally, almost the whole world was combined against the evil-doers, who are cowering and retreating before us. Our gratitude to our splendid Allies goes forth from all our hearts on this Island and throughout the British Empire.

We may allow ourselves a brief period of rejoicing, but let us not forget for a moment the toil and efforts that lie ahead. Europe is still under the Axis boot, and the Pacific is also suffering the damning glare of Japanese aggression. The Axis, with all her treachery and greed, remains unsubdued.

The injury it has inflicted on Great Britain, the United States, and other countries, and her detestable cruelties, call for justice and retribution. We must now devote all our strength and resources to completing our task, both at home and abroad.

Advance, Britannia! Long live the cause of freedom! God save the King!" (...)

.

## Knife fight on the Dnieper
### The Russian offensive grinds to a halt, August 8th- August 27th

The powerful Summer 1944 offensive came in and crashed hard into the defensive wall prepared by the Germans on the great Dnieper river. The body of water, large and deep enough that an army needed either bridge or serious engineering to cross it, was a perfect defensive barrier.

Adding to that was the fact that the Wehrmacht had extensively fortified the western bank of the river. For months now, tens of thousands of workers from Romania, Hungary, and most importantly, Russian prisoners of war had toiled to erect the concrete bunkers, machine gun nests, and large trenches by the river's banks. From the Black Sea to the Pripet Marshes, the river was manned continuously by defensive positions and troops.

Theater commander Erich Von Manstein had put everything into its completion, marshalling, every scrap of resources and reinforcements that the Reich could call upon. Most of the troops evacuated from the British Isles and Ireland were transported right on the Dnieper defensive works. German industry had also been busy shipping tanks, anti-tank guns, mines, barbed wire. Stockpiles of oil, ammunitions, reserve panzers, and spare parts were also assembled in the rear areas to sustain a long and intense fight.

In particular, the artillery had significantly been bolstered, from the gigantic K-51 guns 30 kilometers behind the lines on their railcars to the 15 CM and 10.5 CM heavy howitzers that equipped every German division on the Eastern Front. So now the troops operating the Dnieper line had their regular complement of artillery battalions. Thousands of guns had thus been added all along the lines and at the clear lines of approach that the Red Army would take, like at Dnepropetrovsk or Kiev.

The Luftwaffe was not to be outdone, either. From everywhere in the German Empire, planes had been mustered, and everything that could be reasonably spared from the uneven fight with the Allies in the Iberian Peninsula had been shipped to the area. So many ME-262 had been flown and railed near the large airfields of Kiev and near the Black Sea Coasts that it had affected air defenses all across the Reich. But Manstein had been adamant. The Wehrmacht must stop the Soviets in such a convincing way, and with such force, that they would throw them back into confusion. The sheer force of the planned blow would, hoped the great general, break the 1944 offensive power of the damned Yvan's.

And so, for the whole month of August, the Russian steamroller crashed hard on the Dnieper line, like a tremendous successive wave of might and steel. Every assault was a powerful combination of tanks, planes, and the famous artillery barrages that the Red Army was so dreadfully renowned for. But on each occasion, the brave German forces pushed back the Soviet hordes.

Losses mounted on both sides for the whole month, but they rapidly rose to uncomfortable levels in the Russian camp, while the Axis was comfortably protected in their trenches and bunkers. Then a couple of weeks into the attempts to cross the river, the casualties became unsustainable even for the USSR.

Eventually, the orders came from high above in Kuibyshev to stop the attacks. On the morning of the 27th of August, the beleaguered German defenders of hard-fought areas like Kiev and Dnepropetrovsk woke up to the first quiet night they had had in a long time. The Russian artillery had retired further East.

Manstein had won his bid for a stalemate in southern Russia.

# The other members of the Axis alliance
## Balkan States, Italy, Spain and Turkey

### Italy, August 1944

When Italy entered the war in 1940-1941, it was far from asking to be engulfed in a world-spanning conflict. But it was lead by the bombastic Benito Mussolini, and so it had limped along. The Duce, as the Italian leader liked to be called, had linked his destiny to the one of Third Reich. The war, so far, had been splendid to the country. The Roman dream of the "Mare Nostrum" (our sea) had been completed. If one did not consider that it had to be shared with the senior partner in the Axis alliance, Germany, it was a significant accomplishment. The Italian flag stood alongside the Reich in Bagdad, Cairo, and the Caucasus. For a time, it had also stood proud as far as Southern Morocco, at the height of the Axis expansion in 1941.

Greatly strengthened by plentiful oil and new resources, the Italian industry had produced more and better weapons of war. The Germans had even shared several panzer and plane blueprints with Rome, and some of them, mainly Panzer IV and FW-190, had started to be produced by the beginning of 1944. Slowly but surely, the state of the Italian armed forces was improving, as better and more reliable equipment arrived to equip the Duce's soldiers. As they phased out their older equipment, the Germans shipped several trainloads of the PAK 41 anti tanks guns (that were being replaced with PAK 43 in the Wehrmacht), Panzer III, and BF-109. While still starting to be outdated in terms of technology, they were a hell of a lot better than most of the weapons that Italy possessed.

The Regina Marina, or the Italian Navy, had had an excellent war to date. The eternal problem of oil had been solved by the successful Axis campaigns of 1941 in the Middle East, so the Fleet had been able to operate at will when needed. While it had not fared well against enemy ships in several surface battles in 1940 in the Western Mediterranean, it had been beneficial to support the many land campaigns with shore bombardment. The Russians remembered the Italian shells quite well from the battles of Odessa and Sevastopol. The Fleet had been instrumental in the long siege of Oran. And finally, it had suffered in four years of war but battered as it was, it was still an essential weapon for the Axis. It was now preparing itself for the last battle, for it was not a matter of if the Allies would retake Gibraltar and burst again in the Mediterranean, but when.

The Italian land army had fared a lot better than what the onset of war showed. The humiliating defeats in the northern African deserts were far away. Well stiffened by German forces, it had fared well in a supporting and reserve role. In Russia, where the Duce had decided to send several corps, the Army had been very useful, again as a reserve and rear-areas partisans battles. The biggest test for the armed forces had been in North Africa and Spain. Most of the troops were engaged there since 1942 to resist the Western Allies. They shared every heavy battle that the Spanish and Germans also fought with all the bitterness they could muster.

The big worry for Rome and the Duce himself was what would happen when the Allies came in their multitude with their ships. The enemy was already present in strength in Tunisia, so it would not take much for these forces to transition to Sicily and Southern Italy with a strong fleet to protect them.


### Spain, August 1944

Francisco Franco, Spain's Fascist dictator, had no room for maneuver left. The Spanish forces, already pretty battered by the civil war that was fought just before the onset of the Second World War, had depleted them quite heavily. He still had men, but training, materiel, and modern weapons were lacking. Nonetheless, the forces had been useful in 1941, 1942, and even 1943, again supporting the Italian and Germany Armies.

The losses had been terrible, as the Spanish divisions' lack of mobility made it that many of them had been encircled and destroyed in the North African campaign, in the Siege of Oran, and the final evacuation of Tunisia.

Franco had tried to talk to the Allies to end the war for Spain, but the negotiations had been cut short by the Germans, and ever since then, the Claudillo was not master in his own country. A full division of German SS infantry was stationed in Madrid, the capital. He was "protected" at all times by many a Gestapo unit. He had resigned himself to his fate and hoped for an Axis final victory. But he didn't harbor much hope for the future of his country.

The Germans had already written off Spain from their ledger. They only considered the country and its forces as a delaying fuse against the Allies, for an imposing line of defensive fortification was being built in the Pyrenes. That is where the OKW planned to do the real fighting. The next six months would still see battles in the Iberian peninsula, but the Axis as a whole was living on borrowed time in the theater.

### Turkey, August 1944

Ismet Inonu, the Prime Minister and successor to the great Mustapha Kemal, (the Turkish state's father), had never really been for Ankara's participation in the conflict. Outside events, mainly the major Axis successes of 1940 and 1941 in North Africa and the Middle East, had created the opportunity for the war party within the country's government and elites to push for entry into the conflict. At the time, even he had even been a little inclined in somehow believing that it was a good move for Turkey to side with the Axis. The Germans were masters of most of Persia, Iraq and promised much of those lands would go back to Turkey as a rebirth of the Ottoman Empire. The demise of the great Turkish Empire had not been too far removed in the past, and the lure of it had been still very strong in most nostalgic power circles in the government.

So, in exchange for territorial concessions, Turkey had entered the war in 1941. It would get Syria, all of Northern Iraq, all of the lost territories of the Caucasus since the 17th century, and would even get its dominion back over the Crimea, lost to Catherine the Great, the 17th-century Russian Tsarina. Crete, parts of Greece had also been included.

The Turkish Army, while not entirely a modern force, had still boasted French and Czech tanks, several cavalry divisions, and a substantial 45 infantry divisions. Helped by several arms shipments from the Germans, the forces had been significantly bolstered. The Army feared very well alongside the Germans in the Caucasus and northern Persian campaigns. It had fought, bled, and conquered like its forefathers. Morale and national pride reached new heights in 1942 and 1943. And then the major reverses and losses of freshly conquered territory had come. The Red Army was at the gates of newly conquered Turkish territory. They had re-occupied the whole of the Caucasus north of the mountains and were pushing hard to fight their way across.

The Axis outlook did not seem so good in Russia itself, where the Wehrmacht, alongside several Turkish corps, had been forced to retreat to the great Dnieper line.

Inonu had reverted to his old thinking and Mustapha Kemal moto of not involving the country in any more European war. He'd already started to recall several Russian front units to bolster the defenses in the Caucasus and had also secretly contacted the Allies. Negotiations were ongoing, and the results of the coming fights in the east would very much influence the direction where Turkey would swing. If it left the Axis alliance, it would completely un-hinge the Middle-Eastern position for the Reich and pretty much cut the flow of oil since over two-thirds of it was being shipped by rail through Turkey via the Bagdad – Constantinople rail line.

## Romania, August 1944

The Romania Army, from the onset of the conflict with the USSR, had given all it had to the Eastern Front. Marshall Antonescu, the de-facto Fascist dictator, had sided very early in 1940 since his country was under intense pressure from Stalin. They'd have to give Bessarabia to the Soviet Union and give even more concessions in 1941. So, it was clear for the Romanians what the Russians wanted of them: To be a client state. Antonescu, being a fervent anti-communist and a Fascist, had gotten along really well with Hitler.

The country had contributed three full armies to the conflict to date. While equipped mostly with World War One weapons, it still had been much-involved in the heavy fights against the Red Army. As they phased out their equipment for better ones, Germany had also been able to send a lot to Bucharest. A host of Panzer II and Panzer III were shipped, alongside many 1916 Mauser Riffles that had been sitting around in old depots deep in the Reich. The Luftwaffe also send several squadrons of fighters and flight instructors to get some kind of Romanian air force. In 1944, it numbered a small 150, efficient fighter force that had been very useful to Manstein in his desperate southern Russian theater defenses.

The Romania land army had significantly contributed but equally suffered to the same level as their heavy involvement in most major land campaigns south of Moscow. It had recently suffered a catastrophic defeat on the Volga, where it had lost most of a whole army (six divisions). Antonescu looked at the Russian steamroller with much dread. With every passing day, it was nearing his country. However, hope was still there, as the Dnieper defensive line was strong and manned by powerful units. Antonescu gave his all to the defense of it, and most of what was left of his forces handled the lines near Dnepropetrovsk with a German Corps.

## Hungary, August 1944

Hungary had contributed everything it had to the war in the east. Regent Horthy, an avid Fascist and anti-communist, had thrown in his lot with the Third Reich as early as 1940. The two armies of the country had marched alongside their German cousins in Barbarossa and the subsequent campaigns. In 1944, it was but a shadow of itself. The land was small, and its army's World War One quality at best. Several arms shipments had also been given to Budapest by Berlin, but it had failed to provide the needed strength to the Hungarian forces. Regent Horthy kept all his troops in the east and hoped, like his Romania counterpart, that the line that Manstein had drawn would hold.

## Bulgaria, August 1944

Bulgaria had never been, from the onset, a staunch supporter of the Axis. King Boris III, for his part, did not enthusiastically fight the war for Germany. The country had been motivated enough against the Greek in 1941 in operation Marita and had given its all to the invasion and subsequent conquest of their hereditary enemy. But the Turkish entry into the Axis had been received like a cold-water shower in Sofia.

Since then, Bulgaria still participated in the war and sent some units abroad but kept about half of its forces near the capital, Sofia. Boris was the leader of a tiny country and, as such, could not defy the Reich and its allies, but it tried very hard to fend off German demands to send more troops abroad.

## Yugoslavia, August 1944

An artificial construction of the Treaty of Versailles in 1919, the country was simply impossible to hold together once the gates of conflict poured in it. Croats, Serbs, Slovens, Muslims all hated each other with a passion and had only awaited the right moment to attack the other. That moment had come. The rife and unstable World War Two proved too much for the new state.

In 1939, the Kingdom of Yugoslavia found itself surrounded by countries that had joined the Axis as allies of Nazi Germany. Prince Paul's decision in 1941 to sign a non-aggression pact and then a full military alliance with Nazi Germany resulted in severe protests in the country, which led to a government crisis in March 1941. A coup was attempted with British help, but the United Kingdom could not correctly support the rebels, having other, more significant problems in their own country. So, Paul was able to keep power after several days of uncertainty and some German help.

With its small, nationally fragmented army (there were two main factions in it, Croats and Serbs, that hated each other intensely), Yugoslavia was initially able to participate in the Greek invasion and send some forces abroad to support Germany at her request.

But it did not take long for the internal forces within the country to tear it apart. Since 1942, the Croats and Slovens had declared themselves independent, and the Reich had quickly recognized them, while Montenegro and Bosnia, mainly of Muslim faith, rose against the Serbs. From 1943 onward, the country was in a severe state of civil war, and the only contribution it made was some Croat volunteer units. The rest of the men within Yugoslavia were simply too busy fighting each other. The Reich had also pretty much written off any contribution from it and just left the country alone to implode on itself. At least it was one area it didn't have to garrison.

## Patrol over the Channel
### August 29th, 1944

The Mk XII model was the first Spitfire powered by a Griffon engine to go into service. The first of 100 Supermarine company-built production aircraft started appearing in October 1943; The first test flights were done in Bagotville, Quebec (Canada). That first run of 100 units was done in the company's new Windsor plane factory. By summer 1944, they had been transported to the United Kingdom, amidst the British home country's successful reconquest.

The single-stage Griffon engine (II or IV) gave the aircraft superb low and medium level performance, although it declined at higher altitudes. In fact, at lower altitudes, it was one of the fastest propeller aircraft in the world. It was a fact that many of the MK XII had outpaced the super fast FW-190 German planes in recent fights over the Channel and Northern France.

All in all, it was a magnificent plane and scores more powerful than Gaston's older Seafire. The unique carrier plane had been the mainstay of Gaston's war to date, but recently orders had come in for the whole Bonaventure air squadron to be transferred on land. No reasons were given as generals admirals needed to do no such things, but the pilots had their theory. The recent and overwhelming victory over the German fleet had significantly reduced the needs for full-fledged fleets in Europe. The Bonaventure had been ordered back to Canada to train another batch of fighter pilots. Several senior aces had also been kept aboard, but Gaston had been lucky and had been in the group that stayed in the fight, on the best plane available to British forces.

Pushing his plane speed to maximum, he immediately felt the rush of speed that coursed thru his body. He was above the water somewhere between the Dover Cliffs and France. He could see land approaching fast. He was on another reconnaissance mission over the Channel Coast. He veered the aircraft toward Cherbourg, hugging the beach to take as many pictures as possible, as fast as possible.

The mission was not to engage in a fight with a German plane; it was to understand the Wehrmacht's defensive dispositions in the area. For even if the Allies were not ready to cross the water and invade France yet, they could still plan to do so as best they could. His orders had thus been clear. Avoid enemy planes.

Not that Gaston had thought it would be difficult, for Luftwaffe fighters were a rare occurrence these days. From generals to fighter pilots, everyone in the UK wondered where the numerous planes they had fought and bled against in the naval Battle North of Scotland had gone. No one knew for sure in the Western Power's camp, but the overall accepted theory was that they'd been transferred to Russia, for no surge of planes had been reported in Spain.

Another minute and he veered right in the general westerly course his flight plan dictated. He flew over a large bunker complex over a non-descript Normandy beach. He completely surprised its German defender, just zipping by. The flak soldiers did shoot at him, but the red tracer shells arced high and far in his plane's grey wake. And in a couple more instant, he was gone.

He repeated the gesture several times, at one point taking pictures of a beached U-Boat, another bunker complex south of the fortified city of Cherbourg. When he got in sight of the French town, he turned his plane due north, in the UK's direction. His mission was done, and he'd taken the pictures the brass wanted.

The flight home was uneventful, as most were these days. Gaston knew this would not last, as he'd seen the newspaper's news about Russian defeats in the Soviet Union and a great fight won by the German near the Black Sea. The damned Germans would be back, and he would have to fight them again.

Just droning over the seagoing back to his home airfield, his thoughts strayed to his civilian life, which seemed so far away now. It only had been three years, but it felt like a lifetime ago. He wondered if his sweetheart Anna would wait for him. She was beautiful, and many a boy had wanted to date her back in the days. He dearly hoped she would still be there when he came back. He also wondered about his brother Jean-Paul, that was in the army somewhere in Portugal. He knew he was alive, but in his last letter, JP, as everyone was affectionately calling him, had said that it had been very rough fighting. Gaston dreaded to fight the Germans on the ground. He felt quite lucky to be flying.

Intellectually, he knew he was killing someone when he downed a plane (some at least were able to parachute themselves, thank god), but at least he didn't have to do it face to face. He also didn't have to see the gore, the horrible injuries, and mutilations. He thanked God for this and also gave a prayer for his brother to keep him safe.

As he angled his plane to approach and land it, his last thought was about hockey and if he would be able to play again when he got back in Canada. War was not a game, and he did not enjoy it. It was just a job he had to do for the liberty of the world. But hockey was something else entirely. He and his brother Jean-Paul were quite good at it, and he fantasized about coming back to Alma and play again to beat all his rivals in Jonquière, Chicoutimi, and Port Alfred the nearby towns that he and his buddies entertained a fierce rivalry with.

Such were the thoughts of the fighting man. Very much dedicated to the present to win a war and survive, but always projecting to a better future somewhere away from the horrors of battle.

*Noumea, New Caledonia*
**September 1ˢᵗ, 1944**

The titanic fight between the USA and the Japanese Empire spanned the Pacific as a whole. After the twin American victories with the reconquest of the Hawaiian Islands and Midway's battle, Japan had switched to the defensive. Admiral Yamamoto still had a pretty sizeable fleet at his disposal, even if he'd lost several of the country's fleet carriers, namely Akagi, Hiryu, and Kaga. But the US fleet had grown so much in size that Japan could no longer win a head-to-head fight, as had been amply demonstrated by the battle of Hawaii in February. Six months later, it was even less of a contest, Japan having received one fleet carrier (the brand new Shinano), while the USA had received no less than 50 ships, with at least ten capital ships.

After the brief fight in the Marshall Islands, where the Japanese had again won a tactical victory, the Imperial Fleet still had retired to the Carolinas, leaving the area to the numerous Allied ships. In may 1944, the Americans had landed in force on most of the islands. Kwajalein (main base) had fallen at the end of June 1944 in a bloody fight that saw the US marines kill almost every enemy soldier on the island since they would simply not surrender.

With the Marshalls' fall, a significant dent had been created in the imagined Japanese defensive perimeter. The Marianas and all of the central pacific position was in danger of falling to the Allies, that reached far with their ships, planes, and submarines.

Ever since the loss of Oahu in 1943, Admiral Yamamoto had seen the writing on the wall and had correctly guessed that the American industrial giant would out-produce his country to such an extent that there was no hope for a military victory. And so, he'd given the orders to start fortifying the major islands in the southwest, the Philippines, Borneo, and the Celebes.

The central base for the whole Pacific Southwest theater was located on the island of Truk, in the middle of the Carolina Islands. Apart from the Kure Naval base near Tokyo, it was the most significant base that the Japanese sported. Ever since 1943, five major airfields had been built around it, and many naval canons had been added for its defense. To cap it all, a sizeable portion of the Imperial Fleet was operating from that area.

For this was where the war on sea would play itself out. The Japs had built more bases in New Britain, mainly around Rabaul. Again, in the Solomon Islands, several airfields and small ports, where numerous planes and submarines operated, all to interdict Allied shipping to Australia. New Caledonia, which had fallen amongst the Japanese conquest of 1942, formed the other end of the barrier against Allied communication lines to the Australians and New Zealanders.

That large island represented the eastern-most limit of    the

Japanese Empire. It had been difficult to supply, hence the chain of airfields that spanned from Truk to Rabaul to Guadalcanal and Vanuatu before arriving in Noumea.

Admiral Nimitz, commander in chief of the US Pacific Fleet, had thus ordered Admiral Spruance to lead a major effort to retake the island before they would concentrate on liberating and occupying the Solomon and New Britain. The island liberation was critical to re-opening an easily workable link with Australia and New Zealand, which had been fighting pretty much on their own since 1942.

After all, the Allies would need to do something about the Japanese presence in Darwin. The damned enemy had landed there at the height of their expansion (1942-1943) and was still occupying a sizeable portion of central-northern Australia. While the Anzac (Australians and New Zealander combined army forces) had blocked their advance, they had not been able to push them back into the sea. The brave Allies from Oceania lacked good equipment, ammunition, and men. They'd sent a lot of their troops to help the beleaguered British Empire in Europe, only to see Japan stab them in the back while most of their divisions were away fighting the Nazi hordes.

Not that the Noumea battle would be much of a contest. Sure, the Japs had many planes to defend the island, but no ships had been reported by the recon planes and the intelligence service. The Japanese strategic mastermind had correctly guessed that it would be plain hazardous to send the fleet so far from its base and, more importantly, from the critical Mariana and central Pacific position they were currently holding. The Imperial navy was nowhere to be seen and would not intervene.

For Spruance had at his disposal a mighty fleet that harbored a full Marine division, one Canadian division, and one Australian that had transferred back on ships from North Africa to the South Pacific. The vessels that were gliding along just 300 kilometers north of

Noumea numbered, amongst others, the aircraft carriers Saratoga, Wasp, and Hornet, surrounded by the battleships California, Tennessee and South Dakota.

Seeing the planes taking off in succession from his vantage point on the Saratoga bridge, admiral Spruance hoped that the first strike would demolish Japanese airpower on the island. He would also approach the Japs with his big gun battleships and pound their defenses to oblivion.

Then the next day, the troops would land. The admiral was a bit worried about enemy strength, but he should not have concerned himself with it. The Allies would utterly destroy all Japanese resistance within three days and reclaim the island for the forces of liberty. The Americans were simply too strong in the area, and the Japs too far away to do anything significant about it.

## Truk Atoll, Caroline Islands
### September 4th , 1944

Admiral Yamamoto stared intently at the last, laconic and desperate report from the Noumea defense force. Three days. They'd lasted only three days after the landings. Even if they, according to the report, fought to the last man. The Americans had just been too strong. Powerful air strikes by hundreds upon hundreds of American B-29's bombers had started with shattering the defenses and the airfields for ten straight days at the end of August to nicely soften the area for the coming of Admiral Spruance's fleet.

Then, the carriers' airstrikes had hit the defenders on the 1st of September, to be followed by an intense shore bombardment. When all of that was said and done, the troops had landed. By then, the Imperial Army was only able to offer token resistance to the invaders.

A scene that was almost a repeat of the Marshall Islands campaign. Bombing, bombing, then more bombing with the B-29's, then attack by the battleships, then the carrier planes, then the troops. Yamamoto did not see how this formula could be defeated on any of the fortified islands that Japan held at the moment. The only way any area could be defended was with enough planes, ships, and anti-aircraft guns.

Laying back on his chair in the large room that was his HQ on the battleship Musashi, he seemingly looked at empty air, thinking. The cabin was lavishly decorated, as befit the Grand Admiral of the fleet. The pictures on the walls were of some of the Navy's battleships. There was also a picture of Admiral Togo, the grand national hero, victor of Tsushima's battle, the naval victory over the Russian Imperial fleet in 1905.

His thinking always came back to the same conclusion. Japan would be destroyed, island by island, if the Americans willed it so. It would be overwhelmed in every battle it would fight, and the death would be slow but certain. Death by a thousand cuts, though Yamamoto sourly.

He'd been thinking about a plan lately, and the report from Noumea solidified the idea in his mind. The whole southwest position could not be defended piece-meal. By the Emperor, it could not be guarded island by island. The Allied material and numerical superiority would overwhelm them at every turn.

Unless he did something bold, something audacious. The concept was taking solid shape now in his thinking. There was a chance for a defensive victory. One battle so big that he could make the American bleed enough for them to check their advance. That was a plan that did not include any retreat or force-preservation thoughts like he had been doing for the last few years.

It would involve the very heart of the whole Imperial navy, and its commitment would be until death – or victory. The planes, scattered all around the southwest and even in their Australian occupied lands, would be concentrated in one area. The army would also focus its troops and flak assets in one location. Planes from the Philippines, Japan, Borneo, and from their Indian offensive would be recalled. Every boat that could float would also be committed.

He suddenly stood up from his chair in enthusiasm, walking over to the large map of the southwest theater that was pinned on his cabin's walls. He would await the American here in Truk. There were enough atolls and islands here in the Carolinas to effectively house the planes he planned to bring forth for the ultimate battle. The base's large lagoon could also harbor the fleet's entirety, and its extensive oil facilities had enough supplies for it all.

Yes, the Truk atoll would be the stage for the Pacific War's last battle and either be the Japanese Imperial Navy's graveyard or the location of its greatest victory.

*Extracts of Heinz Guderian 1952 book, Panzer Leader*
## The battle for Southern Spain and Gibraltar, Mid to end September 1944

The brief glimpse of success in the summer, where the Army Group had been able to repulse the Allied offensive, was very far away, in those lovely sunny days of the Spanish fall. The needs of the disastrous situation in Russia made it so that we had only received a trickle of reinforcements. The United Kingdom's added battles further depleted the overall bad situation with supply, replacements, and, most importantly, air cover.

While I accepted the situation as an unavoidable problem to be juggled with, it did not make for a favorable Southern Spain position. The enemy had finally been able to regroup after my successful offensive, a mere three weeks later resumed the offensive. The already worn down and depleted units in front of them in the Badajoz area rapidly either got overwhelmed or were ordered to retire in a swing north-east. The Army Group's armored elements were also quite reduced in strength and numbers since not a lot of replacement had come forth in August. I had to resolve myself to use precious few panzers in stop-gap and fire brigade roles. Open-air operations were so dangerous for our mobile force (because of enemy planes) that most movements were at night, and when we attacked, we made sure we called on what Luftwaffe planes could be mustered.

And so, for the whole month of August, it was a battle of back-and-forth between our brave forces and the Allies, but always we would retire east and north. The city of Seville, former HQ for all Southern Spain, fell on the 15$^{th}$ of August. After a whole Spanish corps was encircled and destroyed in the area, the theater commander, Von Rundstedt, ordered me to retire to a more defensive line that ran east-west from Malaga to North of Seville.

His general idea was that the Allies would plunge toward their real objective, Gibraltar. While this was not the desired scenario, it was hardly because we could choose to defend the place. We simply just didn't have the troops to do it. At a conference at Rundstedt mobile HQ on the 21$^{st}$ of August, we both agreed, along with the rest of the commanders on the ground, that the current situation did not permit us to defend everywhere and that the only way we could have held the south of the Iberian Peninsula would have been with significant reinforcements.

The fresh troops not being available (most were earmarked for Russia), we resolved ourselves to play for time. After all, the Gibraltar defenses had been upgraded after the 1941 conquest and were considered quite formidable. This decision did not go well with our beloved Fuhrer, however. As our original plan went, we only planned to put a division of troops into the Rock for its defense, but Goering ordered Rundstedt to cram a full corps in it.

To both our dismay, direct orders were sent to put the Wiking SS division and the sole remaining heavy panzer battalion we had, composed of 32 Tiger II's, into Gibraltar. To complete the forces, the 11$^{th}$ and 23$^{rd}$ Infantry were also explicitly mentioned in the orders. Again, the two units containing our best anti-tank guns. Sometimes our Fuhrer did behave like his predecessor. He clamored for a stubborn defense of Gibraltar and ordered the defenders to fight to the last man. This did not bode well for the future when things could get really desperate.

By then, the coastal guns and the heavy artillery used earlier to attack ships in the straight of Gibraltar (at the naval battle of Gibraltar) had been repositioned. New bunkers dug either directly in the Rock or else near it. Only 3 K-51 guns had been moved away to be re-installed in the tremendous defensive line built in the Pyrenees.

For there was no mistaking our mission. While this could not be said officially, our task, as amply emphasized by general Paulus from OKW on his visit to Rundstedt HQ on the 12$^{th}$ of September, was to gain time. Time that the Reich needed to complete the fortifications in the mountains. Time it also required to produce and move the units to their positions.

While the troops in Gibraltar were ultimately condemned, the strength of the defensive position and the Allied resolve to take it would create one of World War Two's biggest siege battles. And it would also serve its most important purpose. Fix the enemy's attention, so we'd have time to regain our balance and finish the Pyrenes defense line.

*Army Group Dnieper*
**Tank marshalling yards, end of September, 1944**

Tank commander Erich Walder finished his cigarette and threw it in the water maelstrom that was the churning puddle of brown water at his feet. It was raining so hard that the whole tank yard sprawled in front of him only seemed to be a blur. Dozens of tanks were almost invisible because of the heavy falling rain. The damned Russian fall was upon them all. Everyone on the German army felt miserable for it, for it was a time when one would always be wet and dirty.

But it was also a time when offensive operations stalled to a trickle. It was simply impossible for a modern army to move in this gigantic bowl of mud and water. So, after the summer's dreadful campaign, every sane German soldier in Army Group Dnieper did not mind so much to be physically miserable. At least the chances of being killed had lowered considerably.

Not too far in the distance, Walder could still hear explosions and sounds of fighting, which was expected since the front was relatively static on the Dnieper front. Both sides were entrenched on their respective banks and fired at each other for whole days and nights. It was mostly an artillery battle at this point, but Erich knew better. When the cold weather returned, he knew that the damned Russians would try to send their armies over the frozen river.

He was standing on the Kiev St Sophia orthodox cathedral's front entrance, about a kilometer from the actual Dnieper and thus the main frontline. Erich was quite happy to have a roof over his head, for not many a soldier near the frontline could boast that level of luxury. The cathedral was a grand white building. Built in 1037, it was old but sturdy with golden cupolas, in the pure Eastern

Orthodox style. The heavy battalion, 40 units strong again after the very welcome and recent reinforcements, was stationed in the religious building with other Panther and Tiger I tanks units. The area had been chosen because first, it was, as said before, close to the front, but also because it had a large grass yard circling it, with huge trees scattered all about. Camouflage nets had been installed, so the panzers were entirely invisible from the air. And, as a rule, the Russian soldier was reluctant to hit religious buildings. The USSR didn't have an official religion, and in fact, was against all of them. But the reality was that the people were still very religious, their Tsarist-Orthodox dominated past not being far away. All in all, it was as good a spot as any, and Walder was grateful for not being shot at for a change.

The rest of the Panzer Lehr division, Erich's battalion parent unit, was stationed a bit further west, to another marshaling yard. Southern Russia's frontline had pretty much crystallized during August after the powerful Soviet offensive had run out of steam. Nonetheless, the Red Army had pushed the Wehrmacht back hundreds upon hundreds of kilometers to the west. It had forced Manstein to resort to desperate counter-attacks and build the final defensive line that could reasonably be held, the great Dnieper river.

While all was relatively quiet at present, only fanatical fools (like the SS) still believed in the fact that they had finally stopped the Yvan's. The cooler-headed and more experienced soldiers that had been fighting the Russians since the start of Operation Barbarossa knew that the Red Army was simply re-accumulating its strength and would surely be back at it at the earliest possible moment.

Leaning on the side of the great double door, Erich was looking at the rain falling and plunged into his thoughts. He wondered what was happening with Ingrid, if she was all right. According to some rumors, the first Allied flights had been detected near and over Berlin. Nothing serious yet, but it announced trouble. He hoped, dearly, that nothing terrible would happen. He started to daydream about what he would do after the war and fantasized about getting married to his sweetheart.

# The siege of Gibraltar part 1
## September 15<sup>th</sup> to September 27<sup>th</sup>, 1944

There could be no shadow of a doubt that the assault on Gibraltar would be more challenging than that of the previous campaign in 1940-1941. The Axis had had over three years in which to tighten up its fortifications, bring the manpower up to strength, stock up with stores upon stores of ammo and weapons. It was, to say the least, filled to the brim with guns, canons and other heavy artillery.

The previous battle damage had been mostly repaired and compensated with extensive concrete strengthening works, dozens of new tunnels dug into the Rock itself. Naval guns from scuttled ships had also been installed directly into these new fortifications, and while the Allies had been bombing the positions non-stop, most of them were still in workable conditions.

The fortress strength consisted of up-to-date fortifications – since many had been added by the Germans and their famous Todt organization – as with its unique location within a minimal area. Simply said, maybe a division or two could attack the northern defense simultaneously, and frontally at that. Such was the narrowness of the only access to the Rock itself: less than half a kilometer. So, the size of the army did not matter very much. What mattered was the size of the guns and amount of bombs a besieger could bring to bear on the position, as the German had amply demonstrated in their successful storming of the fortress at the beginning of the war.

One simply did not blast quickly into something as hard as Earth's bedrock. After their victorious drive (on their second try) in Southern Spain, the Allies finally arrived within view of the formidable defenses of Gibraltar, coming on its outskirts by the 12th of September.

General Patton and Montgomery had naturally called in every gun within reach for the attack, and the Allied high command had made available the heaviest pieces available. In all, 54th Corps (artillery commander General Westerland) had at its disposal fifty-six heavy and medium batteries, forty-one light and eighteen mortar batteries, in addition to two battalions of assault guns. This made a total of 121 batteries, supported by two observation battalions.

The heavy siege artillery, the guns that mattered for this type of battle, were brought forward by the Americans, in the form of the 240 mm howitzers "black dragon," that were the most potent artillery weapons deployed by the US in the war to date. It could fire a 360 lb (160 kg) high explosive projectile 25,225 yards (23,066 m) and was designed to batter against heavily fortified targets. It was to be the largest field piece used by the US Army during the siege of Gibraltar.

And then there were the battleships. Over ten of them were brought just in front of the Rock, which could be considered point-blank range in naval terms. For the Allies, this was feasible since there was no real contest in the sea after the Battle of the North. There was also the fact that the Italian Navy (Regina Marina) was nowhere to be seen because of Allied air superiority. The US president had even ordered the king of Allied big ships, the brand-new BB-67 Montana, sporting 63 000 tons of displacement and twelve 406 mm guns, to the scene. The boat, designed to go head-to-head against the Yamato class battleships that the Japanese were operating in the Pacific, would have to wait for its duel with them. It was needed first to demolish the Rock of Gibraltar.

To complete the array of destruction that they would employ against Gibraltar, the Allies, of course, had their airpower. 500 B-29's were called in from the Pacific War, over 300 B-19, and several hundred medium bombers. 150 British Halifax were also brought to contribute.

So, to say that the Allies would bomb the place to oblivion was not an overstatement. But sheer power was not the only thing that mattered in siege warfare. One also needed to attack and control the area it was bombing. For it was a fact that rubble and broken terrain had a way of giving the besieged soldiers good cover, as was amply shown throughout the war in many a demolished cities and fortresses. It would not be the first time in World War Two that bombing while destroying standing buildings created more opportunities for the defenders.

The opening bombardment on September 15th was something to behold. In a coordinated attack, all ten battleships fired from their positions out at sea, while above a flight of over 800 planes dropped their bombload. All the while, the 121 artillery batteries and the 240mm black dragons also fired into the Maelstrom.

The shelling went on for most of the 15th and the 16th, until such time that the Allies simply ran out of ammo. The destruction on Gibraltar was hard to describe. To the observers and soldiers laying eyes on the Rock on the morning of the 17th, it seemed like the whole area was now a lunar landscape. A thick dust cloud was also covering the site to a radius of a couple of kilometers, the result of pulverized Rock blown into a fine powder.

Several hours later, general Montgomery, by then named commander of the besieging forces by the Allied high command, launched his attack. Optimism was high. Never in the annals of war such a powerful bombardment been inflicted on so small an area. But it rapidly became obvious that the German defenders retained much fighting capability as the assault was bloodily repulsed. Casualties were so high that the Allies decided to wait for more ammo for their artillery. The battleships would also be replenished in naval ordnance.

Another bombardment was thus executed on the 21st thru the 23rd. And again, the Allies sent their troops forward, again to be repulsed. Admiral Tovey, commander of the combined Allied fleet, even tried to cross over into the Mediterranean with his fleet but got hit by several shells from concealed naval guns at the base of the Rock, while several of his ships hit mines.

By the 27th of September, it was apparent that the fortress would not fall easily.

# Fast bombing
## September 28th, 1944

At 870 kilometers per hour, the ground below for the high-speed German bombers was just a blur. The Arado Ar-234 Blitz Bomber was the fastest operational combat aircraft in the world, slightly faster even than its cousin, the Messerschmitt Me-262 jet. And it was finally making itself heard in the war. Since May 1944, German industry had been making about twenty-five units a week, making for a very respectable 400 operational units. While half of them had been sent to the Eastern Front to face yet another crisis with the Red Army, the other 200 planes had been personally ordered to Spain by Goering himself. The Fuhrer was much worried about the state of affairs in Gibraltar and had wanted to make a daring and powerful raid on the massed artillery batteries reported to pound the Rock to dust.

Of course, Allied air patrols had seen the jet bombers, but as the German flyers zipped by, they had been unable to either hit any of them or catch up. They were just too slow (comparatively speaking) to do so. The ground units had some time to scamper away to cover, but the poor batteries of black dragons 240mm howitzers never stood a chance. The men operating them had been busy piling up the new shells they had just received for the next planned bombardment.

In a thunder-like boom, the Arado bombers lined up neatly toward the obvious canons pointing at Gibraltar. As they made their approach, Allied tracers shells pierced the skies in every direction but were generally fired after the planes had passed by in the blink of an eye. It made for an impressive show and gave the Allied soldiers the impression that something was done about the impossibly fast enemy. Still, again it amounted to nothing, apart from an explosion-riddled sky.

The bombers flew overhead, dropped their bombloads one after the other over the target zone, and then climbed again in a vertical arc, with powerful speed and noise. Allied planes followed in their thunderous wake a long while later. They never caught up to them.

Explosions immediately ripped thru the neatly arrayed canons, destroying or seriously damaging several of them. Luckily for the Germans, one of the ammunition dumps stacked near the artillery park was hit, which created a gigantic cascading explosion that echoed for tens of kilometers around.

In the German jet engines' dying noise, Allied artillerymen and soldiers started to come out of their makeshift cover to a scene of unimaginable destruction. The large enemy raid had transformed the black dragon battery into a pile of destroyed metal.

There was also the yelling and moaning of numerous wounded. Medics and everyone available ran to the scene to assist and help. The best and smartest American and British aviators, mostly aces (five or more air victories in the war), had already figured that their only chance of hitting one of the fast Arado jets would be on their way back to German airfields. Several squadron commanders radioed between themselves to assemble on the most likely return path of the enemy. Most of the pilots took up altitude, so when they spotted the Germans, they could plunge, thus increasing their speed significantly with gravity.

The Arado was an incredible instrument of war. Fast, deadly, and just downright miraculous a weapon for the fledging Reich. But it had one weakness. Jet technology was not well developed in these early days, and so its engine was ravenously hungry. This made for a very limited range. The blitz bombers (as they came to be called later) needed to come back the same way they had flown in, and this played precisely into the Allied pilot's hands.

They spotted the enemy from far away with their high above vantage point and a beautiful, southern Spanish cloudless day. The 75 assembled fighters thus started their dive to try to catch the Arados as they passed by. Most pilots miscalculated their dive and went too short or arrived too late. But some of them succeeded in making it right.

Those that did level their planes in a downward arc toward the enemy were able to take a worthy shot. The Allied airmen's downed seven jet bombers, that went down in flames just over the tip of the German frontline. Most of the shot down jets exploded loudly on the ground, some even just into or on top of Axis trenches.

Amidst climbing flak tracers and exploding skies, the Allied fighters turned around and went back to their lines. At least they had made the enemy pay a part of the billowed for their day of killing.

In a general sense, warfare had just changed on that day. Ever since the Germans had started to bring forth jet-powered planes to the battlefield, the balances had been tipping their way in the air war. The only reason the Allies had kept an edge thru 1944 was because of their numbers. But the Third Reich had been hard at work making more of their revolutionary planes, and while the Arado Blitz were still few in numbers (less than 500), the ME-262 Jet fighter was being made at a rhythm of 1000 per month.

The days of Allied air superiority were thus numbered, and over a little bit more time, the Axis would finally even the odds and give a much-needed boost to their fledgling hopes for final victory.

## Swastika over mother of freedom
## New York 10ᵗʰ October 1944

From the start of the US involvement into the Second World War, the Third Reich had looked across the Atlantic Ocean in impotent rage. At the time, Hitler had even entered into a fit worthy for the ages on the news of the American "dastardly attack," as he had called it. Immediately after that, meetings after meetings had been held at the highest levels of the Nazi leadership, with the Fuhrer and Hermann Goering, at the time head of the Luftwaffe, presiding. The two men had wanted (and as fast as possible) a long-range heavy bomber capable of hitting America's cities.

The idea was to bring the horrors of war to the US civilians, and in Hitler's own words, "break their feeble will to fight." "Only one bombed city will make them ponder," was Goering's favorite saying during those optimistic times.

Several aircraft companies had been invited to present design as early as October 1941. The project, code-named "Amerika Bomber," was followed up by a flurry of designs from Messerschmitt, Junkers, and Heinkel. They all presented a plane, and out of all of them, the Junkers company was chosen for its quality of its work.

The Junkers JU-390 long-range heavy bomber project was thus born. With 112 feet long fuselage, a wingspan of 165 feet, and a height of 22.6 feet, it was a mammoth plane. It was armed with a pair of 13mm machine guns in the ventral gondola and two 13mm machine guns on its beam.

It also sported six gigantic engines to provide for 314 miles per hour and a range of 6030 miles (9700 kilometers). The Junkers JU-390 was also equipped with **20mm cannons** in a dorsal turret and a single canon on the tail. All of this hardware was handled by a crew of ten. These were spread between the flight crew and dedicated gunners.

Like its smaller brother, the Heinkel 111 (arguably the Wehrmacht's workhorse bomber during the Second World War), it could carry twenty 50 kg (110 lb)bombs. Seemingly small a load for a plane this size, it had been decided to keep it that way to increase its range to the maximum given by the 6 x BMW 801D radial piston engines that delivered 1,700 horsepower each and to leave room for the gasoline to make them work for so long a distance.

The first operational flight for the Junker 390 was made on January 4th, 1943, and was cause for much optimism. At the time, the project designers had promised the Fuhrer and his Luftwaffe deputy that it would be ready in 1944.

After several confirmed long flights across the Axis empire, the plane was deemed ready for limited production by May 1944. It was a very complicated machine to make. The Germans did not have the capability to mass-produce them like the excellent Boeing company was doing out of their huge Seattle factories. Production started in earnest in mid-July, and by the end of September, the Junkers company had been able to make 40 of them.

It had taken even longer than the original design called for because German leaders and designers had taken good notes on the matter of the American B-29 raids on the Hawaiian Islands. It was there in 1943 that the US planes had chased the Japs away from Pearl Harbor with a host of range-boosted planes. The B-29 sported additional tanks of fuel to carry them to their destination.

The 40 Amerika Bombers made for this very first raid on mainland North America had the same kind of modifications done on their machines, making them slow and cumbersome planes and reducing their top speed to 200 mph and the bombload to ten 50kg bombs. This would not make for the most potent raid in history, but the Reich's leader's goal was to hit American's morale, not burn its cities to the ground (not yet, at least).

The 40 units were quietly flown or assembled directly on-site at an airport near the small Spanish town of Santiago the Compostela, on the Atlantic Coast. The city was what could pass for the closest approach to the American city. It made for a journey of 3285 miles (5288 kilometers) one way. It almost made the JU-390 fly without modifications, but the 500 missing miles were completed with the additional fuel tanks.

A vast airfield was also built-in great secret, with camouflage nets above to hide the works, since the Allies were not very far away in Northern Portugal and many planes patrolled the area. The 40 gigantic bombers took off at night, with no lights on, and specially trained crews for direction in the night. They flew on instruments only for the first part of the trip.

The Allies never saw it coming. The 10th of October was a very crisp day in New York City. The dock area was bustling with activity even at this early an hour. It was six-thirty in the morning, and the workers on the docks started to hear engine noises coming from out to sea. They turned, curious about it, but they saw nothing on the horizon, so thick the morning fog still was. They went back to work. After all, there was a war on, and they could hear and see military planes every day. Only a couple of the workers, a little bit more curious than the others, mentally registered that it was not common to see planes coming from the sea at that early hour. They usually flew above the city, but never really from out to sea to the city.

Fifteen minutes later, a large flight of bombers, with an enormous wingspan and six engines, could be heard and seen flying over the Statue of Liberty. Many a civilian mistook the planes for B-29's. Everyone had heard of the brave airmen pounding the hell out of the Axis armies on every front America was fighting on.

So confident were the military authorities that they were safe on their mainland home country that not even a single patrol was scouring the skies that day. The German aviators, motivated, eager even, concentrated on their task at hand. Under half a minute or so after the large bomber flight had approached and flown over the Statue of Liberty, the German bombers opened their bays and let drop the bombs.

The more curious onlookers then slowly started to register that something was wrong. The planes had dropped what seemed like small black dots before veering hard, back from where they came. Following the dots, a whistling sound was heard. Not many New Yorkers knew of the sound. But most Europeans had learned by now to be wary of the characteristic whistling sounds of incoming bombs from airplanes—but in this case, no one scattered in the targeted area, to their great misfortune.

A few milliseconds later, all hell broke loose in Manhattan. Multiple explosions rocked the buildings, the ground, the docks. The Empire State skyscraper was even hit by a bomb, leaving a gigantic hole on its side.

On their way back above the Statue of Liberty, the German flyers let loose a flurry of their 20mm canons. The horrified bystanders, military men, and dock workers all saw the red tracer shells sprout from the German planes and hit the Statue multiple times, splintering its metal frame. After the German bombers were thru, it was riddled with holes, smoke dust surrounding it.

The German bombers left rapidly, disappearing over the horizon. The P-51 fighters of the home defense forces were sent after them, but too late. They almost caught up to them over the Atlantic but had to turn back for lack of range.

The Nazis had finally struck at the heart of America. They had succeeded in their goal of profoundly shocking America. But not in the sense that the narrow-minded leaders of the Third Reich thought. The consequences for the Germans would be far-ranging, from the increase in the fighting spirit of an enraged United States, to the more specific new priority that their president gave to the multitudes of B-29's operating worldwide: Level every Germany city standing.

From now on, and that for most American citizens, there would be no quarters given to the damned enemy.

## Thru the Straits
### U-181, October 11th, 1944

Since ancient times, Gibraltar's narrow straits separating Spain's southernmost tip from North Africa have been known as the "Gateway to the Mediterranean Sea." From a geographic standpoint, one can easily see the area's military significance only by its "choke point" feature.

Axis shipping had been able, after their conquest of the Rock, to pass between Atlantic and Mediterranean freely. But at present, it was apparent to see why U-Boat 59 was in a deep dive. The sea's surface was choking full with Allied ships, and the sky above was vigorously patrolled.

They were almost to the bottom of the sea and about to attempt a crossing. They'd briefly surfaced earlier to replenish their air and look around the general area at the Mediterranean's mouth to have an idea of the number of enemy ships.

The sailors were tired. Worn even. It had been a very long voyage. They also had had several close calls with air patrols near the Azores and been attacked three times by destroyers hunting them with their sonars and depth charges. Their mission had brought them all the way to the shores of Mexico. There they had picked up one of the most famous men in the Third Reich. Otto Skorzeny. The man had been back from a critical mission within the United States.

The man himself had not been comfortable in his first U-boat voyage. First, there was the constant feeling of being confined. The dampness. The rank air. Human odor. All things that Skorzeny could work with if he'd been in a situation he could control. But that was just it. He was crammed aboard a rickety underwater boat.

He was no sailor and could do nothing about his survival. His right-hand man Sturm also seemed to feel the same way. They spent their days milling about, and once in a while got to go on the bridge when the ship briefly surfaced at night to give a little bit of fresh air to the crew in a rotating schedule. After a few days, they'd finally been accustomed to the weird noises that the hull made. They both decided that it wasn't sinking, it was just the way it was. But overall, never in his life had Skorzeny felt so helpless about his fate. He resolved to never again step into such a vessel.

U-Boat Ace captain Wolfgang Luth, the second-most successful German submarine commander of the war to date, with to date 34 merchant ships sunk plus the French submarine Doris, had sent 187 000 tons of enemy shipping to the bottom of the sea. He'd been sent on patrols off South Africa and even had a successful foray into the Indian Ocean, where he sank four merchant ships. As to the straits of Gibraltar, he'd crossed them twice before the Axis conquered it, once submerged and once on the surface, at night, using the tide's currents.

He'd long pondered how he should cross the straits. The Allies heavily patrolled the area, and there seemed to be an enormous battle underway against the Gibraltar fortress itself, as every time he surfaced at night, he saw the explosion. The presence of numerous battleships, constantly firing in the Rock's general direction, also gave him a clue that a large battle was underway in Southern Spain.

So, a surface crossing would be almost impossible to do since there were so many ships around that something was bound to happen, and the U-Boat spotted. There was also the fact that the Axis had heavily mined the entrance of the straits and into the Mediterranean with one of the most extensive minefields ever laid down in the history of warfare.

A submerged crossing also challenged Luth by the unique environment of the area. The strong underwater currents, and the presence of Sonar-equipped ships that would indeed ping him while he crossed. The sea was relatively shallow in that area, and one sub commander had to be very familiar with the seafloor's varying depth. And if depth charges were hurled at his U-boat, there was not going to be much evading maneuvers he would be able to do. The Germans' saving grace was that the prevalent ambient battle noise would severely hamper the Sonar's capability to detect his boat.

In the end, he'd chosen the best of two bad options. U-59 would cross underwater. He'd gone to the SS man and told him of his decision. Skorzeny just nodded and told him to try and do his best. Luth could tell that the big man was not in his element. He promised him that they would succeed in bringing him home unscathed.

The length of the strait was about 25 to 30 miles long. Having submerged quite far because of heavy Allied surface traffic, the U-Boat was in for a 6 hours ride. Once the U-boat was underwater, Luth ordered the all stop for the engines. He'd decided to rely only on the entry current for the passage into the Mediterranean. With a three knots speed, it took a long time. The boat seemed almost unmoving, but this was the best way to reduce noise and look like part of the water to avoid being detected by the damned Sonars from the ships on the surface. He started his move when the tide was flowing the fastest and ordered the boat in "silent running" mode. The all quiet was imposed across the ship.

For those long hours, no one spoke, slept, and even moved, looking up at the hull's ceiling, to watch in impotence for whatever the enemy could throw at them. Sonar, depth charges. All the while, they heard the overbearing noises of dozen upon dozens of propellers milling about.

Then several hours into the crossing, the noises reduced to a distant vibration. Luth announced thru the in-board communication that they were thru the Allied ships but could still not surface because a large minefield covered almost every meter of the area. But the stress level aboard the submarine dropped significantly. Another two hours and they were thru.

By that time, the air in the submarine was rank on a level that was edging on the dangerous, so Luth ordered the boat to surface to replenish its air reserves. On the way up, he moved the periscope up, turning as he did into the direction of Gibraltar. No enemy ships within easy range of his U-boat. There was a minimal chance he could be spotted since they were in the dead of night. He ordered the boat to full speed. "Head for Italy at best speed," said Luth in his most relieved and commanding voice. His men were only too happy to proceed.

Within the submarine's depth, Otto Skorzeny and his right-hand man Marco Sturm heaved a breath of relief. They immediately felt the air rush in the ventilation system, consequently telling them that the submarine had succeeded in crossing the Straits of Gibraltar and surfaced. They would, after all, make it to Germany.

# The siege of Gibraltar part 2
## Last call of the SS Wiking Division, October 27th, 1944

Before the death of Adolf Hitler and Himmler in Russia in 1943, the SS were on a meteoric rise within the German armed forces and the Reich as a whole. They were given the best equipment, the best posting, and the best recruits. In fact, since their appearance on the battlefield, the SS formations had rapidly gained an elite reputation, for their fighting power and morale, amongst others. Formed from volunteers only and with the strictest criteria's, they did very well in the fighting.

But at the same time, most of its members were the most enthusiastic Nazis, so they were prone to fanaticism. They were also very likely to kill prisoners, Jews, and anything else that their twisted ideology did not like. Consequently, the SS did not entertain a positive reputation.

Everything was set for the SS forces to eventually replace the regular army within the Nazi state. But the death of Hitler and Himmler changed their fortune dramatically, for the SS were not on Goering's love list. The rivalry between him and the head of the SS had been very bitter before the man's death. Both men had jockeyed for Hitler's love and attention for years before the war, and the fight had continued in the war.

The new Fuhrer wanted nothing to do with SS armed forces, but at the same time, needed them because they were so good. He had consequently allied with Himmler's successor Reinhard Heidrich when Hitler's plane went down in flames and had been able to keep the peace within the German armed forces. But there was no mistaking who was the strongest partner in that alliance.

Subtly at first and then very obviously, Goering changed the equipment priorities of where the best of it would be sent, and the regular army started to get its fair share again. The SS dropped in the priority order. Many recruiting stations were closed, as most new recruits were drafted into the regular army. Consequently, not many SS divisions were created in 1943, and in 1944, not even one was levied.

Not many of Germany's henchmen disagreed with their new master. The SS had been a very problematic force within the country, and many a Nazi official had been worried about what would happen when they'd be more numerous than the regular troops. And after all, the world as a whole would be a better place without the fanatic SS soldiers.

Goering last somewhat subtle move had been to make sure the SS forces would always get the most challenging jobs. It was hard to argue against it since they had elite status. And so, they got to face the brunt of the Russians attacks during their 1944 summer offensive. Several SS battalion-sized units had also been left in the United Kingdom as part of the token force to hold the island while most of the Wehrmacht was evacuated. The Allies swept these SS formations in their reconquest of the UK. In short, the elite force was sent wherever a situation was boiling. So, by the end of 1944, while the SS was still a force to be reckoned with, it was dwindling rapidly.

Instances like Gibraltar, where strong forces were needed to hold the fortress, were the perfect opportunity for Goering to continue his work. It would be encircled and cut off from the main German front, and there was no hope of rescue. The Fuhrer enthusiastically ordered what was arguably the best division in Guderian's army group: The Wiking SS division. It was to hold Gibraltar to the last man.

SS Wiking division story began after the invasion of Poland in 1939 (and before his death in 1943). Heinrich Himmler, the former head of the SS, sought to expand the Waffen-SS (the organization's military branch) foreign military volunteers for the Nazi state. The enrollment began in April 1940 by creating two regiments: the Waffen-SS Regiment Nordland (for Danish, Norwegian, and Swedish volunteers) and the Waffen-SS Regiment Westland (for Dutch and Flemish volunteers). Interestingly enough, men from these countries flocked to the German recruitment stations.

The SS Infantry Regiment Germania of the SS-Verfügungs-Division, which were formed mostly from ethnic Germans, were transferred to help create the nucleus of a new division in late 1940. In December 1940, the new SS motorized formation was designated as SS-Division Germania, but after its formative period, the name was changed to SS-Division Wiking in January 1941. The division was formed around three motorized infantry regiments: Germania, Westland, and Nordland, with an artillery regiment. Command of the newly formed division was given to Felix Steiner, the Verfügungstruppe SS Regiment Deutschland former commander.

Of course, the unit had participated in the Barbarossa operation and, as such, had seen much fighting. It had eventually been transferred back to Guderian's command for the western campaign. It had been part of all the heavy action in Tunisia, then Portugal. It also had been at the tip of the spear during the German counter-offensive in the summer of 1944.

As its last act, it had been worming itself thru the demolished trenches of the fortress of Gibraltar for the whole length of the siege. Its ranks had been depleted severely by the heavy battles of the last few weeks. It also had been bombed relentlessly by Allied battleships, bombers, and canons. But it had endured. The Allied 4th army, composed of a Canadian corps, an American, and a British corps, had been attacking it for over a month. The other units fighting along with the SS, the 11th and 23rd Infantry, and the 3rd heavy panzer battalion had also suffered much. All of the Tigers II had been destroyed, while some of the brave tankers had picked up riffles and continued the struggle on foot. The 11th was, by the 20th of October, amalgamated with the 23rd, as it did not have enough troops to continue the fight as an independent unit.

With this setting, the German defenders fought their last battle, amidst the trenches, demolished rock and bunkers, pumping rounds after rounds after the advancing Allies. The enemy had progressed well in the previous weeks. The gains were measured in meters every day, but it was relentless. Once they'd taken a part of the fortress, that was that. The defenders could only fight a losing battle.

Felix Steiner, commander of the Wiking division, was sitting down in one of the last standing bunkers. He was looking absently over a table that had a map covered with dust. He'd stopped trying to remove most of it since the enemy bombing and shelling from above always brought more as the 10 meters thick rock over it was frequently pounded. From the embrasures, he could see red tracers flying from both sides. Explosions everywhere. The ground shook repeatedly. Behind him was the embrasure facing the sea since the besieged defenders had their backs to it and were clinging to their last few meters of the Rock. Allied minesweeper ships could be seen milling around, working on the large Axis minefield laid months before.

Steiner had relayed that fact to HQ to let them know that the enemy would soon break out into the Mediterranean. The Luftwaffe and the Italian air force had mounted several airstrikes, making for intense battles in the sky, but the Allies had progressed toward the end of the minefield nonetheless. He'd even ordered some of his remaining anti-tank canons (all his big guns were gone by then) to fire on the ships. They'd dueled with the enemy for several days (and did their fair share of damage), but most had been destroyed by the end of the siege.

The SS man felt like there were not many options left. He'd stopped ordering troops around since they were now confined to such a small perimeter that it was stand in place, defend and die. The commander of the 23rd infantry division, Alex Faterman, had radioed him the day before that his command bunker was about to be overwhelmed. He'd been north of Steiner's position, on the rockface facing the Atlantic Sea. The operator had not been able to raise him again since that time.

A large explosion shook the bunker to its core, extinguishing the oil lamps and lifting a large could of dust all around. For several seconds nothing could be seen but grey smoke. The other soldiers and Steiner coughed for a while. It was desperate.

It was so desperate for the beleaguered defenders that the battle for Gibraltar would not even endure one more day. In one last-ditch push, the Canadian 3$^{rd}$ corps, with French-Canadian Regiment de Maisonneuve in its lead, stormed the last German redoubts by the end of the 27$^{th}$ of October. No quarters were given to anything that was remotely resembling a SS uniform, as the French Canadians exacted their revenge on the massacre that the Wiking men had done to one of their captured units back in the summer offensive. And thus, ended the fighting career of the SS Wiking division.

The Allied flags of the USA, Canada, and the United Kingdom were hoisted on the Rock's highest part at 16h00 on the 27$^{th}$ of October. Gibraltar's fall was a major strategic success for the Western Allies and a disaster for the Axis.

The numerous and powerful Allied fleets would eventually enter the Mediterranean, and there was no limit to the mischief they could do with the troops already posted in Tunisia. Italy was now very much in danger, and amphibious landings could easily flank the whole Axis position in Africa. Then there was Egypt and the entire oil convoy system.

The Axis's final victory was as far a reality as it could be in these dying days of October 1944.

# EPILOGUE

Frank Whittle, the born-again president of Powers LTD, a British aviation company developing jet engines, walked right beside the top man in the whole British Empire, Winston Churchill. The new Powers LTD factory was built within a large aluminum complex that had seen the light of day in 1942-1943. The reason for the building's location was because of the presence of one of the biggest electric dams in the world, the Isle-Maligne power complex, that had been built at the turn of the century. Many factories had sprouted around it. And then even more, after Nazi Germany occupied the United Kingdom.

The plane factory itself had been built as an annex to the large Alcan factory in Alma. A long section had been added just to the side of what was called the 405 alloy production unit. Since its opening in May of 1944, much work had been accomplished. Allied engineers had flocked to Alma, from American to British and even Australian ones. They'd all cooperated toward one goal. Make the power LTD jet engine concept a reality and as fast as possible. The American Boeing company had also invested tons upon tons of money to help out Powers. Whittle would have loved to keep the concept to himself and make the planes by his means, but the fall of the UK and the destruction of his industrial capability had seen to the disappearance of his business. It would have stayed that way but for the appearance of the jets on the enemy's side.

For the Germans had stolen a march on the Allies by developing a plethora of jet-Powered planes and were fast evening the odds in the air. Already, Allied air patrol couldn't cross anywhere near the Pyrenees defensive line without taking severe casualties. B-29 air raids over Germany, sent in retaliation to the New York attacks, had miserably failed. They'd been intercepted by hosts of ME-262's and even other jet-powered variants. The result had been nothing short of disastrous, 90% of the planes being destroyed. The Luftwaffe had even started to employ high-speed jet-powered tactical bombers. The Allied fighters could not even intercept them.

For German industry had been hard at work, making as many jet fighters as possible. And their jet-bombers production was ramping up at an alarming speed. The Allies didn't have the exact numbers produced, but if they'd known that the Reich was making over a thousand ME-262 a month, they would have been even more worried. It would get really bad before it got better.

Hence the personal visit from the head of the British Empire at war, Winston Churchill. It was not the man's first visit to the area. He was on his fourth trip since May 1944. The Prime minister insisted on making sure the first meteor jet fighters would roll out of the factory before the year's end. To that end, he often visited Whittle's factory to make sure he and the Boeing people had everything they needed. It also helped that the big freshwater lake near Alma, called the Lac-St-Jean, sported a great variant of freshwater salmon called ouananiche that was a good sport to fish.

For the Allies, it was simply not a matter of money or resources. Their airmen in Europe were dying, and time was running out. There was a moment where the Axis would reclaim the skies' mastery if nothing was done about it.

"So Frank, tell me how things are developing," Churchill said, pointing to a bridge crane that was moving one of the two jet engines on a plane awaiting its assembly on the factory's floor. "This should be the first operational jet.", said Whittle proudly. "We're finishing it today, and it will be transported to Bagotville for its test flights." Churchill nodded. They were accompanied by a  host of uniformed officers, generals for the most part. There were Canadian, American, French, and British officers. Everyone smiled. All around them, the big factory was bustling with activity. Showers of sparks flew in all directions, for the workers were busy welding and assembling the all-aluminum frames for the future Meteor Jet fighter.

"Good, good," said Churchill, taking a cigar from his pocket to lit it. Taking a bit of time before talking again (he was busy with his cigar), he said: "Frank, great work. We'll be in Bagotville to see the test flights". Churchill paused, looking at Whittle with a grave face. "We need these planes, Frank. We need hem dearly. Our boys are dying by the troves over in Europe, and there won't be a victory over the Axis if we don't even the odds in air technology", finished Churchill. Powers LTD's boss just nodded approvingly.

In the next few days, the first official flight of an Allied jet-powered engine would be recorded. They were still months away from production, as the planes needed refining before entering into the mass-building phase, but some hope was in the air for the Allies.

# Extracts from Von Manstein's 1958 book, LOST VICTORY
## The Eastern Front at the onset of winter 1944-1945

The unmistakable feeling of relief that we all felt at HQ East in Smolensk had been palpable for weeks now. It was one cold day of November 5th, 1944, and I was, along with my staff officers, taking a stroll along a long line of recently arrived Tiger II panzers and Elephant mobile guns. As we walked under the rifled gun barrels canopy, we bathed in the cold and felt oddly confident.

We were in the gigantic supply and assembly yards of Army Group Center located within and around the train depot. The place had grown in size by exponential margins since my arrival at the height of the 1942 winter disaster that had befallen us in Moscow.

There had been no reported attacks, nothing serious really, on Army Group Dnieper along the river-defensive line that bore the same name. The Red Army had, slowly but surely, been winding its relentless attacks in Southern Russia to a trickle. As more and more forces arrived in that sector, I felt confident that we had stabilized the front for a long while. We had enough troops to man the whole length of the frontline, helped immensely by the manpower of our allies, and the ample availability of German weapons that were finally starting to be plentiful enough to equip some Romanian and Hungarian divisions with real, modern weapons.

I remember the ground still being muddy and wet on that day. It was still at the annoying threshold between winter and fall, where wetness and cold-worked side by side to make us soldiers miserable. Light snow was falling slowly in big flakes, and the skies were cloudy. Above us roared a squadron of jet fighters, bound for the frontline near Moscow to battle it again with the Red Air force. ,

From the Baltic to the Black Sea, the rush of ME-262 reinforcements had finally started to tell and had evened the odds across the east. We didn't master the whole of Russia's airspace yet, but where we chose it so, we could remove any Soviet presence from the air. This made for a lot easier defense than I expected even in my wildest dreams. From the moment the Russians would attack in force somewhere, we would send the ME-262 to remove their bombers and fighters from the attacked spot, diminishing the Soviet offensive power by a notch. One that was achieved, I would then send the Stukas and the very few Arados jets we had to attack the Russian multitudes on the ground. More than one attack had been broken this way.

As I continued to walk between the tanks, gesturing to the soldiers and stopping once in a while to discuss with them, I could not help but look worryingly at the skies above. It was a given fact that in winter, and especially the Russian winter, there would be days without it being possible to have planes in the air. This, I felt strongly, would be utilized by my opponent, general Zhukov.

He would attack in bad weather. During a storm, even. More than one report of troops concentrations in the Yaroslavl-Kazan sector, north-east, and east of Moscow, respectively. I had felt sure about the time and place of attack at the time, and I would be proven right. The coming offensive would again test the will of the Wehrmacht and push it to its utmost limits.

But unfortunately for the Russians, we were no longer in 1942, where lousy supply and lack of rear reserves had created the perfect conditions for a significant victory on their side. They'd retaken Moscow while the German Reich was at its weakest. This time, I vowed that the story would be different, for I had modern equipment in its multitude on my side. My forces were rested, at full strength, and with high morale. The future would prove me right. The might of the German army was not yet broken in 1945.

## Pentagon building
### Meeting of US leaders, December 1ˢᵗ, 1944

The President seemed to be in one of his good days, thought general Marshall, listening to Roosevelt talking about the Pacific's recent advances. The old man was pleased about the gains in the Solomon Islands. The 4th marine division had already claimed the airfield on some non-descript place called Guadalcanal in the middle of the Island chain. Nimitz and his admirals were making good time on his naval campaign, and the full supply route to Australia was re-opened again. Already three infantry divisions had been landed in Eastern Australia to help beef up the Us army Pacific theater commander in chief, General Macarthur. The offensive to reclaim Darwin and the little corner of Australia that the Japs were occupying was near.

The discussion just before the Pacific one had not been as pleasant. They'd talked about the recent failures of the bombing raids over Germany and the growing Axis air power. It now seemed that while the Reich was not attacking the Allies on their ground, it was difficult to fly over their airspace without being intercepted and received significant casualties.

The decision had also been taken to stop the bombing raids over the German industrialized Ruhr, pending better fighters. The Allies hoped to bridge the technological gap with their enemy soon, thanks to the very promising meteor project of the Alma factory in French-Canada.

"Also, gentleman, general Marshall confirmed to me in an earlier meeting that the nuclear development project would restart soon." The mention of his name brought general Marshall out of his daydreaming. "Hum…" he cleared his throat to gather his thoughts and give him some mental time for a right answer. "Yes, Mr. President. The project will be restarted in a different location since the Axis learned of the one we had in Mexico." He shuffled thru his papers. "We found some scientists still alive after the raid and some that were not at the facility when it was attacked. General Groves had also survived the attack and has assured me that the work would restart shortly."

The room listened, apparently in a somber mood. They all had in mind the recent German propaganda film they'd seen, portraying the damned commando that had attacked the nuclear research facility. Otto Skorzeny, the same man that had abducted general Clark earlier in the war, receiving the Knights Cross with Oakleaves, one of Germany's highest decorations, for his mission in America. In the short movie, he received the medal directly from Goering at some grand phony ceremony that the Nazis liked to organize. Not something wholly heartening to see. At least not for the enemies of Germany.

Several prominent people were about in the room. General Patton and Eisenhower, army commander and European theater commander-in-chief respectively, had been recalled to Washington for this very conference. The secretary of state, Cordell Hull, was also present. They were in one of the secure meeting room at the Pentagon. Smoke occupied most of the space, as people in the room smoked—some the cigarette, some the Cigar, like Patton.
The mood was less festive than initially anticipated for this time of the year. Hopes had been relatively high when they had successfully landed in Portugal earlier, and the fall of Gibraltar had also created many hopes that the war would soon be over. Or that at least they were getting into the last year of it.

But instead, the Axis forces had shown a great reluctance to abide by these hopes. Resistance to the Allied forces had gradually stiffened to a point where it was quite difficult to advance. The loss of complete air supremacy had something to do about it, but it also seemed that the Germans had increased their fighting units' combat-effectiveness. No wonder, with the multitudes of powerful tanks delivered to the frontlines.

The Allied fleet had yet to enter the Mediterranean. They'd gone thru the minefield, but the first foray into the sea in November had been met by a rugged Axis air raid, comprised of hundreds upon hundreds of ME-262 fighters, escorting bombers crammed full of the new rockets or missiles that could be thrown at ships. The fleet had retreated amidst heavy casualties and several capital ships damaged, while the air force (American and British fighters alike) had tried to regain control of the skies. But to no avail. Axis air strength-based in Sardinia had been too strong.

In the North, the Allies were slowly building up the United Kingdom into the great springboard it would be for the liberation of Europe. Still, there were not enough forces available yet to entertain a significant campaign in the Iberian Peninsula and also land in Northern France or the Low Countries.

In the East, the Soviets had won great victories over the summer of 1944, not unlike their western counterparts. But it also seemed that the Germans had been able to solidify the frontline, again because of airpower and those damned mighty tanks. In a visit back in October, Molotov had told them not to worry and that the planned winter offensive would break the back of the German on the Eastern Front.

"We need to keep the faith, gentlemen, said Roosevelt in his most reassuring tone. The same tone that had won him many elections. "The forces of liberty will triumph over the empire of evil," he said again. "We just need to keep doing what we are doing. We have advanced far into their realm, and while we currently are experiencing some setbacks, the power of our industrial base will win over their might eventually", finished the President smashing his cigarette in the ashtray to emphasize his point about final victory.

While every man in the room intellectually agreed with them, at this very moment, it wasn't easy to see the end of the long tunnel they had just entered into.

## Masurian Woods
### The Wolf's Lair, December 8th, 1944

General Halder, head of the OKW, was presiding over another meeting of the Oberkommando Der Wehrmacht, the supreme command of all German Armed forces. Three other men were present at the meeting in one of the gigantic bunkers. General Von Paulus, the former army commander in Turkey and Persia, and general Walter Model, another front line general that had been at the Eastern forces head before Barbarossa. The last person attending the meeting was not a military man, but nonetheless critical to the Reich's war effort. Albert Speer, the country's minister for armament and production.

The Wolf's lair was located in Eastern Prussia, in the deep Masurian woods, about 200 kilometers East of Konigsberg. It had its airfield near and sported all the defenses the Reich could muster for its beloved Fuhrer and the men assisting him. Since 1942, it was the place where the war was directed from. It had all that was needed for a modern HQ—top of the line communication equipment's, protective bunkers, proximity to the Eastern Front. Adolf Hitler had it built, and while it was not the perfect place for an HQ, it had been decided to keep it operational after his death. The time had not been ripe for significant command changes, while the Reich was reeling back on every front.

One important man was absent from the meeting: Hermann Goering, the leader of Germany. Halder wondered what or where or how he was. The Fuhrer had, according to rumors, relapsed into one of his morphine spells. It was not ideal for the country, but the head of the OKW had learned that military affairs were best left to military men to manage during the war. His absence was not that much of a problem for the conduct of operational and grand strategy, it was even a blessing.

They were sitting in one of the big, concrete-reinforced room that sported the main command bunker, called the Fuhrer Bunker. It was quite bland, for it had no decorations, just two doors, and a large table. For once, there were not even maps laid down for the discussion. Halder did not want to talk about operational matters but rather an overall strategy.

"Gentlemen," he opened the discussion with a smile. "Welcome," he finished looking at everyone. For it had been a long voyage for the three men. Speer had come directly from Berlin, so he had about a full day of travel under his belt. Model was just back from the main Eastern theater HQ in Smolensk, while Paulus had just arrived the day before from his long trip to Madrid. The two generals had been ordered there to appraise the general situation for the OKW for the meeting.

Halder continued: "We need to discuss the conduct of the war for the next year. It appears we have been able, in the last few months, to slow down or even stop Allied advances on most fronts. We must now make sure we continue to do so, while at the same time start looking for a favorable outcome to the war for the Reich".

It was a fact for all the men in this room that the Allies had declared that they would not settle any peace with Germany short of their unconditional Surrender. This was most unacceptable for these proud men, mostly since the German army had conquered large swaths of territory. There needed to be a purpose for all these deaths, victories, and sacrifices.

"General Paulus," said Halder looking directly at the man. "Please give us your report of the Iberian Peninsula theater." He sat down while Paulus sat up. "Thank you, general. I must report that my trip was most enlightening to understand the state of the situation in Spain.", He paused, walking to the head of the table. "It is obvious from the ratio of forces we entertain against the Western enemies will force us to retire completely to the Pyrenees defensive line sooner than later. Guderian and Rundstedt have played a game to gain time, and they've succeeded wildly. But as we all agreed earlier, the objective is to husband our forces, and so by retreating into the defenses, we will greatly lower our present casualty rate. Also, the longer we keep the Spanish in the war, the better. But there will come a time when we will have to evacuate central Spain. Franco's government will surely not survive, and we must expect most of his armed forces to surrender to the Allies." He paused, expecting some questions.

Model had one. "General, what is the state of readiness for the fortifications in the mountains?" "They are ready, General. More than ready, in fact. I was pleasantly surprised at the quality and strength of the whole area. We have a lot of fortified positions and the guns to operate them in great quantities. The arrival of these two brand-new panzer divisions will bolster the defenses like never before with their full complements of Tigers II". He looked thankfully at Speer for his excellent work in getting the weapons to the frontline. The minister of armament nodded smilingly.

"What is your level of confidence that the Pyrenees line will hold?" asked Halder expectantly. "It will hold for as long as we can keep the mastery of the air." Our current operational strength for the ME-262 and Arado blitz bombers is strong, and the Allies are not even venturing over our lines anymore unless they absolutely have to. In my opinion, the enemy will have to do something significant to change the actual balance we have so carefully achieved.". He paused again before changing the subject. "Kesselring also visited me when I was in Madrid to give me an appraisal of the central

Mediterranean situation. The air reinforcements we sent to Sardinia has checked any serious Allied naval foray into the sea. The Fritz missiles are working wonders. The general believes that again if the enemy does nothing significant to change the current state of affairs, he can hold the area indefinitely."

"Good. Thank you, General Paulus", said Halder, turning toward Model. It was the man's turn to speak. "My trip to Smolensk has also given much to be optimistic for," said the officer with a smile. "The attacks on the Dnieper defensive line have altogether stopped, and we have gained mastery in the air. In the north, the front is quiet as it has been for three years now. In the center where we hold Moscow, our forces are powerful, well supplied, and strongly entrenched. Manstein has at his disposal many panzer divisions to bolster any beleaguered part of his frontline. We also have mastery of the skies in that area, thanks again to the miraculous ME-262 fighters. There is no reason why the front should not hold for a long while." He paused to make his next point a little more dramatic. "However, large troops concentrations are reported to be assembling in the Yaroslavl and Kazan areas. It appears obvious that the Soviets will launch another powerful winter offensive. But general Manstein is confident that he will be able to hold the line."

"Thank you, general," said Halder. "Minister?" he gestured smilingly at Speer. "Thank you, sir," said Albert, in his is respectful voice. "The Reich's production has reached new heights and continues to grow. We are now making 1200 ME-262 fighters a month and about 100 Arado blitz bombers. Tigers (I and II), panthers, and tracked canons production is also well within the projected figures. We are even accumulating some units in large spaces in Germany for lack of casualties or trained men to use them." He paused, clearing his throat uncomfortably. "I believe that at this point, manpower is our biggest weakness," he said, letting his word hang in the air for a little moment. Everyone in the room looked at him worriedly. They were all aware that there were not enough men for the Reich to do all it needed to do. Since the start of the war, the casualties had been nothing short of horrendous, hence the primary reason they had resolutely switched to the defensive. They had millions of war prisoners toiling all across the Nazi empire to make the tools for war, but they needed more. "There will be a time where the main reason for not making new units or air squadrons will be manpower shortage, of which we are already experiencing. I need more men". Speer finished bluntly.

Halder interjected. "The class of 1945 will soon make it to the military training yards", he said with a reassuring voice. "It won't be enough, general. We have the means to make more weapons, but just not enough to operate them. Maybe if we can stay on the defensive for a while and husband our forces properly, we can start thinking about seriously growing the size of our armed forces in 1947 or 1948". Everyone didn't know what to say to this since Speer seemed to be serious. Go on with the war for another three to four years to have an eventual chance at victory? This seemed, even to pure military man, impossible to bear.

For the military situation, remarkably improved to a point where the Reich had a tiny hope of victory, did not change the fact that the country was warring against most of the planet, and that eventually, it would only run out of warm bodies to throw at the enemy's multitudes.

Germany was sufficient for now since it was on the defensive and its units mostly at full strength. But once offensive operations resumed to the level seen in the first four years of the war, losses would mount to a point where a critical mass would be attained, and everything would fall apart.

Wishing for the Reich's survival was improbable, at best. But these men would try as hard as they could, along with the masses of brave German soldiers and other Axis countries all across the European and Middle Eastern frontlines.

THE STORY WILL CONTINUE IN BOOK 5 OF THE BLITZKRIEG ALTERNATE SERIES:

# STALEMATE EUROPA

## Thank you very much for reading my work.

\*\*\* Please go and review my book(s) on Amazon and Goodreads.com.
\*\*\* It really helps me out and motivates me to write more books.
Thank you in advance.

Made in the USA
Las Vegas, NV
29 May 2021

23849474R00173